Malpractice

Malpractice

A NOVEL BY

Eleazar Lipsky

William Morrow & Company, Inc., New York

PZ3
L6688
Mal

For Joshua and Jacob

Primum non nocere.[*]
       —the first principle of Medicine

* First, no harm to the patient.

Malpractice

PART ONE

1

"All right, lady?" a voice said.

Dimly she understood. A familiar thing was happening. She was in safe hands. She was a camera, she thought, and the shutter had clicked, leaving her in darkness.

"Just hold on," the voice said.

The scream was an ambulance siren, making its way through the industrial section of the city. It was an old ambulance in poor repair. Its exhaust was noisy, its springs were stiff, but it had a respirator. In this it was unique in that city. The respirator was not needed for this woman. Her breath, coming in long slow gasps, was enough to sustain life, but barely, as blue lips and fingernails showed. The siren required police permission and that had not been given, but the driver had made his own decision and was clearing the way ahead. He was skilled in the work, trained in first aid to give oxygen, to give heart massage, to drive with skill and speed through the heavy traffic. Occasionally he called back to the attendant, giving directions and encouragement. The woman was fortunate. The men were reliable and conscientious. They were able without supervision to help her in her need.

They were driving west toward the river. A crimson sun lay ahead in a hazy, smoke-filled sky. A factory was passed, then a sharp turn brought them to the emergency entrance of a hospital. Even as the motor died, men and women, alerted by the siren, were running out to help. Nurses and a burly male aide rushed into the sun. A stretcher rolled swiftly through a crowded recep-

3

tion room into the treatment room. An intern ran along holding the patient's wrist. On the other side, a nurse ran, reading a slip of medical instructions pinned to the patient. A sheet thrown over the stretcher jerked convulsively. "Let's go, let's go, let's go," the intern said. The woman was brought inside to an empty cubicle and lifted to a bed. A nurse drew a curtain and the room went back to a slower tempo of activity. A rasping snore could be heard. A nurse called for someone to come down from neurology.

"Dr. Tatum. Dr. Tatum," the loudspeaker called.

A week earlier at a point in space and time not known to her, an electrical storm had begun to fire in the woman's brain. Manya, as she was called, had been asleep in her bedroom in a shabby frame house on Treacy Street in an old section of the city. That she was fairly young could have been seen from the delicate white skin and clear features. That she was sick, from the medicines on her bureau. That she was troubled, from the groan that shook her body. The room was poorly furnished but neat. A sorrowful Virgin hung over the bed.

The billions of neurons were at ebb, discharging at weakest voltage, electrical activity measured in millionths of the smallest unit of measure. They fired in organized synchrony, in the long slow waves of sleep. The tiny currents passed through the outer layer of gray cortex. They flashed along the branching connections of white matter beneath, through the brain stem, through the spinal conduits, scanning the woman's life. Of this she knew nothing.

A pathway shifted. The firing was irregular. The disturbance grew.

She sat up suddenly. Her head was heavy with a strange feeling in her eyes and ears. There was something to remember. She could not remember and was afraid to try. Voices were coming from her right. It was not the voice of her child. The jolly song came from the radio, she thought, but that was not possible. Men and women were singing. She felt excited and nervous and tired. She heard the song but could not remember what the song was. "Manya," she heard. "Manya, go into the closet. Manya. Manya." The voice was quiet but urgent and of course not real. No, she thought, no! That way lay the horror.

But then she got up and looked in the closet. Her dresses were crowded by a man's work clothes and a hunting jacket. A stench came from that place. She went back to bed and turned to the wall. A design of rosettes ran up the ceiling and into space. Inches times inches times inches would give the cubic volume. She shrank back. Must not multiply. That way danger, she thought.

"Manya, hurry," the voice said.

The singing died off. It was an illusion, she knew. Still, it felt real. There was often a dream, when she would seem to be in a small garret room, crouched and trembling, and the music would always be the same, a song of jovial men. They were singing in German. It was a beer-hall song.

She was choking. She was sick, sick to death. A bolus was rising in her throat. She cried out and her voice was small, it hid like a mouse, got swallowed by a mouse. A drum began to boom.

Her hand convulsed. A force gripped her body and thrashed it aside. She lay staring at the wall. My child, she wailed. The wail was silent, locked in her mind. Her eyes were bursting. Her skull split in twain.

A groan filled the house.

The door flew open. A man in underwear came to the bed with a glass of medicine. "Call the doctor," he said to a child in the next room. He tried to give the medicine without success. "Oh, Jesus, oh, Jesus," he said.

And now eight days later the electrical storm was still flickering in the woman's brain.

Meanwhile in Treacy Street, a police officer made entries on a card showing time and circumstances, and dispersed the curious. Neighboring women shook their heads at the visitation.

"It's that kid I feel sorry for," one said.

They sighed and left, crossing themselves, feeling guilty—not one felt anything but relief to be quit of the afflicted woman, if only for the moment. The street life resumed.

Upstairs under a couch the child lay hidden. A wan face, turned to the wall, was smudged. She was small even for her age, or she could not have crawled into the cramped space. She was mute, listening to the house. A motorcycle roared past. Barking could be heard. A cat meowed. She smelled matted dust. A heavy tread shook the house and a man's voice called out.

"Betsy? Betsy, honey?"

The man ceased to call and the house was empty. Perhaps the pets were fed, perhaps not. The child did not move.

The call could not have come at a more tiresome moment. Percy Tatum was resting in his room in the flood tide of fatigue, smoking one of the innumerable brown cigarillos he would consume during the day. A towel covered his eyes against the glare of the late afternoon sun. The day had begun at seven in the operating room working on a boy of nine to repair the results of a botched ventriculogram—a blood clot that had plugged a vital area of the cortex would leave its necrotic effects forever. The ventriculogram could have been avoided, he thought, with more time and care. And Bellinger—well, with the usual recriminations Bellinger had left him to run the service. The burden was heavy for the staff was small. Interns were not easy to attract to Lewiston Central Hospital, and since only three had been recruited the doctors' load was heavy. Tatum had his own hot temper, and a flare-up during rounds with the second-year resident—Dr. David Levin, a surly Israeli—had left him shaking with anger. But about what? Really, he could not say. The bell rang again. He picked up the telephone and listened.

"What's the woman's condition?" He heard his own irritation and controlled his voice. He repeated the question, staring without pleasure at the wall. The room was a monk's cell furnished with only a hard bed, a bureau, and a closet, but it had its own shower and john—a fringe benefit Bellinger had wangled for him for which he was not especially thankful. Privacy was his due. A photograph of a young woman in mortarboard and graduation robes was the sole decoration. Several medical texts were stacked on the bureau. Penfield and Jaspar on the basic mechanisms of the epilepsies was a reproach. It was Bellinger's gift. Bellinger had passed it on as useless and surpassed; but it was not surpassed; merely, at his age, difficult. Too often he had fallen asleep over the maze of graphs and maps and statistical discoveries. The suspicion that he had started to focus on a complex aspect of his

6

specialty of medicine somewhat too late in life haunted Tatum's thoughts.

"I'll be right there," he said. He lowered his head and breathed purposefully. He was bone-tired. Eight hours in the operating room, two in the clinic, grand rounds, teaching rounds, and only a chocolate bar for lunch had left him drained; and now that he longed to leave for the farm, this call had to come. He put on a fresh white coat, affixed his gold-rimmed bifocals, studied his appearance in the mirror, and left. He was careful to lock the door.

Bellinger's office was open. John Howard Bellinger, M.D., director of the service, was jaunty in a recent photograph of himself with a sailfish trophy against the blue skies of the Caribbean. It was a characteristic pose: cigar stuck high, captain's cap at an angle, one arm clutching the fish, the other encircling a young woman's waist. The young woman, a quondam concert pianist, was peaches and cream, stout and breasty in an interesting way. Bellinger was magnetic and light-skinned with a strong curved nose and lanky black hair and a look of assaultive challenge that made him handsome as Billy-be-damned, Tatum thought, and too disorganized for his talent.

An Egyptian queen in Afro hairdo—Lurene Storrs on the payroll—was dusting the photograph. There was no love between her and the girl in the photograph. She glanced at Tatum with studied insolence and went on with her task.

Tatum sniffed. "Where's Dr. Bellinger?"

Lurene slid a glance of mockery. "New York," she said. "Vital dinner conference at the Ford Foundation. If the magic works, we might start breaking ground soon for the Dream." The duster flicked at an architect's projection of a proposed medical complex of concrete, glass, and aluminum. The Dream—sometimes irreverently called Bellinger's Non-Violent Coordinating Medical Center—had been incubating for a decade. "There's a Brandeis chick down there with real good influence, he says. Very attractive by candlelight. Full of pity for the poor and swings millions." She dropped into dialect. "So it is the Cause—it is the Cause, oh my soul, that draws him on."

Tatum hated the dialect. "What about the call from emergency?" he asked.

Lurene put on her eyelashes. "Dov was notified. It can wait till he gets there."

"Dov? Do you mean Dr. Levin?"

Lurene was amused. "I suppose I do. He's on the ward now. He switched with Rikki. *Doctor* Rikki," she added, stressing the title. Rikki was their first-year resident, Dr. Krishna Rajagopolachari, a graduate of Monghyr Medical College in Behar, India.

Tatum pressed his mouth to a thin line and took a chart from a filing cabinet. Insubordinate snots, he thought. At least the interns took orders without backchat, although that was small comfort. "I'm damn annoyed," he said. "When I make out a schedule, I have a reason. How can I run the service properly when this goes on? I should have been told about the switch."

An eye pencil was applied. "What's the difference so long as it's covered?"

"Don't be cheeky," Tatum said icily. "If my wife calls, put it through to emergency," he added, and strode off. Damned insolence too, he thought. It was something definitely to take up with Bellinger, but to what use? It would only mean another scene, and he'd had enough of those to last a year of Sundays. Bellinger was still sleeping with the girl and would raise not a syllable of reproach. It was quite intolerable. He walked with a long stride, hitting the worn linoleum with hard leather heels, and the clacking preceded him, echoing from the walls. He nodded to nurses and aides, greeted other doctors and felt better. He enjoyed the ceremonial rites of passage. His coat was starched to extra stiffness, and he enjoyed its sanction and protective comfort. He was a doctor and aware of that role. He wore a habitual sneer. His manner was humorless and impassive, one of dignity, courteous to all. "Doctor," he said, bowing to a passing group.

"Doctor," came an indifferent reply.

He smiled fixedly at retreating backs, and then the smile vanished into something bleak and wistful. He was conscious of a high vaulting nose, small brown eyes sunk in deep craters, a cloud of steel-wool hair jutting from his temples, and tight black lips. He could have cursed himself—the snub had thrown him into a mood of gloom and there was not the slightest reason. He disconcerted them, he knew, but did not care. Still, it hurt. He threw back his shoulders and went on, swinging an academic key.

He paused at the neurological ward, tempted to enter. He made rounds as often as possible, sometimes at hourly intervals. It was excessive, he knew, but away from the service he felt restless and anxious, and the close attention to the patients—a pleasant and friendly manner, laying on of hands, touching the mute and comatose—was always satisfying. The ward was almost tranquil. The day shift of nurses had left the patients cleaned and bedded for the night. Some patients were complaining that it was still daylight, too early for sleep—but the late shift were busy rushing trays to the wards to get the feeding done. An octogenarian was yelling for a bedpan. Dov Levin was writing out an order on the chart, he saw, no doubt prescribing something to knock the old man out. Tatum had an impulse to intervene, to assure the patient that he had indeed been on the bedpan throughout the day, but he went on to the street level instead.

Emergency was the usual hubbub and disorder. What once had been a basement corridor with a single nurse was now virtually an outpatient clinic for the neighborhood. Every conceivable ailment and situation could be expected to show up. The traffic was heavy. But the service was still the orphan of the hospital, much neglected. The bloody victim of an automobile accident, being carried to the treatment room by two attendants, was shouting. "No interns! I can pay! For God's sake, no interns! I live at—" The commotion ended.

Tatum felt a hand at his sleeve.

"Help me, Doctor," a woman whispered.

Tatum studied the woman's eyes. They were bloodshot and yellowed. Her hair was thin and white. Her mouth was blue. "I'm busy, madam," he said. "Let me call a doctor for you."

"I feel bad. I'll faint," the woman said, reeling.

Tatum picked the woman up like a child and strode to the reception desk. He said, "Mrs. Ponsonby, can't we take patients by the severity of their complaints, not in the order of arrival? This woman's very sick."

Mrs. Rebecca Ponsonby, a dour black woman, looked up. "Sorry, Doctor, but she's not emergency. She's on home care. She's been told to wait there for her doctor."

"He never comes," the woman said. "He says he does, but he doesn't. I can't wait anymore."

9

"I'll give her a number," the nurse said.

"Never mind that," Tatum snapped. He carried the woman directly into the emergency-treatment room. The room held a dozen cubicles divided by curtains, filled with patients in various states of sickness and distress. There was a smell of vomit and antiseptic. The intern on duty found it important to busy himself with a respirator. It was astonishing, Tatum thought, how people found reason to fiddle. "Don't stand around with your hands hanging. Let's not be afraid of sick people," he exclaimed. He turned to the desk. "Team thirteen!" he said, and beckoned. "And you there! Doctor! Come here at once, man!" The intern reluctantly came forward.

"Team thirteen," the loudspeaker said.

Tatum clapped his hands. "Let's start the goddamned IV. Let's go. Let's go. Where's everybody?" Equipment began to arrive. An RN came running. Eventually, a cardiac resident, licking mustard from his mouth, entered with a shuffle, half running, half skipping, and took over the lifesaving devices. "Okay, Doctor, I've got it," he said, adjusting a monitor. A dot of light danced on the oscilloscope. "You can go now. I've got it," he repeated.

The black vaulting nose above him tilted with outrage. "Be damned sure you have," Tatum exclaimed. "I hope you had time to finish your meal." He parted the curtain and left the cubicle.

Dr. Louis Goldfarb, chief of the emergency service, was examining the admissions log. Tatum strode over and began without ceremony. "Lou, since you took over, this service is a disgrace. Just bloody horrible. If we can't give these poor people prompt treatment, by George, let's go out of business." He was shrill with rage.

Work came to a halt. Everyone stared as the strange-looking black doctor, using his spectacles for emphasis, berated the older man for the unconscionable delays in the ambulance and emergency services, citing all sorts of untoward episodes glossed over by the sloppy record keeping of a demoralized staff.

Goldfarb, a wiry, hatchet-faced man with tired eyes, was unimpressed. "I don't think you should be carrying on like the wild man of Borneo in front of people, Doctor," he interrupted. "You're not satisfied to fight with Bellinger in the operating room? You have to fight here too?"

"I won't tolerate—" Tatum began.

"You won't tolerate what?" Goldfarb said. "Doctor, let me run this service, hey? You've got a woman with fits waiting for you? So see her."

Tatum drew back, blinking. "I'm sorry, but I'm tired out, overworked, Lou. I haven't slept—"

Goldfarb cut this short. "Where do you get this 'Lou' stuff? Maybe you're overage for a resident, but that doesn't carry privileges. What's this everybody-is-equal thing?"

"I said I was sorry," Tatum said.

"I don't want you to be sorry," Goldfarb snarled. "This hospital isn't your private domain, nor Bellinger's, though you both seem to think so. If you've got complaints, bring 'em up to the medical board. But I'll have my own complaints. Your indiscipline is atrocious, Doctor, and that's the least of it. You've got no monopoly on this pity-the-poor crap. I was poor before you were born. Now excuse me while I try to help a patient, hey?"

There was the silence of embarrassment. Someone stirred, and the hum and noise resumed. Tatum was left slick with sweat. He was conscious of averted eyes. A bad taste was in his mouth. Why had he staged that scene with Goldfarb? He had promised his wife better control, but it was too much, really too much.

A nurse was beckoning. "Dr. Tatum, we're ready for you."

He smoothed back the sprouting horns of hair and snuffed deeply, quelling a licking flame of anger. When he entered the emergency cubicle, it was with an air of grave concern.

The woman lay unconscious, breathing slowly and heavily in labored gasps at long intervals. Tatum picked up an admission slip and noted that a city ambulance had been called on request of a private physician. "Who's Dr. Gates? Why isn't she here?"

The nurse said, "She sent word she's detained on a hard delivery on Joseph Street. It's a changing neighborhood."

"I know the street," Tatum said. "Well, let's see what's here." The sheet stated that the patient, a Mrs. Maria Shroeder, was referred to Lewiston Central Hospital for eight days of seizures of some gravity with a prior history of the same. She had received sodium amytal, he observed. "Amytal? What good is that?

She'll start up again like a Mexican jumping bean when she wakes up." The right side was contracting spasmodically. "Do we know this patient?"

"Glory, yes," the nurse replied. "She's been coming off and on for about five years. The social workers know her too. Family situation, husband and a little girl."

Tatum pushed back the woman's hair, then examined her eyes with a pocket flashlight. He did not like her breathing. The pulse was slow but satisfactory. Other vital signs seemed normal. The tongue was pale but intact. He slipped a hand under the hospital gown. He felt a slight rigidity of the right belly. "Does she wet herself?"

"No, she's always kept dry," the nurse replied. "At least so far as I know."

"Does she fall?"

"Not to my knowledge. Maybe so."

"What's her Christian name?"

"I think Maria. She's called Manya."

Tatum leaned forward. "Manya," he said. "Manya. Manya." The woman groaned. "Manya," he repeated. The eyes opened and turned aside to the right. He spoke firmly, explaining that she was in a hospital and safe.

Deep in the woman's brain, myriad cells fired a minuscule electrical charge. A faint current oscillated, stabilized, discharged uncountable millions of ions along millions of pathways. A thought flickered. There was light and a dark form in the center.

"Manya. Manya."

Voices were real and not real. A hand had prodded at her belly. ". . . wet herself?" it had said. Sun blazed, danced, searched.

A lion breathed in her nostrils. A face swam into vision gigantic beyond belief. High vaulting nose, steel wool radiating, blue-black lips, thoughtful eyes behind spectacles, and a strange manner. There was thunder.

"Singing . . ." she said.

"You hear singing? Who is singing?"

She struggled. "Men."

"So you always hear singing?"

She was silent for the interminable moment. She raised her right hand, then her left. The hands were delicate and tapering and equal in size. The face was pleased and said things. A voice spoke. It was, she knew, her voice. "Black," it said.

"That's right. I'm black," the thunder said.

"My baby," she said. "Is my baby all right?" The voice echoed within her skull. She did not know tears were on her cheeks and, knowing, would not have cared.

"That's right. I'm black," Tatum said. He wrote an order in a fine precise script. He wanted the patient upstairs as soon as possible.

"Isn't she going home?" the nurse asked. "She usually does after rest and medication. The real trouble is these people won't stick to their medication. I think she does that to get away from the house."

"Suppose you mind your business, Nurse," Tatum said. "Maybe we'll do better this time. Maybe she's gone through the revolving door long enough." He returned the chart and left.

The nurse put hands on hips. "Glory! What did I say?" She signaled a student nurse. "Help me, dearie? They want her up in Bellinger's service, poor soul. What that doctor thinks he can do for her beats me."

"Right! What do I do?" the girl said. She touched the snoring woman. "Oooh! She's warm! Ugh! It's so uncanny. If she starts to throw a fit, watch me fly!" Quickly and efficiently, the woman was prepared for removal to the fifth floor. Dress, slip, bra, stockings, shoes, pocketbook were examined. Stockings had runs. Shoes needed heels. The purse was empty except for a grocery receipt for small items of food.

As records would show, Manya Shroeder arrived at the neurological service after a delay of six hours. It was past midnight. The resident on duty saw a note that Tatum had retained the patient for his own further examination. Next day Tatum met the patient and reviewed her medical history. Her husband was seen and the social worker consulted. Tests were made. A departmental conference was held at which Dr. John Howard Bellinger, the chief of neurology, presided. Opinion, divided as to diagnosis and treatment, had an edge of antagonism. Tatum stood alone, but that was not unusual.

Tatum saw his patient daily on rounds, and often with greater frequency. A good relationship was established. Eventually, she was brought to the surgical service where brain surgery was done. She returned home apparently improved. She took care of her child, shopped, made curtains for her kitchen. She sent Tatum a Christmas card of effusive gratitude. She told neighbors that sexual relations with her husband had been resumed.

A month later, early in February, she fell into violent convulsions and was found unconscious by a neighbor. That neighbor, Mrs. Ingrid Czeisler, placed a handkerchief in the woman's mouth, sent the child from the house, and found a telephone number pinned to the kitchen bulletin board.

A woman's deep, almost masculine voice answered. "People's Clinic. Dr. Gates here."

"Dr. Gates? Come quick. She's at it again," Mrs. Czeisler said.

2

Flight 326 was circling in a holding pattern when the delay in landing was announced. Perhaps fifteen minutes. Perhaps an hour. The pilot was cheerful about it. The stewardess brought news that the cause of the delay was ice at the Huron County Airport. A groan went up.

William Mahler stopped the girl. "Miss, did you people know about the ice when we left LaGuardia?"

The girl said brightly, "I'm sure it was clear. The ice must have formed after takeoff."

Mahler said, "I think that ice was forming when we took off. You people are hanging on to every ticket and to hell with us. Can I buy a whiskey?"

The smile remained fixed. Sorry, but regulations put a limit of two drinks to a passenger. Mahler was unimpressed. He wanted a drink or he'd make a row, he promised. The girl shakily went forward with this message.

Mahler turned to a pleasant, handsome woman in the next seat. He said, "Sorry about that, but it's one for our side."

The woman had been reading a novel since takeoff. She looked up. "Well done," she said in a flat upstate accent.

Minutes later extra drinks were announced.

Mahler said, "Can I buy you a drink, ma'am?" He had waited for that opening since takeoff.

She was amused. "Thank you, Mr. Mahler, but not this time."

Mahler was surprised. "How'd you know my name?"

15

"You gave it to the stewardess. And you're going to Lewiston, which interests me. Will you stay there long?"

"I'm not sure," Mahler said.

She smiled. "I don't blame you for being doubtful. Lewiston thinks it's the center of the universe, but when you come to it—what's Lewiston? Nothing. You're on law business, aren't you?"

Mahler followed her glance. He had been reading the *Syracuse Law Review*. "I'll know when I get there," he said. "I haven't been to that city for years. I played football once against the college."

"Yes, I know. You played halfback for Hamilton. Our high school class had a rooting section for Lewiston. Home team, you know. I remember a great end run, if you're the same man."

"I'm the same man," Mahler said. He added, "Not quite, but roughly."

"Well, you should remember me then too. While you ran, I watched. Hoping you'd never make it." An appraising stare took in a strong jaw and knitted brows. She saw a hard-muscled man with a broken nose and a strong, humorous mouth. "Yes, of course, Will Mahler. I'd have expected someone taller after all these years. I think they called you—what was it? Indian Mahler?" They were in abominably narrow economy-class seats. "I think I'll have that whiskey," she decided. She slid over a glance of cool interest. "You're well known, you know. You were in the New York prosecutor's office. After that last murder prosecution of yours—what was that woman's name?"

"Alice Kent?"

"Yes, Alice Kent. Rotten situation, even for a prostitute. Did she really murder her lover?"

Something cold gripped him. It was not a case he had any pleasure to remember. "If I didn't think so, I'd never have asked for the verdict. It was a job and I did it, if that's your question, Mrs.—?" He paused.

"Sorry, I'm taking advantage," she said. "I'm Mrs. van Loon. You may remember my husband—Judge van Loon. He sat in the Appellate Division, Third Department?"

Mahler nodded. Van Loon? Some vague recollection stirred. "Yes, of course. Judge van Loon. Anyhow, Mrs. van Loon, to answer your next question, I had no fun out of that trial, though the newspapers might have said so. I was always very cautious. I never initiated a prosecution without being certain of my ground, in all those years."

"You never made a mistake?"

Mahler paused. "I'll say this. None that I know of. They said I was brutal in that case. I don't think I was, but if I was, it was to get at the truth, not because I liked it. And the victim wasn't her lover, he was a pimp. He wasn't just killed, he was stomped to death. I tried to help that woman but she wouldn't let me. Does that answer all questions?" He concluded with a grunt.

"Dear me," she said, "I'm sorry I raised the question." Somewhat disconcerted, she swept back a hair and returned to her novel. Mahler turned to the window with no idea why he had been so rude. Perhaps because of his unhappy situation, perhaps bad social habits. He was not sure, but then he was not sure of many things these days. An impulse to apologize was quenched —or rather deferred.

Dark, leaden clouds extended to the horizon and, above, feathery cirrus clouds obscured the sun at noon. A translucent light of winter filled the world. With luck the flight would return to LaGuardia. He was not enthusiastic about the business in Lewiston and had taken the case with misgivings. Except to send an investigator ahead, he had made no real preparation for the trip. Now what, if anything, would the man have to report? He was longing for winter to end and for summer to come with his small beach house at the shore.

The aircraft made a long, slow turn and a swishing noise filled the cabin. He opened a briefcase and took out a set of notes of a conversation a week earlier in his office in New York City. He did not need the notes. He had the interview committed to memory. Landowski's nagging voice instantly came back to mind.

He had returned that day to his office on the fifteenth floor of the old building on Madison Avenue after a long and desultory luncheon downtown at Dino's. Dino's was a Mulberry Street hangout for lawyers and politicians from the Criminal Courts Building. It had been an established eating place for twenty years, and he was a fixture there. Or should have been a fixture. He had felt comfortable sitting at his regular table in the fellowship of the criminal bar. But over the years the others had left for

Washington, or had gone into private practice, or had got bench appointments—well, many were now judges before whom he appeared. New people, younger lawyers, long of hair, slovenly in dress, now filled the tables. He felt less than comfortable with the new vocabulary that filled the air. He was a fish out of water, and he felt blue as the afternoon dragged and the last cup of *cappuccino* went down. It was late when the subway took him back to his office in midtown.

The switchboard was empty and buzzing. The reception room facing the bank of elevators was empty except for a tall blond man with vaguely familiar features sprawled in a chair under the large gilt shingle that bore a dozen legal names including Mahler's own. He nodded and went down a dark hall to his office in the rear and stretched out on a sofa. The winter sky, gray and overcast, was not far from his mood. The years away from private law practice had left him unprepared for its difficulties. He was waiting for real law business, but although the press had carried his picture upon his resignation as chief of the New York Homicide Bureau with stories of his celebrated criminal prosecutions, nothing really big or satisfying had yet come in—nothing beyond more civil business than he cared for: some fair matrimonials, a few theatrical-partnership agreements, a routine brokerage-house embezzlement, and, of course, personal-injury matters of poor liability and no great value. He had the usual letter of regret from the district attorney, but that was small consolation. Apparently the presumed brutality of that last big trial downtown—that woman charged with her lover's murder, a trial that had ended tragically in her suicide—had alienated too many people. Too ironic! he thought. He had done everything to save her life and still felt shaken by the outcome. Always unwise to get caught up, he reflected. He felt like a novice, starting out on the long difficult business of putting a law practice together.

The telephone rang. It was Mrs. Garabadian to announce that a Mr. Landowski was waiting to see him.

"Landowski? Who's that?"

"He says he wrote he'd be in the city sometime. He's from Lewiston. Lewiston, New York."

"Send him in." Mahler replaced the receiver. He recalled that letter of course, but what Landowski had in mind had not been stated. He stood with a professional smile as the visitor entered. "Hello, Gene," he said easily. "So what's the Rule in Shelley's Case?"

Landowski was a muscular blond man well over six feet tall with wide shoulders and enormous hands. His eyes were mild and troubled. He smiled at the law-school joke. "I still don't know," he said, and refused a cigar.

"Pull up a seat," Mahler said.

Landowski threw a fur-lined overcoat on a sofa and took a chair facing an oversized oak desk. The dark paneling and array of certificates and signed photographs of judges and politicians and newspaper stories of courtroom trials evidently made an impression. Mahler sank back in a large leather swivel chair. He remembered Landowski well enough. They had been classmates at Syracuse Law School, where they had taken their degrees. Landowski had been the one always sure to wave for attention, sure to confuse the simplest fields of law—sales, agency, torts, negotiable instruments—with contentiousness and literal reliance on textbook gnomic wisdom. More than twenty years had passed since graduation, and so far as one could tell, barring a growing paunch and thinning hair, Landowski had not changed much.

Landowski's gaze wandered. "Nice layout," he said.

"Yes, it is."

Landowski said, "Well, you've had a career, Bill! You know we've been reading about you. Nice thing about the *Alumni Journal*. It keeps the class in touch."

"I suppose it does," Mahler said.

"How big is this firm?"

"It's not a firm really," Mahler said. "We share overhead and services but we're independent. I'll show you around later. I had my first job here as a clerk for Thayer Connolly, active in real estate and tax work. I got that job downtown for trial experience and didn't come back till now. That was twenty years and now look at it. That terrace"—a gesture took in a terrace decorated with frozen potted vines on smudged trellises—"was used for office parties in Thayer's time. Not anymore. The pollution's taken over. So here I am and where'd it get me?"

"You got the experience," Landowski said.

"Sure, but sometimes I think I made a mistake. I should've located in some small town with a shingle on Main Street. Write wills, draw up deeds, home at five, lots of fishing. This city's getting too much."

"You've got a funny idea of small-town practice."

Mahler laughed. "So how's it going with you?"

Landowski hesitated. He had done well enough as an upstate lawyer in a small industrial city with a mixed population, he supposed. He was active in local politics and had ambitions for the city council. He and his wife tried to be good citizens, but, of course, a Polish-American lawyer had no real chance, he complained. The other ethnic groups had it sewed up—Yankees, Irish, Jews, Italians in turn—and now blacks and Puerto Ricans pouring into the inner city with crazy and strident demands were making things hard. It was impossible to serve even on a school board in a Polish neighborhood—what with demands for decentralization and community control and a supposedly liberal administration in City Hall and all the rest . . .

It was instant boredom. Mahler's smile was fixed, but he had gone lackluster at the litany of ethnic grumblings. He had almost forgotten Landowski's activity in Polish-American affairs. His own family, so far as he knew or cared, had sprung to life in a gangster-infested section of Brooklyn which was still subtly the center of his universe. He waited for an opening, and said, "Gene, what brings you here?"

Landowski plunged into the purpose of the visit. The matter had come out of a neighborhood situation—a family sent to him by Father Zator, their priest.

Mahler's expression did not change. "What sort of case?"

Landowski waited. "Malpractice," he said with feeling. "Medical malpractice, to be specific. Would you be interested in coming in?"

Mahler felt something stir. He was relieved that the matter was not criminal. "Maybe," he said, "but I'm too old to fool around. Is the defendant good for a judgment?"

"Well, sure. I don't know if the doctors are personally insured, but that won't matter. They both left town. But I wouldn't even want to sue 'em. The action would be primarily against one of our city's hospitals. The city's responsible if there's a case."

"If? Don't you know if you've got a case?"

Landowski rubbed his face uncertainly. "Of course there's a case. It just needs to be investigated and developed. I hope you're interested. If not, I've got a call in to Charles Seidman. He thinks it has possibilities."

"Charlie's a good man." Mahler's tone was neutral. "Writes good books. Let me know what he says, eh?"

"I thought I'd talk to you first."

"I appreciate that. Why me?"

"Well, there are aspects here."

"Oh, aspects. What's the catch?"

"No catch. Well, nothing really." Landowski broke off. "I should tell you something, I suppose. The doctors were black. Negroes, in fact. Both graduated from a medical college in South Carolina for colored doctors, so you can imagine the training. That's one of the problems. With all the uproar, nobody wants to reflect on them professionally. I thought you might not mind." He paused, trying to read the expressionless mask. "Or does it bother you, Bill? If it does . . ."

Mahler seemed amused. He lit a cigar and sank back in his chair. "Gene, I was raised in a Jewish neighborhood. We weren't brought up to dislike the black man. So I'm not afraid of him. And I'm not afraid of my feelings for him." A cloud of blue smoke went up. "In my experience he's just like any other son of a bitch I meet in life. What's color got to do with it?"

"Nothing, of course," Landowski said uncomfortably. "Sorry I mentioned it." Then with some cunning ventured, "But don't you think that might affect a jury?"

"Yes, it might," Mahler said. He let a moment pass. "But you don't know what I think. What was the malpractice?"

Landowski seemed relieved. He glanced about conspiratorially, then leaned forward and cupped his hand. "Brain surgery," he said dramatically. "These people have suffered horrible damage, and they're entitled to a big recovery. It could be worth your while."

Mahler faced the terrace on which grit and dirt were swirling in an icy wind, thinking how little he had to show after twenty hard years in the public service. He said, "Okay, I'm impressed. What was the reason for this brain surgery?"

"Supposedly to remove a tumor."

Mahler paused to tap the cigar in a battered leather-covered glass ashtray. The ashtray had been his mother's gift on the day he had begun law practice. It had stood on a dozen desks since.

"Come on, Gene. What was the reason? Doctors don't just go around grabbing people to operate."

"Don't they? Come on yourself, Bill," Landowski retorted with feeling. "Lewiston Central has a bad reputation in the community for slipshod work, but I'm not depending on that. I know this family. There was no reason for this operation. Do you want to hear about it?"

Mahler sat back with a dead stare, chin in palm. It was a studied pose and quite disconcerting. He said, "Did she have any earning capacity?"

"Not since this operation. Before that she was a librarian and sang in the choir. Of course it's affected her husband too."

"What does he do?"

"Not much, I'm afraid. He's got some kind of disability. He tries to run a small repair business, but it's tough with this problem. Taking care of his wife, I mean. Their kid, a girl of seven, is disturbed. Manya is intelligent all right, more than her husband. She'll make a nice impression. Reads a lot, or she did before this happened."

"What about the marital situation?"

"Oh, that. Yes. Tragedy there. Wrecked the marriage."

"You seem to like this woman very much."

"Manya? Yes, of course. She's a fine individual. What about it?"

Mahler shrugged. "These things aren't easy to accept and if you get too involved, you're likely to see malpractice under every rock. Of course, if any part of this is true . . ." A gleam of interest flickered and disappeared. "Well, tell me about it." He dropped an ash into the tray. "And, Gene? There's no jury here. No crap, eh?"

He listened with intensity, sucking his cigar. His glance was unwavering. He was intent not on what was said but on a thread of meaning and truth not easily seen. The main claim was that the woman had been reluctantly persuaded to accept the operation to determine the cause of her seizures—or spells, as Landowski put it—and it was only after the event when she saw her bandaged head in the mirror that the horror became clear. It had been in vain. The infrequent spells were now violent seizures, more frequent, more difficult to control. Far from being cured, the poor woman was in misery, tormented by headaches and neurological afflictions of unbearable intensity as well. It was all criminal, a great outrage, Landowski concluded with deep anger.

Mahler stirred. "Where's the malpractice?"

"Where's the malpractice?" Landowski echoed.

They were back in law school, Mahler thought, and Landowski was still low man in the class.

Landowski gathered his thoughts. "I just told you. She was virtually normal when she went in. She was a wreck soon after she came out, mentally, morally, physically. She was completely changed. Why can't she claim *res ipsa loquitur?*"

Mahler would always recall a moment of professional wonder and irony. Landowski had stated the elementary rule of evidence to allow the court to infer negligence from the thing itself. Well, yes, certain things were self-evident. Forceps should not be found in the belly after surgery. Nor should towels or sponges or spectacles or cuff links show up after the event. In such cases someone clearly must have been careless and the courts required nothing beyond proof of the event itself—such were the advances both of law and medicine. Nor should surgeons amputate wrong limbs nor dentists extract wrong teeth. Anesthetic gas should not explode in a patient's lungs. Minor skin surgery should not lead to general paralysis of the entire body. The spinal cord should not be severed by the careful surgeon—and when such mishaps took place, as unfortunately they did more frequently than generally realized, the law did indeed put the burden on the doctor to explain negligence away. But was this such a case? He studied the broad, obstinate Slavic features of an honest man and sighed. "It's not that easy, Gene. Doctors aren't supposed to be infallible. They've only got to use their best judgment. They're not liable for mere errors—"

"I know *that!*" Landowski interrupted.

"Sure you do," Mahler replied.

"Some error!" Landowski said after a moment.

"Well, suppose they made a mistake? The best make mistakes.

23

We both know it means nothing unless you show the diagnosis and treatment were below standard. You don't just claim malpractice. You've got to prove it. And prove that the malpractice actually caused the damage."

"Well, that's easy."

"Is it?"

"Sure! She's got a hole in her head. And—and she's got this suffering." Landowski frowned, puzzled by the irony. "What else but the operation would cause that? It's obvious."

"Nothing's obvious," Mahler said. "Maybe she ate some bad dandelions. What does her medical file show?"

"I don't know. I haven't asked for it yet."

Mahler looked up. "Why not? What are you waiting for—Christmas?"

"I was afraid to show an interest. Something funny might happen to that file if I did."

"That's true, of course," Mahler mused, "but without that history, you might find a jack-in-the-box too." He was almost enjoying the moment. "It's not like finding a bag of peanuts in the belly after surgery. We've got to assume that this team made the usual tests and that they used their best judgment. Who says they didn't?"

Landowski drew a breath. "I know that the old family doctor, Dr. Schlomm, always told Manya she could be stabilized on medication, that she could be kept under control. So did her present doctor. She objected to this operation."

"She?"

"A woman doctor. Dr. Jane Gates."

"Oh. Well, go on."

"But she was brushed aside. In fact, she got threatened and was told to shut up or face charges—"

Mahler frowned. "Just a minute. Threatened by whom?"

"These people in neurology. The resident, Dr. Tatum, told her to keep her long nose out of it—that's a quote—or she'd be sorry. Manya was their patient, not hers, he said, and so was the decision. Dr. Bellinger, who was chief of neurosurgery, agreed. There was nothing she could do, she told me."

Mahler said, "What else did Dr. Gates tell you?"

Landowski's laugh was scornful. "That's another thing that

smells here. First she was helpful. Then she told me to forget it. Now she's not taking my calls. But three months ago she sent Manya to the Luzzatto Institute for a psychiatric consultation. A doctor named Herlihy studied her. So that tells you. But the fact is Dr. Gates raised hell before the surgery. She had a reason. What was it? Frankly I think she's covering something up for these doctors and the hospital."

"Really? You surprise me," Mahler said without tone. "I didn't suppose that sort of thing went on in American hospitals, not with all the dedicated people running around." He swung about, digesting the matter. "Okay, so the family doctor got temperamental and the specialists got rough. What's novel in that?"

"Well, you don't have to look so skeptical."

"I'm not skeptical. I'm just asking."

"I see," Landowski said. "Look, maybe I'm wrong, but it's the way they went about it that's so suspicious. This resident, Tatum, told Manya she had a malignant tumor in her skull. Cancer. He said it was causing the seizures, that it had to come out, or it'd kill her."

Mahler looked up. "He said a thing like that?"

"He certainly did. You can imagine her state of mind." Landowski wet his mouth. "But suppose there was no tumor? And no reason to think so?" He was beginning to tremble. He leaned forward, placing large hands tufted with blond hairs on the desk. The chair creaked under his weight. "I've lived with this case, Bill. I *know* there was malpractice. If she had cancer, she'd be dead by now, so obviously the diagnosis was wrong. Why isn't that a case?"

Mahler stared. "And that's your proof? That doesn't prove a thing. Tumors can be removed with success."

Landowski shook his head. "But it *wasn't* removed. The next day Tatum told her the tumor was malignant just as he predicted. He even seemed pleased that he was right about it. He also said he hadn't got it all out and she'd need another operation. So if it wasn't removed successfully, she shouldn't be alive, right?"

Mahler frowned. "You also just said there was no tumor?"

"That's right. I did."

"Which is it then? Was there a tumor or not? Exactly what's your point?"

"Don't you see? It was a contradiction, a cover-up to hold the patient under his control. It was too much double talk to be on the level." Hope faded, suspicion was renewed. "What do you want, Bill? Guarantees?" Landowski exclaimed, stung. "I've told you what I know. I'm sure there was malpractice, but I can't seem to get at it. That's why I'm here. You know how and I don't. What must I do to get help?" He swallowed convulsively. "How do you think it feels to live with cancer? She's in a terrible state of mind, Bill. No one can persuade her she hasn't got this thing growing in her skull. It's an obsession, a phobia, impossible to live with whether or not it's true. She lives in agony and how can that be justified—especially when you see what's happening to that little family? All right, so I'm a country lawyer and a dumb hayseed and anything you like—I know my limits—but what do you call it? Or maybe you don't think feelings count?"

"Oh, no. Feelings are important," Mahler said after a pause. He stared dourly at the agitated lawyer. "Gene, I honestly don't think you've shown me anything. A big verdict sounds good, but how many are there? Nine out of ten cases end right here in the office. And those that go to trial? Three out of four jury verdicts favor doctors, not patients. Think of those odds. And suppose you win. The judge can cut you down or knock you out entirely. Above them you've got the appellate judges whose bunions hurt when they can't reverse. You're only thinking of framing the complaint. I'm thinking you can spend years of time and effort for nothing. This is the hardest kind of case to prove. It's not one fact you need but the cumulative effect of lots of facts and their evaluation in the light of medical knowledge and experience. So unless you're on solid ground, it's ridiculous to start." He paused, facing a plaster cast of Lincoln.

"Of course . . ." he said.

He stood, shaking his head. "Seidman turned you down, didn't he?"

Landowski flushed. "I'll be honest. Yes."

"Others have too?"

"Yes, others."

"Why?"

"I have no idea."

"I have. Those lawyers have all they can handle. They can

pick and choose. They've all got better cases than yours, I'd say."

Landowski faced reality and sighed. "Mr. Seidman was nice enough. He told me to get the files and a medical expert, preferably one who'll be ready to testify, then he'll consider it. But I haven't got either. I've talked to every doctor I know, and no one wants to get involved." His voice was touched with wonder. "Jesus, Bill! Why is it almost impossible to get doctors to testify against each other? And without an expert witness, people like Seidman won't bother. Where does that leave us? Manya's crippled and tortured and she can't get a day in court. What am I supposed to tell her? That she's the victim of two professions? If there's no case, forget it. But can't you at least help me look into it?"

The silence was profound. Mahler began to stride the room, chewing his cigar to shreds. Son of a bitch, he thought with more respect. Landowski had built to a nice effect. He stared dubiously. "I don't know, Gene. I haven't heard anything but guesswork so far. Have you got a good compelling legal reason for me to get into this flypaper?"

Landowski brought his hands together in supplication. "Please?"

Mahler laughed. He turned and opened the door to the next office. "Oh, Jim? Can you come here a minute?"

A dignified white-haired lawyer, rosy-cheeked and twinkle-eyed, entered. James P. Curtayne, formerly dean of the criminal bar, was almost eighty but still erect and ruddy and good-humored. He wore a gardenia in his buttonhole with aplomb. He was about to leave for home. Mahler introduced the two and explained the problem of finding an expert witness. Curtayne considered the matter carefully, frowning as he conned his memory of names. It was surprising how many eminent doctors he had outlived. Still! "Good case, why not? I'll think about it in the morning. Delighted to have met you, sir. Good night."

"Real lawyer," Mahler said with affection when Curtayne had left. "Okay. We'll see what that turns up." He was torn by the view ahead—the toil of a massive lawsuit, hostile climate, doubtful records, upstate jury, little evidence, much surmise, a contentious Polish-Americanski associate, poverty-stricken plaintiffs dependent on the lawsuit to rehabilitate their lives. He noted the time with surprise. Almost five? The Old Timers' Bar would be filling up and the prospect was fair. Perhaps the drought was past, the rains would come, the voice of the advocate would be heard in the land. Every aggressive instinct was alive. And yet, and yet! "What was the name of that medical school they went to?"

"Gorham."

"Gorham? Never heard of it."

"There, you see! Nobody has."

Mahler drummed. "All right, but I'll want to make my own investigation before I jump into this swamp."

"I'll be glad to help," Landowski said eagerly.

Mahler yawned. "This is no commitment," he cautioned. "I'll want to meet the family, see that doctor first, sniff around. Okay, kid?" A bleak smile appeared. His decision, limited as it was, could have been foreseen, he suspected, the moment Landowski had opened the door. "Now let's hear the rest."

Landowski's face was a van Gogh sun on a blaze of canvas.

An hour later, Mahler showed the visitor to the elevator, then returned. After an irresolute moment, he put through a call to a newspaper in Harlem. Cinabelle Webster, feature writer, came to the telephone.

"Hey, man," she said with pleasure. "What can I do?"

After a good-natured exchange, Mahler said, "Can you get anything about a doctor upstate named Bellinger? Also one named Tatum? I'm looking for leads."

"Johnny Bellinger? What's he into now?"

"Do you know him?"

She chuckled. "Oh, sure. I met him way back at a sorority dance. Smooth talker and dances like a snake. One of these new types—big and bad. Scares the hell out of Whitey. I don't know Tatum. Anything special you want?"

"Not yet. Later, maybe," Mahler said.

She laughed. "You buy the drinks, honey."

After further expressions of mutual regard, Mahler hung up. Cinabelle Webster was a resource, a secret weapon developed over the years. He jotted a list of points to cover, locked his desk, and left for the day.

•   •   •

Mahler had lived for years in the same bachelor-style quarters in a housing complex overlooking the United Nations. His apartment was cheerless enough except for an expensive stereo hi-fi almost never played and a color television set without charm. The walls were covered with bookcases—novels and scientific works to ease the sleepless nights—but the place now had no attractions at all. After calling at the Academy of Medicine, he had stopped off at a medical bookstore with a list of texts on neurology and brain surgery. Then, following a gobbled dinner, he had returned to his flat with a set of notes. The Shroeder case was churning in his mind. He put through a call to Curtayne.

"Jim? Have you given any thought to a neurosurgeon for that matter in Lewiston?"

Curtayne sounded irritable. "Yes, I've given it thought. Is it that urgent at this hour?"

"Sorry, Jim. I didn't realize the time. I called because I found something peculiar at the medical library. Neither of these doctors is listed in the New York State Directory."

"What does that prove?" Curtayne asked. "They may be listed out of state. Or neglected it. I haven't been listed myself for years."

"It's got me thinking," Mahler said. "I really called because I need an informal peek at the medical history before the hospital knows what we have in mind. I know reams of ex-cops but none I'd put on this. Have you got someone to suggest?"

Curtayne said, "I'll see what I can do. But really, Bill!" He rang off.

Mahler was left in an empty room. He wandered fitfully and made a pot of coffee. Sleep was impossible. He got into pajamas and settled down to a text in neurology bought earlier in the day. The illustrations of the brain with all its pathologies had a horrid fascination and the text only less so. What special kind of men were they, he wondered, who could enter and mutilate the moist and dangerous convolutions of the human brain? When he looked up, it was almost dawn. He closed the book and stared at the sky.

The following day Curtayne suggested luncheon at an old Bavarian restaurant on Madison Avenue across the street. It was a busy eating place with friendly old waiters. Bratwurst and cabbage were in all their glory. Mahler pursued the last glob of gravy with a last morsel of black bread. Curtayne was full of congratulations on the new case. Most encouraging, he thought.

Mahler was not responsive. "I'm uneasy about this matter, Jim. I've handled medical issues before, plenty of them, but mostly straightforward criminal-law situations. Gunshot wounds. Stab wounds. Poison, maybe. Psychiatric defenses and all that. But this is a specialized field. I have no special expertise."

"You're a trial man," Curtayne said. "Work it up like any other case."

Mahler scratched his chin. "The usual issues won't throw me, I suppose. Who forgot the oxygen? Who dropped the patient? Was the needle sterilized? Who forgot to crossmatch the blood? Common-sense questions. But brain surgery has got to be something else. It's a mixture of physical and psychic, of brain and mind. Lots of uncertainties. Lots of conflicts of opinion. How can I be sure I'd be on solid ground?"

Curtayne was sipping tea with relish, subtly amused. He said curiously, "Is it so important to be sure?"

"It is to me," Mahler said. "I've never once walked into court with a lie. I've never misrepresented a fact. I've always worked with the truth. I did that all these years because I had a public interest in mind. I had nothing personal to gain or lose. And here I'm caught up in a matter where I can hurt, or even ruin, those doctors, perfect strangers, and on what? On the flimsiest damn story you can imagine. They say I'm a perfectionist. Maybe so, maybe not. But if this were a criminal matter, I'd throw it out. So why am I itching to get into it?"

Curtayne returned to his tea, puzzled. As a prosecutor, Mahler had been fair but seemingly hard and cold-blooded. What evoked these qualms was hard to imagine. "But this isn't a criminal trial, Billy boy, and nobody goes to jail. You can turn up the worst malpractice imaginable, and no medical license will ever be put into jeopardy. The malpractice action is the only remedy the patient has—and why shouldn't a moneyed corporation shell out? Come on, Bill. You agonize too much. Bad for the blood pressure." The genial smile brought no response. "That's what the investigation will prove. And speaking of that, I've got your investigator." He turned to the entrance and waved. A swarthy man with sharp features came over. Curtayne introduced Jean Baptiste Beaupré, a former client.

Beaupré sat and jerked a thumb at Curtayne. "Greatest lawyer in the world. Never sends a bill. I respect that," he said in a marked French accent. "My card, sir."

Mahler looked up from a business card of the Beaupré Investigation Bureau. "Executive Vice-President?"

"That's the thing these days," Beaupré said. He sat and launched into small talk about law-enforcement friends. People in the Treasury. People in narcotics. Federal people. Interpol people. An international fraternity known to few. A brandy came and went before he came to business. "Now, sir. You have this problem, I'm told. Something about this hospital in Lewiston?"

Mahler nodded. An air of cunning and a crooked grin appealed to him. "Do you know anything about hospitals?"

Beaupré repeated the question with surprise. "Do I know anything about hospitals? Sir, do you know Dr. Manfred Weissblatt of this big hospital in Massachusetts? A superb specialist?"

"No, I don't," Mahler said.

"Well, there you are," Beaupré said. "How can I be helpful?"

Mahler made known his wishes.

Beaupré cocked an eye. "Through the door? Or through the window?" he said obliquely. Mahler's blank expression was his answer. Beaupré burst into laughter. "Eh, sure? Why not? I've been in hospitals all my life. Cook, dishwasher, patient, plumber, security guard. Maybe some secretary's sister talks. Or a supplier knows the details. I tell you, sir, when it comes to details, I respect suppliers."

"I respect suppliers too," Mahler agreed. "What about lunch?"

Beaupré expressed regret. "*La foie, la foie,*" he sighed. "Now I should tell you I'm busy. I can give two days, no more. I charge two hundred dollars a day. Plus expenses."

Mahler said, "That's money."

Beaupré looked pleased. "Yes, isn't it? Well, think about it, then let me know. It's a great honor, sir." With a wink and a grin he was gone.

Mahler said, "Who's Dr. Manfred Weissblatt?"

"I have no idea," Curtayne said dryly, "and I wouldn't ask. Beaupré's a fantastic undercover man. Mentality of the underworld, but his record's clean. I know, because I got it cleaned up for him fifteen years ago. Very independent. His methods are complicated but you can't do better. Okay?" Mahler nodded warily. "Now you asked why you're doing this?" Curtayne went on. "I'll suggest an answer. You're looking for a big case. Only you want to be sure of the merits for your own moral reasons. Well, that's not for trial lawyers. In an uncertain world, who are we to be sure of anything? And why would we want to be?" Curtayne struck a match, chuckling. Mahler's strength as a trial lawyer, he reflected, was a blind tenacity that had carried him through the years. Once he had his teeth in a matter, he would not let go. It was also his weakness. His present uncertainties, considering his career and record, struck the old lawyer as perverted and inane, and no doubt they were.

"And of course, if you win, there's big money," he added in afterthought. "That's the rub. Who knows what lies in the hole in the bottom of the sea?"

"Lewiston! Fasten seat belts."

Mrs. Sarah van Loon smiled. "Give in, Mr. Mahler. We're coming down. No-smoking sign went on."

She began to make up her face, smoothing powder on a thin, high-bridged nose. She applied a lipstick and studied the mirror. "You must be coming here on the Shroeder matter," she said with a shrewd glance. "I hope it'll be a good visit for you."

A blank expression did not change. "Shroeder matter? What's that?"

"Oh, don't look so surprised," she said, snapping the compact closed. "Lewiston's a small city with only a handful of lawyers. It's been full of rumors for weeks about a trial lawyer coming from New York for that lawsuit against the city. When I see a text on epilepsy and the functional anatomy of the brain sticking from your briefcase and the *Syracuse Law Review* with that article on medical malpractice on your lap, it's a fair guess. I'd be delighted to be wrong," she concluded cryptically.

The plane dived through the murk, bumped to a stop, and taxied to the gate. They put on coats and left the plane through falling snow. A nervous Landowski was waiting in the terminal.

"Hello, Eugene," Sarah said cordially. "Mr. Mahler and I just had a nice talk. You couldn't have picked better trial counsel, I'm sure." She turned to Mahler and put out a firm hand. "I'll be interested to know how you make out," she said, smiling. "Feel free to call on me for anything you need. Eugene knows how to reach me. I'm at the Municipal Building. Good luck." A stocky young man who could only be a policeman in plainclothes led her out.

Mahler turned to Landowski. "Municipal Building? What's she doing there?" he asked.

Landowski recovered from a measure of surprise. "Oh, Sarah? She works for the city attorney. Trial Bureau. Steel hand in a velvet glove. Good lawyer. She'd be handling our case."

Mahler followed a slender back out of sight. "I thought she was an opera singer or actress or something. What happened to all your secrecy?"

Landowski looked embarrassed. "Small town, nothing's secret. We can stop off at the office first or go directly ahead. The clients are expecting us."

Mahler glanced at the busy scene. Huron County had come far since his last visit. The crowded airport now served two national and three regional airlines. An exhibit of machinery showed the stamp of industry on the region. Quite a change from the upstate college town of his memory. "I'd rather meet the clients. And on the way let's pass the hospital. Okay? I want to see what we're talking about."

"It's just a building. Later, you'll have dinner at my place. Polish meatballs. With a little vodka, they're out of this world."

"With vodka, what isn't?" Mahler grunted. "Another time, Gene. Thanks."

They drove along a road lined with gaunt black trees, sentinels of winter, into the bleak inner city. "Hold up," Mahler said at the approach to Lewiston Central Hospital. The red brick, eighty-year-old institution stood eight stories high over the surrounding slums. It was an enigma. Threatening. A mouse tower on the Rhine.

Landowski was talking a blue streak.

3

Frank Shroeder was at work in the cellar when the front doorbell rang. He switched off a hand drill and walked painfully to the stairs. "Manya? Answer the door?"

A child answered. "She's resting, Daddy."

"Answer it then." His voice was thick and hoarse, tinged with a slight guttural accent.

"Must I?"

"Yes, you must."

"All right." The child left, then came back. "Mr. Landowski's here with a man."

"Why here? Why not at his office?"

"Gee, I don't know."

"I'll be right up."

Shroeder clenched and unclenched his hands, knotted and distorted with arthritis. Every movement was agony. He could barely manage the tools of his small trade: furniture and upholstery repairs. Aspirin had no effect. He was never really without pain. He was a factory worker who could not keep a job and had fallen back on a home workshop. He worked slowly, taking three hours for an hour's work, but it was extra cash and he kept it up. He washed with pumice in hot water and changed to a jacket and went upstairs to the front parlor. The visitors, who had been talking in low tones, broke off as he entered.

"Where's the kid?" Shroeder asked.

"She went to call Manya." Landowski rose and introduced his companion.

Shroeder wrinkled his forehead. "There was a Mahler in our outfit at Bastogne. Joe Mahler. From Plattsburgh. Any relation?"

Mahler said, "Not that I know."

Landowski said, "Frank fought at Bastogne."

Shroeder sat and studied the stranger. "You look like you seen service, Mr. Mahler. Not that it matters. I just feel more confidence when a man's been in the service."

"That so?" Mahler said.

Landowski filled an uncertain moment. "Frank, Mr. Mahler's interested in Manya's case. He's a specialist in these matters."

"Everybody's a specialist," Shroeder said. "That's why Manya's like this. She did fine until the specialists got at her. Sorry, Mr. Mahler, but I've been through this. There was that lawyer from Rochester, Mr. Peckham, I believe. Then Mr. Vale from Binghamton and those other trial lawyers. Not one was interested. Even Gene here didn't want the case at first. Father Zator really made him take it. You heard of Father Zator?"

"I have by now," Mahler said.

Landowski looked annoyed. "Frank, change the record, huh? Nobody made me take it. I'm here because I want to help."

"Don't kid me, Gene," Shroeder said. "Father Zator plus a soft spot for Manya. Everybody's got a soft spot for Manya." He turned about, wincing as the thick neck muscles stiffened. "I understand you're basically a big criminal lawyer, Mr. Mahler? So what actually brings you to this zoo?"

Mahler said, "I'm here to see if you've got a case against the hospital."

"Why? Don't you think we got one?"

"Not so far you haven't. That's why I'm here."

"And if not?"

"We'll see if we can make one."

"What's that mean? Make a case?"

"Just what I say. It's like a chair, or desk, or piece of machinery. It has to be made."

"I see," Shroeder said. In fact, he saw nothing. He was confused by a brutal manner of amused cynicism. He felt at fault somehow. The lawyer's eyes were fixed on him, cold and disconcerting. "Or you don't play? Is that what you mean?"

"I don't play," Mahler said. He glanced at the street. It had been snowing heavily since his arrival at the Huron County Airport, but a warm southerly wind had melted the snow and the traffic had plowed the drifts to mush. It was dirty outside and gloomily overcast. Small winter birds were snatching suet from a feeding station on the porch. He turned back to Shroeder. "It takes too much work and time to fool around. Getting at the records. The medical proof. It's going to be especially tough."

"Why especially?"

Mahler stared at the man. How much could he explain? "You've had it explained. We need a doctor who can testify for us. What do you think are the chances?"

"I don't know."

"Then you'd better know. We also need a specialist who knows the local practice. Preferably in good standing in the local medical societies. Who won't be pressured or persuaded in some damned locker room not to testify. Huron County is a small county. How many specialists are even available, for Christ's sake? So I'll see how this looks, and if I bow out, you'll understand." He started a cigar. "Right now I want your view."

"My view? That's real funny." Shroeder sat blinking. "The doctors stick together and so do the lawyers. My view is: I don't trust any of 'em."

"Do you trust Gene Landowski here?"

Struggling against his thoughts, Shroeder studied the swollen painful knuckles. "I'm going along, mister, but nobody's kidding anybody," he said hoarsely. "Manya's got a hole in the head and my lawyer has got himself a healthy piece of the action. Have you got your piece too?"

"I will have."

"What piece will you want?"

"Enough to make me satisfied."

"Then we all know where we stand?"

"Except that you're riding on us, mister," Mahler said. "If we fall, you fall. Nothing for nobody. Too bad. Will you trust me?"

"Will you put meat and potatoes back on my table?"

"I'll try."

"Then what choice have I got? It was definitely malpractice. But how else can I prove it without a lawyer? I got no faith in this crap."

36

Mahler turned to Landowski with a grim smile. "Tough son of a bitch, isn't he?" He came back to Shroeder, amused. "Okay, but don't give us a hard time and we'll get along. What makes you think it was malpractice?"

Shroeder sat blinking, rubbing his knuckles nervously. He was startled at his own boldness, but something in Mahler's deep voice, in the humorous demanding manner had drawn him out. He was not ordinarily so frank. A gesture took in the room. "Take a look," he said. The small parlor had a nice touch. It might once have been attractive, but it was now unkempt. A cat's feeding plate was in a corner. A mop and pail stood at the doorway. A child's fingerprints smudged the walls. "You think this is Manya?" he said with burning feeling. "When we got married, she was immaculate clean. You could eat off her floor, in a sense. She sang. She was up and down the house all day, cleaning, sewing, laundry, the baby. You never ate better food. And with all that she took time to read and paint. She gave her life to those paintings."

Small watercolors, minutely painted primitives, were askew on the walls. The concepts were fanciful, expressive of Old World village life.

"I'm an old man. I'm almost twice her age," Shroeder went on in a suddenly trembling voice. "But her? How did I rate a princess like that? She was a lovely girl with a whole life ahead of her and not this—this *thing* they left me with. You ask was it malpractice? What else could it be? The thing speaks for itself."

"Yeah. It speaks for itself." Shroeder pondered, deep lines furrowed his brow. "She was all right before she went into that hospital. Sure, she had this tendency, but she was all right. I mean, nothing I couldn't handle, not in that sense. She was okay on medicine. Getting along. She came out changed. Why? What explanation did they give? What else but malpractice?"

"Exactly," Landowski said.

Mahler continued to smoke, studying the other man. A dogged, complaining note of discontent and resentment did not quite fit. "Even removing a wart can kill you. You must know that."

"Maybe they shouldn't remove the wart," Shroeder said. "If she'd have died, all right. That'd be better than this. She talks about killing herself—and what's that doing to the kid? The kid's being ruined in the process. My God, my God," he muttered. "How's it going to end? What's the way out for us?"

"What do you want?" Mahler asked.

Shroeder looked up. "Money, I guess. I want a good boarding school for the kid, away from her. And she needs help, a private psychiatrist maybe. I'd get it for her myself, but how can I? I'm a charity case. That's what she's got against me now—that I can't help her, and because I'm no man."

"What does that mean?"

"I'm ashamed to say."

"You'd better stop being ashamed."

Shroeder went silent. He grasped the mantel and stared at the grate. It was dirty, heaped with cold ashes and litter, but he saw nothing. "I mean I got a wife who's no wife," he said despondently. "At least not with me she's no wife. Gene here knows what I mean. And I got to take it, I'm told, because of her condition." He looked up with a grimace. "I swear, sometimes I could kill those doctor bastards. But how would that solve anything? If I was in the can, who'd take care of the family? The charities?" He shrugged. "Maybe if I got her fixed up I could go away from her. Florida, maybe. I'm entitled to live too."

"Does your wife know about this?" Mahler asked.

Shroeder turned a burning glance. "It's her own idea. 'Frank,' she says, 'get rid of me. I'm no good to you. I'm dirty, I'm worthless. I got a cancer growing in my head,' she says. 'Take the baby and put me away someplace!' She's full of that, Manya, and maybe she knows something, but without money what can I do? It's driving us both crazy. It goes on, and on, and on." He paused. "So what's to know? How we make out in bed? I tell you something. That day—that goddamned day—Mrs. Czeisler found her out cold on the floor, shaking, turning blue—I was praying for her to live. Now I ain't so sure it was a good idea." He turned to the wall. "Actually I blame myself. I helped those doctors talk her into the operation. Do you want to know about that?"

"Later, Frank. Right not I'd rather talk to your wife," Mahler said.

Shroeder went to the foyer and called, "Hey, Manya? What's keeping you?"

•   •   •

38

It had been one of her poor days. She had awakened late with a painful headache—a splitting pain that went through her skull from rear to front, boring a hole above her eyes. She had a fear of headache pains. She never knew when the demon might not seize her in a mighty fist, shake her to the depths, and his presence gave her dread. There was nothing she could do to shake off his presence. He lived with her forever. And so she lay quietly in bed, turning her thoughts in other directions, wondering at herself.

She was aware of the child's presence.

"Mr. Landowski is here," Betsy said. "With another man. He wants to know are you up to things."

"I think so," Manya said, smiling slightly. Betsy was seven, a pretty child with a pale clear complexion and long brown braids. She was adept at grown-up talk. Everyone now was either up to things or not up to things. It came from the television. "Why aren't you in school?" she said.

"I had a stomachache."

"Not again!"

"I can't help a stomachache," the child said. "You have them too. I heard you last night in the bathroom. Mummy, what's wrong?"

"Nothing's wrong. Go and play," Manya said. She closed her eyes, waiting for the child to leave, thinking of the night. Her mind had been a squirrel's cage, she recalled, letting the sequence reverberate again. Her thoughts had been clear. Morning shall pass, then noon and then evening. Evening meant getting dinner, but she could not make the effort, she knew that. Frank would take over. It was wrong to let him do her work but not to be helped. She thought of the house they lived in.

And another house in another land long ago.

A sensation was rising in her stomach, choking in agonizing constriction. The dream had followed her for nights, part of a series that was identical. In the dream a satanic figure loomed with menace. A sharp implement pointed, possibly an umbrella. No, not an umbrella. It was a goat's tool, black and uncircumcised, unrolling like a carnival whistle toward her legs. It had entered and searched. Oh, please, she had murmured in profound despondency. She had suddenly choked on plaster and dust. She had awakened on a pillow wet with froth . . .

"Manya!" Her husband was calling.

"Coming, Frank," she replied. She sat up, tousling her hair and yawning, throwing off the night.

The staircase creaked. A woman's tread was slow and painful. Mahler put aside a cigar and stood to attention. She appeared at the door and waited, clutching a shawl about her shoulders. She was a plump woman of middle years, blinking behind thick-lensed, gold-framed spectacles. Chestnut hair was cropped close. She was wearing a cotton house dress.

"Come on in," Shroeder said.

She entered with a limp. Every motion was painful, articulated, taken with care. "Manya, this is Mr. Mahler," Landowski said gently. "He's here to ask some questions. He's interested in you."

"How d'ye do?" she said submissively. She sat and turned to her husband. "Frank, I think some of that wine is left? Or maybe they'd like beer?"

A pleasant European guttural blended with the flat regional vowels. Her voice was clear and low and it showed intelligence. She was a surprise.

"Nothing, thanks. We won't stay long," Mahler said.

"Coffee, then? Frank can make coffee?"

"Nothing, please."

She turned to Landowski. "Is it all right to smoke, Gene?"

"If you like," Landowski said.

She glanced at Mahler. "I don't know if it makes a good impression. Which I'm expected to make now, I believe." She turned to her husband. "Frank? The cigarettes are on the mantel?"

"I wish you'd cut it out," Shroeder said.

She closed her eyes. "Does it make a difference?"

Shroeder addressed the lawyers. "It's like talking to a wall." Nevertheless he brought over a package of cigarettes. She filled an amber holder. Each motion seemed to call for concentration. The stranger was a threatening silhouette against the winter light of the window. "You must have a terrible impression of me," she said.

"Not at all." Mahler settled to a comfortable position. This would be something he had done over the years too often to count—feeling his way along a quagmire path of evasion and misdirection. He felt blank under the woman's glance, but that was not strange. That blankness, the trial lawyer's curse, would vanish with the first question. But these uncertainties were not evident in his manner. "Madam, I have only a few questions, not many. Then we'll see how it stands. Do you feel up to this?"

"I'm all right." She struck a match with care. "Have you seen my doctor yet? Dr. Gates?"

"Not yet."

"Ah." The cigarette got lit. "Well, it's the child I worry about. She's running wild and she can't stand me. I frighten her." A smooth round brow wrinkled in thought. "It's a terrible thing I'm doing to my family. Well, you'll have to excuse the mess. I had no warning you'd come here."

"That was the idea," Mahler said.

"Idea?"

"Mr. Mahler means he wanted to see for himself," Landowski said.

She turned about. "See what?"

Mahler said, "The situation. The room tells me things, Mrs. Shroeder. I see books in Polish, French, Russian, English. Good titles, but I don't see anything recent."

"She's not reading much," Landowski broke in.

Mahler turned. "Let her answer for herself, Gene."

"Okay. Suppose you answer for yourself, Manya," Landowski said. "Tell him what you are reading now."

Manya shook her head, coming to focus. "I'm not reading much since it happened. I've lost my languages. Even my Polish is gone. Maybe one day I'll forget how to read or talk in any language."

Mahler ignored the note of challenge. "By 'it' you mean your operation?"

"Yes. Obviously I mean that."

"You read nothing?"

"Well, children's books and comics, but that's the limit. Is that what you want to hear?"

Mahler was smoking his cigar, drawing easily. "I'm only asking questions, madam. I see those watercolors of village life. Poland, I suppose? Has that stopped?"

She shrugged. "That's how I remember that village, but I haven't done anything for years now."

Mahler went on. "And the piano? I see the keys are dirty. I'm told you sang in the choir before this happened. Did you ever study voice?"

A thin mouth twisted wryly. "It wasn't much of a voice. Good for Polish songs. And *lieder*. Father Zator was satisfied, I guess. It's a pity you missed him. He was here this morning for coffee—we have coffee once a week with Polish cheesecake. I still make cheesecake, it's one thing I won't give up. He wants me to come back to the choir. Have you talked to him?"

"Not yet. Maybe later," Mahler said.

"He's ready to go to court for me. He's a wonderful man. Without his help, I don't think I could keep going. And he never makes me ashamed." A sudden giggle was inappropriate. "I guess I give him reasons." The giggle ended in a sigh.

Mahler indicated a heap of song sheets on the shabby upright piano. "Could you manage to sing for me now?"

She shook her head.

"Why not?"

"I'm all doped up. Fortunately. If not, you'd see something."

"Still, you could try?"

"No. I can't remember the words."

"Can you remember the tunes?"

"I think so. I'm not sure."

"Words, no. Tunes, yes." Mahler turned to Shroeder. "Your daughter told us her mother sings to her. Is that so?"

Shroeder licked his mouth. "Sometimes. When she feels good."

Manya closed her eyes. "I can sing when I'm alone. Simple things. When I'm not upset. What are you after?"

"I'm just trying to get the picture." Mahler sank back in the deep chair, testing the sagging springs and webbing. "There's been talk about weakness in the right side. I saw you strike a match and light that cigarette. With your right hand."

She glanced at the hand in her lap. "It doesn't take much to strike a match."

"It does if you have brain damage."

Shroeder said, "It comes and goes, Mr. Mahler. She ain't faking, if that's your point."

"Faking? I never let that thought enter my mind," Mahler replied. The woman's fingernails were rimmed with grime, he saw, her dress was torn, stocking seams were twisted. "But sooner or later, somebody will want to know why it come and goes."

"Maybe it's psychological," Shroeder said.

"Maybe it's anything," Mahler said. "At this point I don't want loose opinions. I want to know what a court and jury would see for themselves—"

Shroeder interrupted. "The woman's no animal, for Christ's sake. She has good days and bad days. Who hasn't?" He turned in alarm to Landowski. "No, say! I don't like this. I don't like the way this is going. He sounds accusing."

"Frank—" Landowski began.

Shroeder burst out, "Don't you 'Frank' me, Gene! Whose side is he on? What's he accusing about?"

"Frank, please! It's all right!" Manya said. "Mr. Mahler wants to know where he stands. He doesn't want to hear it's psychological. He wants to relate it to the surgery. Isn't that so, Mr. Mahler?"

Shroeder's alarm subsided. "Well, okay, in that sense. But what the hell? What's going on in there?"

"Nothing's going on." Mahler turned to the woman. "Are you up to talking?"

A shoulder was lifted. "What else would you like to know? I'm not totally deteriorated yet, but my attention span is limited. I'm forgetful. I can read but not much, and some areas are affected. I can't watch television at all. Perhaps it's a blessing in disguise." A mechanical smile formed. "I have a splitting headache that never leaves me. I have a scar. I feel unreal. Is that what you want to hear?" The smile was watchful, intent on his response.

"What about your spells?"

"Oh, those? There, you see. I forgot to mention them."

"So you did. What about their frequency?"

She held the cigarette holder European style, pinched between thumb and forefinger, smoking thoughtfully. "Ask Dr. Gates. She has my history."

"More frequent since the operation!" Shroeder broke in. "Manya, huh? Tell the man, what I mean. What's this horsing?"

The smile appeared. "It depends on whether I stick to the medication, Mr. Mahler. I'm told that the spells come in clusters now, that I'm worse off since the surgery, but I can't be sure."

"How do you know you've had an attack?"

Manya thought. "Well, once or twice I've noticed that the clock has jumped five or ten minutes or more. Or that my food has gone cold. I'm not sure."

Mahler glanced at the others. "What makes you so uncertain?"

"Is it bad for the case to be uncertain?"

"It depends why."

"I'm confused," she said. "Now they say these might be hysterical symptoms. But I can't believe that."

"What do you think they are?"

"I don't know what to think anymore. Hysterics don't wet themselves."

"And you wet yourself?"

Manya went silent. Landowski broke in. "She's embarrassed, Bill. Manya, just answer the question. Mr. Mahler's here to help you."

She said, "Of course it's embarrassing. That's why I don't like to leave the house."

"Quite a diagnosis," Mahler said. "You seem to know the subject quite well."

A touch of color showed on the fattish pallid cheeks. "Well, I should. After all the doctors I've seen. God! The offices I've sat in! I can't get through the day. I have no feeling for anything, and that's a terrible punishment from God. Not to feel."

"Do you feel that God is punishing you?"

Manya looked about with wonder. A garish portrait of the Sacred Heart caught her eye. "I can only believe that all things, the good, the evil, come from God. Where else can they come from? Gene! You go to church. Don't you agree?"

"Yes, sure," Landowski said.

"So we're all good Catholics! So what?" Shroeder said heavily. "What are we getting at in there?"

She touched the side of her head. "Mr. Mahler, tell me what you want and I'll say it."

Mahler said, "Madam, will you stop this game?"

"Game?"

"That you're responding to my wishes. You just described a serious emotional state. What would you call it?"

Her eyes lowered to the patch of threadbare carpet. Her voice was inaudible. Mahler repeated the question. "I get depressed," she said in a low voice. "Or excited. I don't know which is worse. I feel confused and numb. I cry at nothing. I have dreams and I can't move. I'm no good to my husband, no good to my child. We live like pigs and I can't get myself to lift a finger. I smile but I feel dead. Didn't Gene tell you all this?"

Mahler waited a moment. "When did this depression begin?"

"After the operation," Landowski interjected.

"Gene, please!" Mahler came back to the woman, annoyed. "Is that right, madam?"

She nodded. "I wanted to kill myself."

It was the dreariness, the matter-of-fact manner that gave Mahler a jolt. He felt the pain of desperation. He said, "Did you make an attempt?"

Shroeder answered for her. "No, she didn't. She talked about it."

Mahler sank deeper in the chair, considering the moment. Something was beginning to appear. "Madam, why do you feel depressed?"

"I'm not sure. You really should ask my doctor. Are you planning to?"

"I'm asking you."

A fretful expression appeared. "I don't know why I'm depressed. That's part of the problem."

"Why do you *think* you're depressed?"

"I'd prefer not to discuss it."

"I think you'd better," Mahler said.

She drew a shuddering breath. "Frank will kill me for saying this," she said reluctantly. "It's this thing in my head, I guess."

Shroeder burst out. "Jesus, Manya! You don't have anything there. You were grossly misinformed."

"Frank, please! Dr. Tatum told me the truth. To give him credit, he's the only one who ever did. I've got a cancer in my head." Her eyes bulged, strained beyond endurance.

Mahler spent a moment thinking. "You're sure he told you that? It's quite important."

"It's not something I'd forget."

"Tell me about it."

She stared dully. Well, Dr. Tatum had been more than good, she said hesitantly. He had seen her frequently. His manner had been grave but kind. He had explored her history in detail. He had discussed her family life, her husband, the little girl, and her childhood in Europe with warmth and sympathy. He had built a good relationship, and she had answered all questions about her medical condition. For the first time, she gained insight and hope of recovery and only gradually saw that he was coaxing her to consent to certain tests. He had been supportive through those tests—drugs, electrical measurements, a painful spinal tap, dye injected into a neck artery, X rays taken in a drafty, cold basement room. She recalled a departmental conference with residents and interns and attending physicians. Dr. Bellinger, chief of neurology, had presided. Everyone had asked questions before she was returned to her room. It had not been unpleasant. On the day Tatum brought the results, his manner had been ominously gentle. He had offered a cigarette before coming to the point. Tests confirmed a condition in her brain—most likely, and he was so convinced, malignant. She looked aside as the moment was recalled. Tears filled her eyes. "Sorry," she said drearily. "I'm so sorry I'm a baby. Excuse me."

The silence was uncomfortable.

Shroeder patted her shoulder. "It's okay, Manya," he said roughly. "Just take it easy."

Mahler leaned forward in his chair, staring now with intensity. "What makes you so sure you have this condition?"

"Because I cannot help it," she said. "I don't care what you say now, I know it was the truth. Otherwise, why did they operate?" She turned to her husband. "Frank, wasn't that what you said too? That the doctors have to know what they're doing? To trust them?"

"God forgive me," Shroeder said.

Mahler said, "Then you both gave consent to operate?"

Shroeder turned about, frowning with alarm. "What kind of consent? A doctor misleads? Butchers? Leaves her with this crazy phobia? What did we know? How good were we informed?"

Mahler shot a hard glance at Landowski. Shroeder had touched on an important legal doctrine, the doctrine of informed consent. Unless the patient was clearly informed of the risks, her consent to surgery would not be valid. He came back to the woman. "You say you went along because you were told you had cancer? Otherwise you'd have refused surgery?"

"Yes."

"Very precise position," Mahler said.

Manya glanced at Landowski, who was now staring at the ceiling. She turned back to Mahler. "Do you think we're lying?"

"Not at all. If so, I'd stop here." Mahler sat scowling, chewing a cold cigar. He was aware of muddy pallor, something resentful in the bulging green eyes. "On the other hand, I'm not here to put words into your mouth. Aside from everything else, you couldn't sustain it. One slip and the other side would be at you like sharks."

"Don't be angry with me," she said.

"I'm not angry," Mahler said. He put a series of questions, seemingly aimless, directed at details of her daily life. It was not a happy household. Finally he said, "All right. How do you feel about those doctors now?"

"Is that important?"

"Certainly it's important. We're not collecting a grocery bill." She turned aside, knitting her brows. "I don't know what to feel." She paused as her thoughts turned inward. "I was a baby in Poland in the war. I saw things you wouldn't believe. To this day I can't bear to think what it was like. People were vile, rotten. Who could you trust? I always thought, when things got worst, if I could only find one man, one solitary man to believe in, I could make it, as they say. I thought . . ." She swallowed. "Then Dr. Tatum came along when everybody else gave me up. I was so sick and he was so kind, so warm and concerned in me as a human being, I thought he was that man. I trusted him with my life." She was staring now at a past vision. "Now they say he lied to me—and I've got to believe that too. I'm disillusioned. How can I go on?"

Mahler glanced at the picture of the Sacred Heart. "You had a better man to believe in than that," he said.

Manya turned to the picture. A ghost of a smile appeared,

then vanished. "I don't matter. I wouldn't lift a finger for myself, but I owe something to my family. Frank is a rock, a wonderful man, and I'm destroying him. I'm his misfortune—" She broke off. "It's nothing I want, but what's my choice? I'll do anything Frank says." She hesitated. "Suppose Dr. Tatum was right about my condition? Would it be right to sue?"

Mahler stared somberly at the woman. It was not a question he was prepared to answer. "Why do you ask?"

"Because I still must decide and I'm confused." She clasped her hands nervously. "Will you tell me what to do?"

"Madam, that's what I'm trying to find out," Mahler said. He slapped his knees and stood. "I think that's all for now. Gene, let's go."

Shroeder was taken aback. "Hey, what's the word, Mr. Mahler?" he exclaimed. "Will you take the case? Don't let the woman hang."

Mahler glanced at the woman, then at the others, and the lines of his face cut deeper than ever. "We'll let you know soon enough. You might tell the neighbors not to answer questions if investigators come around."

"I don't get this," Shroeder said.

"I'll see you out," Manya said. She followed Mahler to the outer hall. Snow was drifting under the sill to the tiled floor. Boots and galoshes had a wet smell. She shivered and stood close. She clasped his hands to her breasts.

"Can I trust you?" she said urgently. "Will you tell me the truth? Will you? Will you?" Her clutch tightened, her breasts rose, her breath was noisy. The dry eyes were urgent and desperate.

"Let me look into this," Mahler said. "Then we'll talk about it, eh? Gene? Coming?"

The lawyers drew up their collars and stepped out into the falling snow.

She returned to the dank parlor. The smell of gas and dust was overpowering. She could not meet her husband's stare.

"I thought Father Zator was the one solitary man," Shroeder said.

A grimace of distaste appeared. "Father Zator!" she said.

"Better take your medicine before you forget. I left it on the sink."

She closed her eyes. "I won't forget."

"What a farce!" he said despondently, and went back to his cellar.

A wind from Canada was piling drifts high and immobilizing traffic. The radio announced that the airport was closed down for the night. It meant a change of plans, but Mahler took it philosophically enough. He refused a renewed invitation to stay the night with the Landowskis—the kids were down with colds—and put off a conference till morning. He was distinctly annoyed.

They drove along streets of shabby storefronts and commercial buildings in decay. FOR SALE signs were everywhere. Pedestrians, trudging through the snow, were few. Center City, Anywhere, U.S.A., Mahler thought. He was surprised at the changes which had overwhelmed the city. They came to a stop at the oldest and best hotel in the city.

Landowski sat back with pressed lips, staring at the murk. Except for the whoosh and thump of wiping blades, they were in silence. "Okay, Bill. What's on your mind?"

Mahler scowled at slate-colored clouds, laden with snow, sweeping over the dreary plaza. "Informed consent! Those symptoms! What the hell were you running there? A seminar? Where'd they get all that crap?"

"You can't stop clients from picking up the lingo. They've talked about nothing else for months. What d'ye expect?" Landowski switched off the motor. "You don't think I coached them?"

"I don't think anything," Mahler said.

Landowski was silent. "All right, what do you think of the case so far?"

"What case? I'm still looking for the malpractice—which, if at all, I'll have to get from the records." Mahler paused, plucking a heavy lower lip. His breath was fogging the windshield. "Look, Gene. I've got to be on solid ground. Any hint of monkeyshines and I want no part of this birthday cake. Okay?"

Landowski was stung but, facing a hard stare, he shrugged. "All right," he said sullenly. "What brought this on, Bill?"

Mahler looked off. A snowplow crunched past, forming a path for the slow-moving traffic. Dreary world, he thought. "I feel uneasy. I don't know why." He got out in the snow and watched Landowski drive off.

4

The historic Lewiston House had seen its day. Marble pillars still soared to a high ceiling in a lobby decorated with frescoes of the lawgiver Hiawatha presiding over the councils of the Six Nations —witness to that perfect democracy practiced by preliterates and savages on the dubious principle of deference to age and wisdom. Ghosts of drummers stalked the halls, spit boxes were gone, the glory had departed. A spry clerk with gold teeth could let him have the Governor Cleveland Suite overlooking Oneonta Avenue. There were no messages.

"Front!"

A studious-looking, black youth took Mahler's traveling case and led him to the elevator. He wore dark, enigmatic glasses. A maroon jacket bore his name.

Mahler glanced at the embroidery. "Famous name, Chaka," he said.

"You've heard of Chaka?" the youth said.

"Why sure. Greatest military mind after Alexander the Great. Great conqueror, Chaka. Killed a million people."

"A million people? I never heard of that."

"Killed the warriors and took the women and children into the tribe. That's what formed the Zulu nation. Didn't you know?"

The youth considered the information. "Killed a million people? He must have had his reasons."

The elevator rose slowly, groaning. High above a hoist was rattling in the shaft. Chaka glanced at his passenger. He was bursting to talk. "I'm not really a bellhop," he said.

"I can see that," Mahler said.

"This is temporary," Chaka said. "My real aim is Empire." Empire Corporation, a local conglomerate, made everything from steel girders to greeting cards. "I could get a job there in personnel tomorrow with all the benefits—salary, pension, sick leave, holidays, bowling team, whatnot—but no future. The big boys have it all sewed up. I wouldn't be satisfied."

"What job would you want?" Mahler asked.

"The board of directors at least. But would the big boys stand for that? It's ridiculous to try."

"The answer is to start your own business," Mahler said. "Manufacture a better automobile, for example. I think you passed my floor."

"This way," Chaka said, opening a door. He turned knobs, opened valves, fiddled with television, hung up clothes, and departed for a bottle of whiskey and a bucket of ice. The door closed and Mahler was alone. The overheated suite was a remembered thing. Radiators were painted brown. "The Stag at Eve" looked over a lumpy double bed. A chipped porcelain tub, rust down the center, stood on talon legs in a tiled bathroom. Oak doors varnished black belonged to another age. The scenic wallpaper went back to Governor Grover Cleveland. A notice advised that writing paper, not stinted by the management, could be had on special request. He stretched every muscle and shivered. Every bone was aching from the Shroeder interview and that, he thought, was quite unexpected. He had not been conscious of strain till now.

"Christ," he said wearily. He strode to the window, sunk in thought. Storefronts below were aglow in the darkening street. The interview had not been entirely unsatisfactory, he thought. Manya Shroeder had been the surprise, apathetic but soft-spoken and intelligent, and possibly, as Landowski had promised, a good witness. That last episode in the vestibule . . .

Well, another time for that. He was in motion and there were things to do.

He jiggled the telephone.

An elderly cracked voice answered. "Ayeh?"

"There's no dial."

"Come again?"

"I'm programmed. I dial eight for long distance. Nine for local. I'm not comfortable when I'm monitored."

"Funny feller. What's your order?"

"Let's start with long distance."

A call went through to New York. Curtayne got on the line, sounding pleased with the activity. He said, "How's it going?"

"I'm not sure." Mahler described the interview at the Shroeder home. Curtayne grunted with understanding. Mahler said, "They had no right to tell her she had cancer—hitting her like that in a weakened state."

"Are you sure that happened?" Curtayne asked. "It's not the way doctors talk."

Mahler replied obliquely. "The woman would impress a jury, I think. The husband supports her story."

Somewhere between the cities lightning flashed and the line crackled with static. A bacon-frying sound brought Curtayne back. "Maybe they had to get her to accept surgery? Doctors have different ideas how to break that kind of news. You'll have to find out the practice."

Mahler put a gaudy desk calendar aside with a careful motion. "Sure, and maybe they were hungry for cases. That happens. Weren't you once hungry for cases?"

Curtayne's voice dropped. "That goes beyond malpractice. That almost raises a question of bad faith."

"So?"

A note of worry intruded. "So before I'd impute bad faith, I'd be damned sure of my ground. It could be a two-edged sword." There was heavy breathing. "What are you getting at, Billy boy?"

"I'm not getting at anything," Mahler said. "Except that maybe we're onto something there." He waited for comment, but there was none. "Well, let's hold that for now. How are you coming with those experts?"

"I called the medical examiner, but he's on vacation. I'll have to check some other leads." Curtayne seemed disapproving and after touching upon other office matters hung up. Mahler was left suspended, irritated. Something was on his mind to be done. What was it?

A tap on the door interrupted. Chaka entered, balancing a tray of whiskey and setups and change. "Sipping whiskey," he announced. "Where does it go?"

"Oh, anyplace. Side table's good." Mahler took off his jacket and sat on the horsehair sofa. "Can you raise the window, please?"

"Can do." Chaka complied. "Anything else, man?"

"No, not really. Oh, say! Can I get a taxi in this snow? I've got to see a doctor who works at that big hospital in Front Street. What's its name?"

Nostrils flared with scorn. "Old Central?"

"Yeah, that's it. Lewiston Central. Know anything about it?"

"Who don't? I'm there in O.P.C. myself twice a month for shots."

Mahler looked interested. "Shots? What kind?"

"Some kind of allergy. I got this new disease. B.P.P." Chaka grinned. "Benign paroxysmal peritonitis. Nobody had it until recently. I'm sensitive. I blow up if they're not careful."

"Has that happened to you?"

"Blow up like a frog every last time."

"Who's responsible for that?"

"This guy in O.P.C. They stick anything into you. Why, man?"

"Oh, nothing. I just wonder what kind of place it is."

"What kind of place?" Chaka repeated. "Oh, man! It's no kind of place. It's our biggest disgrace. They treat people like dogs. When my aunt had her last baby, she was in O.B. for sixteen hours with these unbearable pains screaming her head off. Sixteen hours, and not a doctor came except to curse her and the other women out. Those residents were telling the nurses to give any damned medication they pleased because they were going off for the weekend and couldn't bother to sit around. The brutality was too much. Everybody knows those conditions."

"Is it really that bad?"

"Well, man! There was that girl who died because the nurses wouldn't call the doctor after midnight even after she was blue and feverish. The whole community knew that story. Who cared? Nobody cared! It's a racist institution."

"Racist? Don't they hire black people?"

"They overhire them."

"Isn't that good?"

"Yeah, but for what? They get the dregs of the jobs. Cleaning people, porters, clerks, messengers, man! Yeah, and nurses! But what are nurses? Menials. Very subordinated."

Mahler plucked a shred of tobacco from his mouth. "No black doctors?" he asked casually.

"Some, but how many? And for how long? They had a few, but the big boys got rid of them." A sniff expressed scorn.

Mahler was innocence itself. "Oh? What kind of doctors were they?"

"Brain men," Chaka said with satisfaction. "Doc Bellinger . . ." He halted. "Man, you heard of Doc Bellinger? Bellinger Institute of Third World Therapy?"

Mahler looked vague.

Chaka went falsetto. "Damn, man! Doc Bellinger is famous. He was written up in the media. When he left town, he had an I.Q. of a hundred and ninety-six, which is two points higher than Einstein. And you never heard of him?"

"I'm trying to think," Mahler said.

Chaka shook his head. "Well, there you are! Never heard of Doc Bellinger."

"What does that mean? This country's got several hundred thousand doctors. How many can you name?"

"That is different!" Chaka said loftily. "And irrelevant. Bellinger stood for something. He came here to change the balance. We are the unrepresented consumers of medical services, man, and we are excluded entirely from the decision-making process. We have got a disproportionate share of the sick and only two percent of the doctors of this country. That is serious. That definitely has got to change. We need more doctors—but not just any doctors. We need people sensitive to the needs and responsive to the community. And we need them today. Not tomorrow, today. And now! We cannot wait. And we will have them by all means necessary at our disposal. We are tired of being powerless."

"Yeah, I see that," Mahler said, "but I'm bothered by one small point. Doesn't it take time to train a doctor?"

"Naturally. What has that got to do with it?"

"I'm just asking."

"We have waited long enough. We're tired of excuses. Who says black doctors would be worse than those we get right now at Old Central? It's the sinkhole of the world."

Mahler loosened his tie and sprawled on the sofa. "In other

words," he said thoughtfully, "the hospital has a bad reputation in the community?"

"Bad? Bad?" The youth's arms went akimbo. "Man, you cannot believe how bad. People are terrified to go there. They'd rather die than call the ambulance. It's no secret, man. If you don't believe me, ask the nearest child. Doc Bellinger tried to end the genocide, but what happened? The big boys claimed the community was unprepared for the problems. He got eliminated by the structure—as though there's some mystery about running a hospital. Old Central's back where it was." He shifted to another leg. "Well, everything's in order—TV, radiator, setups. Anything else, man?"

Mahler looked up quizzically. "If you needed brain surgery, would you let—what's his name? Bellinger?—do the job?"

Chaka said, "Why would I want brain surgery? That's ridiculous."

"I mean—if!"

"I still wouldn't want it."

"I mean, just suppose. You're lying there. Here comes this man who wants to open your head and poke around. Crunch. Crack. R-r-r! Would you let him?"

"I'll tell you, man. If Dr. Rabinowitz would recommend him as a top man in his specialty, and if Dr. D'Angelo would concur, yes, I'd let him do the job. Provided I was in dire need of the operation and had no way out. I don't see the relevance."

"Suppose he's not a top man?"

"I find that demeaning," Chaka said with limpid dignity. "If I can't have the best, I'd pass up brain surgery. It's simple as that."

"I suppose it is," Mahler said after a moment. "Well, just get me a cab. I've learned something. And keep the change—man."

Chaka pocketed the bill expertly. "Call me anytime, man," he said, and left, whistling.

Mahler laughed and unpacked and changed from a striped shirt to white broadcloth and subdued red necktie, to match his dark suit. He shaved and patted on a special cologne water, Caswell-Massey Jockey Club, and felt its refreshment. He was thinking only of the case. The field of malpractice was larger than he had remembered. During his years away from civil practice, a body of law had been growing in fifty state systems and the fed-

—

eral system as well, but that would be no difficulty. Another week in the library would give a strong retentive mind all the furniture it needed. It was the medical aspect—the vast tangle of texts and opinion and practice that remained ahead—that would hold the uncertainties. Yet something was beginning to emerge, a sense of direction that would lead through uncharted lands. Manya Shroeder. He found himself thinking of the plump white face in the vestibule, the clutching hands drawing him to doughy breasts, the desperation painful to recall that carried conviction. He suddenly felt optimistic and good-humored and in command. It was important to stay in motion, to press forward, to encounter people without preconception, to let fact command theory, to look for the lucky break.

A taxi was waiting in the falling snow.

5

There was a tap.

"Come in, dear."

Edna Crooms, a black woman in a nurse's uniform, entered. "That's the load, Doctor," she said cheerfully. "What about one for the road?"

Jane—Dr. Jane Gates—looked up with a frown. She was a broad-shouldered woman with short hair and heavy, seamed features. She was writing up forms, having spent the afternoon getting rid of patients.

"Not until the last patient's gone," she said. "Isn't someone still out there?"

"Just that lawyer," the nurse said.

Jane glanced longingly at a metal cabinet with its supply of good stock and shook her head. "I'll have to see him. Send him in." She resumed writing.

Mahler had waited in the outer office while a procession of patients—a college girl facing abortion, a case of juvenile VD, a high school couple seeking premarital advice—were disposed of. On the signal he entered the inner room. It was a large doctor's office in what had once been an old-fashioned sprawling mansion in the fashionable section of town. He sat and cleared his throat.

"Excuse me. Forms," she said, writing.

"D. and C.?" Mahler said.

She looked up, knitting thick brows. "You saw the Shroeders," she said. It was a statement of fact, not a question, and anything but friendly. A telephone interrupted. Mahler's eyes wandered.

She followed his glance and without losing the thread covered a fat journal, *Medical Economics*, with a slender periodical, *Community Medicine*. "I'll have to ask my accountant," she said, and hung up.

"How's the market?" Mahler asked.

She continued to write, paying no attention to the man seated across the desk. But she was aware of him. A black briefcase rested on his knees, gripped by strong hands. One had to notice the broken knuckles with their sprouts of black hair.

Mahler said, "Can I get your attention?"

"I'll be right with you," she murmured.

"Doctor!" he said sharply.

She looked up unwillingly. Mahler had opened the briefcase. He took out a diary and thumbed to a page. "Doctor, my file tells me that on three separate dates you declined to talk to Landowski on this matter. On two later dates, you refused to take my calls from New York City. On a third, your nurse promised to have you call me back. I never got that call. Calls went to the hospital, the People's Clinic, and sundry community organizations, without result. I now find myself cold, tired, without dinner, annoyed." He closed the notebook. "I'm sure you know why I'm here."

She folded her arms in support of Valkyrie breasts. It was impossible to tell her thoughts. "I'm afraid there's nothing to discuss," she said in a deep male voice.

Mahler took out a pen. "In that case, I'll need the correct spelling of your name?" He waited. "No answer? Too bad. I'd rather have had a friendly talk. Just call me a taxi." He started to leave.

"One moment, Mahler! What do you want that for?"

He turned. "Because I don't want to have to advise the court that a doctor in this city refused to tell me how to spell her name."

The telephone again interrupted and was snatched up. "Yes?" She listened intently. "My lawyer won't dream of it!" she rasped. She replaced the telephone. "Advise the court? How?" she said dangerously.

"There's a procedure. Be sure of that," he replied. "Now can we chat?"

She thought a moment. "Well, I have a moment. Take a seat," she said reluctantly. She lit a cigarette and sat back with an air of reserve. "Will you be in town long?"

"Not longer than necessary."

"That's informative."

"Yes. Isn't it?"

The seamed eyes were suspicious. "Well—can I get you a drink?"

Tough broad, he decided, not easily impressed—but straight, direct. He said, "No, thanks. I just want to chat. I assume you know what Landowski has in mind. Why are you avoiding him?"

"I'm not sure he's competent to understand this matter."

Mahler grunted. "I'm relieved to hear that. He had some notion that you're trying to protect the surgeons. Ridiculous, of course." A smile appeared but his eyes were hard. "I'm not incompetent. Do you mind answering a few questions?"

"It depends on the questions, I imagine. Is there anything specific?"

Mahler started a cigar. Every motion was deliberate from the snipped tip to the final strong draw. The currents in the room were strong.

"Specific? No-o. Not yet. Later maybe, after I've seen the records. Just now I'd like your general impressions." He blew a plume of smoke at a photograph of a graduating class of a medical school—owlish young men and an oversized young woman in the center. "I was impressed by Mrs. Shroeder as a witness. Severe physical and emotional damage, that's obvious. Whether it's actionable remains to be seen."

"Everybody calls her Manya," Dr. Gates said.

"Yes, Manya. Manya," Mahler repeated, phrasing the name. There was no point in more delay, he thought. "Let's see now? What do you think of that hospital?"

"Really, Mahler!" she snorted. "You can't want me to answer that. I might be misquoted."

Mahler accepted this logic. "I see. Well, a hospital that's always in danger of losing its accreditation, that's constantly warned of sloppy record keeping, that can't withstand medical audit, that struggles to attract interns, that's staffed with foreign residents and dubious attendings, whose nurses scare the population, whose rate of infection is rising, which carelessly substitutes antibiotics for old-fashioned sterile conditions, where unnecessary surgery is rampant—a hospital that's a center of community strife and dissatisfaction, one where politics and petty rackets flourish—yes, it would probably be the subject of misquotations. I see your point."

"Quite a catalog," she said. "How did you get it together?"

"I drove past and sniffed the air," Mahler said. "You don't take it personally?"

"Personally?" She laughed harshly. "As far as I'm concerned, you can take them for every cent the city's got. If you really want dirt, put a microphone in the locker room. Just leave me out of it."

Mahler smiled. "What's your position there? Come on, now, there's no reason not to answer that."

She seemed torn. "I'm an associate attending in medicine," she said. "It means I'm hired to make teaching rounds two days a week. I give two afternoons to the clinic. There's no special attachment, if that's what you're driving at."

"But you know how the hospital functions?"

"In some areas, yes. In others, not too well."

"I see. Can we talk about the doctors? I'll pass over the anesthetist. . . ."

"Joe Ling?" Her mouth opened. "You're not after Joe?"

"Not right now, no. Should I be?"

"I hope not, because he's gone back to Korea. Part of our terrible turnover. Why would you mention him?"

"Theoretically everyone who took part in the surgery might be liable, even nurses. It depends what turns up. But I'm not 'after' anyone. I'm simply trying to get some light on this episode, eh?" It was a note of warning, a harbinger of something to come, but the effect, if any, was not evident in the unusually good-looking hazel eyes. "How well did you know the surgeons?"

She said, "Not well at all."

"Oh? But you were on the same staff?" he suggested.

"That meant nothing. We were in different departments. We met at staff meetings—which I rarely attend. I'm not interested in the politics."

"Didn't you know them outside the hospital? Community medicine. Poverty projects. I understand a lot of that was going on."

"Yes, of course. Ghetto medicine's been our concern. Yes, I knew them." She flushed.

"But you did meet socially?"

60

She said restlessly, "I don't think I want to discuss them without their consent."

Mahler took an easier position. "What's your impression of Bellinger?"

She studied her cigarette. "They say he's brilliant. As far as I know, he did good work. I believe he came here with high credentials. I understand he had a post in Montreal Neurological. He knew his way around the big foundations. I believe he brought in four or five big grants to study how to bring extended care to the public. He started a teaching program. That's about all I know."

"Where could I find out more?"

"Try Dr. Grimes," she said with a grim smile. "He's administrator of the hospital."

"In time, in time," Mahler replied. "What about the resident, Tatum? Manya seemed taken up with him."

"Yes, he made an impression, I suppose. I can tell you he was conscientious. More than conscientious. He took over a great deal of responsibility for the service when Bellinger was off on other things."

"Took over for the chief of service? Can a resident do that?"

"Under supervision and direction? That's what the chief resident does. Why not?"

"I'm trying to learn." Mahler smoked thoughtfully. "What sort of personalities were they?"

"Is that important?"

"Maybe not, but I'm trying to weigh probabilities. Personality always tells a lot. I already picture a high-flying operator, more politician than doctor, with an average drudge of an assistant. Conscientious, you say, but under pressure to get ahead in the field. Am I close?"

She stared. "I didn't say any of that."

"No, you didn't. Will you say I'm wrong?"

She studied her hands a long moment. Then reluctantly: "Well, no. Bellinger was ambitious, but superficial, I thought. Great drive to get his own way. Tatum was odd and unpleasant. Great capacity to antagonize. I'm sure he did his best for all his patients. But these are only impressions. That's all I have to say."

"You mean you'd rather not talk against them?"

"I mean I don't want to be involved. But it is certainly not for personal reasons, if that's your point."

"Is that my point?" He drew on the cigar, staring through blue smoke. The characterizations could not be more sketchy, he thought, but that too was not unexpected. One went lightly at this business. There'd be other occasions. "By the by, did anyone tell you not to discuss this matter with me?"

"Not at all!" she said sharply. "And you have no reason to imply it." She halted. "Well, I *did* have a chat with Dr. Grimes. He called to ask whether I knew what the Shroeders were up to. He'd caught the rumor of your lawsuit. Your friend Landowski has been subtle as a herd of elephants, you know? The whole city's perfectly aware why you're here."

Mahler shrugged. "What did you tell Dr. Grimes?"

"Really . . ." She caught herself. "I told him I'd heard nothing of it—which wasn't entirely truthful. He was too sensible to pursue the matter, except to ask to be kept informed of any legal developments."

"Did you agree to that?"

She glanced at the clock. "Mr. Mahler. Can't we make this short?"

He was well answered, Mahler thought. So everyone was on notice. It was useful information. "All right. I'm told you were against the operation. Why? Fill me in on that and I'll leave now." It was now his courtroom manner, harsh and peremptory.

The stare held a long moment. "I don't think I can discuss hospital business," she said uneasily.

Mahler studied the heavy features. "Well. Perhaps you're right." He closed the briefcase and stood. "Let's call it a night. Obviously you don't want to talk against these doctors—and that's understandable. Okay! We'll meet again—at our office, not here. Or in court. You'll be under oath, if that's what you prefer. I'd rather have a stenographer present. If you'll get me that taxi now, I'll get back to the hotel." He nodded and started off.

"No, wait a moment!" She motioned him back and considered the matter with care. "Look here, Mahler, I had no responsibility for this. Yes, I was against surgery. I want that clear. It's been my position all along. But that doesn't mean I approve of what you're doing. I think this is essentially a medical question."

"To be decided by the medical profession?"

"Yes."

Mahler sat, pursing his mouth. "Might be something there," he said. "Some impartial medical board to receive complaints, make adequate awards, regardless of professional ties, all the rest of that? Have you got such a committee in this county?"

"It's under consideration."

"Good. Then someday it can meet. And maybe it'll be different from every other medical board in the country. Meanwhile, we have a legal problem, haven't we?"

To this there was no reply. A clock was striking—long, slow reverberations of a grandfather's clock at the entrance, reminder that she lived in that house. A second clock responded with a silver chime. She said, "I'm not paid to give opinions, or even information, to any lawyer who barges in. And don't give me law on that because good medical practice comes first."

"Fair enough," Mahler agreed. "But isn't Mrs. Shroeder still your patient?"

"Yes. But that's all she is. She went against my advice. I'm out of any responsibility here."

Mahler waited. "I only want background. Can you tell me when her seizures first began, for example? Or is there a reason not to tell me?"

"Of course not, but I don't have the records. Dr. Schlomm told me—when he turned over the case—as far as he knew they began when she arrived in Lewiston to marry Frank. He noted blacking-out episodes. Fugue states. Vagueness. Going off. And mild, fairly infrequent seizures . . ."

Mahler relaxed imperceptibly. A small trickle in the dam had begun. The next would be easier. She ran a finger through her hair—short-cropped, streaked with gray, he noted—and waited at the desk. He said, "What's called petit mal?"

"Yes, if you like. It's a convenient name for a variety of less serious symptoms. In any case, he said the seizures were epileptiform. That is, one-sided but otherwise *like* classical epileptic attacks. Classical attacks are generalized. The mild symptoms are most deceptive. Anyone can go blank." She eyed Mahler with a tinge of respect. Evidently he had done his homework. "Hasn't it ever happened to you that an eyelid twitches? You hear a voice? You

63

smell something? You feel dizzy? You have a premonition of disaster? You enter a room and don't know why?"

Mahler glanced about the room with irony. "Oh, that last one? Yes, often. Very well. What was her condition before surgery?"

"Reasonably normal life. Pillar of the church, devoted to the child. Mild seizures not too hard to control."

"After the surgery?"

She thought deeply. "More frequent. You should know she's always had problems. Miscarriages. Hormonal imbalance. Stomach troubles. What do you know about seizure disorders?"

"I'm learning," Mahler said. "But I'm willing to learn more."

She glowered. "It's not simple. The epilepsies are convulsive disorders, some mild, some serious, with a variety of causes and manifestations. We know what causes seizures—abnormal electrical discharges of cells within the brain and central nervous system. What starts them off is another matter. Those electrical currents are the basis of all functions of mind and life. When they fall into disorder, those life functions are disturbed."

"Like snow on the television screen?" he suggested.

She frowned but saw no frivolity. "Something like that, I suppose," she said grudgingly, "but you can bang the television set and clear the image. You can't do that with a woman's brain. In most cases of abnormal seizure activity no obvious physical cause can be found. The triggering mechanisms are sensory or emotional —sounds, sights, smells, heat, pressure, excitement, sexual activity —especially where we find emotional overlay and a history of sexual difficulties. And of course seizures, fits if you like, are readily produced by hysterical or psychotic patients—psychoneurotics, to lump them. That's so frequent that we are justified to assume an hysterical or psychotic disorder unless someone can show an obvious physical abnormality of the brain."

"Such as what?"

"Oh, blood-vessel anomalies, scar tissue, cysts, necrotic tissue . . ." She paused.

"And brain tumors?" Mahler supplied.

"Yes, those." She shrugged and returned to her cigarette. "It's all very well to imagine some dreadful danger from a tumor, especially if malignant, but we should be cautious where we have long-standing emotional disturbances linked to the marital situation. Manya's headaches, for example, are typically psychoneurotic—a boring or sharp shooting headache which radiates, or throbs as though bursting. It's not the steady, severe organic headache that comes from the genuine pressure of a growing mass. Then too she doesn't bite her tongue or wet herself either. . . ."

Mahler said, "She says she does."

The heavy brows rose. "Oh, does she now? Interesting. I was about to say that even where the symptoms suggest a physical cause—a tumor, say—we must remember that this type of patient can imitate almost any symptom, especially if she is versed in medical symptomatology. You can't assume a tumor. You need proof. . . ." The short, curt lecture ran on.

Mahler listened with great care. It was information already stored and digested. It was reassuring to follow the language of another art with a sense of familiarity. A sixth sense was tugging.

". . . emotions can do remarkable things to the body. That's it," she said abruptly.

"It? What do you mean by that?"

"I'm trying to emphasize the extent to which seizures can originate in purely emotional or sensory as well as physical causes. There's more to the theory, but I think you know that. I wanted her kept on medication, as I so repeatedly said, to watch and see developments. One does not rush off to surgery at the first sign of alarm. One must wait and see. One hopes for the best."

Mahler considered the matter with care. "How does a tumor cause seizures?"

"It's not the tumor itself. It's that the tumor grows, creates pressure, displaces and irritates normal brain cells, interrupts the electrical circuits, makes them misfire or fire irregularly. A sputtering effect, so to speak." She eyed him speculatively. "Obviously if a mass is growing in the brain, if pressure increases, if more areas get involved, the symptoms would change for the worse. But you must know this."

"But if it's not a tumor or some other physical lesion, surgery would be pointless—right?" She nodded. "Is that why you objected to the surgery?"

She seemed undecided. "I'll say this much," she said cautiously. "I always played it straight with Manya. I always told her I was not convinced, nor was Dr. Schlomm before me, and nobody has satisfactorily proved, that her seizures were organic. Yes, that's why I objected. The case for surgery was not proved. Is that what you want to hear?" she demanded with a trace of contempt.

"If not a physical cause of the seizures, what was the cause, in your opinion?"

Jane hesitated. "Well, I, for one, can't answer that question." She came to a halt, facing a framed license to practice medicine in the state of New York. "I can only say what I did for her. I gave her a regime to control the seizures—medication, a bland diet, mild exercise, limited sex—for both, I should say. They were both my patients, Frank and Manya. Dr. Schlomm had sent them both to the clinic for counseling—just before he retired. Kindly old doctor. German-Jewish refugee, you know, who never knew how to charge fees."

Mahler thought back to the Shroeder household. "Was that for marital counseling?"

Jane stared. "It's part of the problem. Her entire emotional life was being involved and spilling over. Manya's a decent woman, poor and hard-working but apparently still tortured and affected by that convent life in darkest Poland as a child after the war, I suppose. I had no patience for the nonsense. She showed a kind of prudery, or hyperesthesia, or squeamishness that was beginning to affect the marriage. It showed a long-standing situation."

Mahler digested the information. He was being told something, he felt, something guarded and suggestive to note for future use. "Well, all right," he said. "What's been her condition since the surgery?"

The question was repeated. She sat back, weighing her answer. "She's getting along well enough, considering. But she's a fool about herself, as I've told her. I've tried to suggest alternatives to satisfy Frank, but she won't listen. Nor will he. Yet she's too intelligent not to see the nature of her problem—its roots are sexual. Her priest is no help either. Very limited man, I can tell you, with his horizons back in whatever village he came from. There's only one rule for a woman in sex—maximize the friction and invite the best." Wreathes of blue smoke rose in the still close air of a doctor's office. "Now if you don't mind, I've got a clinic waiting. I'm afraid that's all I can tell you."

"One minute, Doctor. You haven't told me anything," Mahler

said. They eyed each other with respect like bulldogs. "Take another minute. I don't want anything unreasonable, but I'm not here to do a slipshod job. I need records, information, names of witnesses, names of those who participated, medical advice, all sorts of help before I even dream of starting. I don't want to go off half-cocked and leave this woman with an untenable case. I want to know precisely where she stands. You say the case for surgery was not proved. The hospital will claim otherwise. Yet you're unwilling to help your own patient against them? Help me to understand this."

She sat scowling. "I simply don't think it's advisable for this woman to go ahead. Manya's being a nuisance about this lawsuit. She's a sick woman—sicker than she knows. I thought I'd got her to drop the idea of a lawsuit, but evidently not. She's been induced to change her mind. Once she gets a notion, it's like talking to the wall."

That had been Shroeder's phrase, Mahler thought. "I didn't get that impression. I found her reluctant to go ahead. She said so."

"Did she now? You're trusting, Mahler. Don't you think she knows all the implications of this business? That a great many things can be had from the lawsuit? Things she wants?"

"Are you saying the claims are false?"

"No. I'm saying one can no longer tell if the lawsuit has not become her sickness—that while the condition is not invented—it's real enough—it is worsened by the strain. I think she can deteriorate. She might break down completely."

"Or improve?" he suggested.

"Perhaps. If she wins. But will she win? Can you guarantee that? Now, I've told you all I can. Since it's against my best judgment, can you tell me why I should help anything so destructive along?"

Mahler considered the question. "Because she needs your help. And if you help her, I'll help you."

The deep voice lowered in pitch. "I'm not sure I like that," she said dangerously.

"I'm not sure I want you to," Mahler said.

The telephone rang. She answered. "Sorry, but my associates won't go along with that!" she exclaimed. She turned in fury. "What the hell do you want, Mahler?"

Mahler studied the heavy mask whose anger matched his own. It was going rather well, he thought.

"I'm told you sent her to a doctor named Herlihy at the Luzzatto Institute. Why?"

She stared. "Weren't you told?"

"Told what?"

"Well, I marvel! Didn't you know she tried an overdose of sleeping pills? No, I see you don't!" She laughed harshly. "These people don't always tell you everything, do they? Well, after that, it was a state hospital or another work-up at Lewiston Central. I wanted another opinion. I hoped Dr. Herlihy would relieve the depression."

"How could she afford it?"

"Dr. Herlihy owes me some favors. He squeezed her in."

Mahler settled deeper in the chair. A path was beginning to open up. "I assume you have his opinion that the surgery was unjustified. Do you accept that opinion?"

There was no answer.

"That was his opinion?" he asked suddenly.

"Yes. So far as it goes." She hesitated. "But the real question, the thing you pointed out, is the depression, the pain, anguish, suffering, the emotional problem. How can you possibly prove that stems from the operation? You'd need expert testimony, and so far as I know, you haven't got it. You certainly won't get Herlihy's. Try him and see."

Mahler waited. "Would you call him for me?"

"I don't think I will," she said grimly. She pressed an intercom switch. "Edna, dear? Get Mr. Mahler a taxi, please? He's leaving." She began to apply makeup, oblivious to his presence. "The nurse will show you out."

Mahler said, "Would you testify, Doctor? You'll get paid for your time, of course." A pause. "I could serve a subpoena, you know."

"Yes, you could do that," she agreed. She studied the compact mirror with dissatisfaction. Mahler might have been dust in the corner. "But I wouldn't advise it," she said, snapping the compact shut. "My opinion wouldn't help, I'm sure. It's entirely out of my field."

"It'd be enough to get to the jury," Mahler persisted. "The rest is my concern. But I'd like a willing witness."

She shook her head. "Please understand. Yes, I feel for a doctor who faces a lawsuit like this, but that's not my concern. I'm thinking of my patient. I know her and you don't." She looked up with some entreaty, and suddenly behind the seamed lines of the face the woman appeared. "Let well enough alone. Manya's a complicated woman with all sorts of problems. You don't know what damage this can do."

Mahler made no move to rise. He blew a haze on his spectacles. "Doctor, I think there's more to your reluctance than you've told me. What does it mean, I wonder, that you were present at the operation? That Mrs. Shroeder was your patient? The other doctors have disappeared, but you're here, aren't you?" He began to polish the lenses with a methodical rubbing motion, holding them against the overhead light. "Maybe I can do more than merely serve a subpoena."

The attractive hazel eyes were suddenly feline, rimmed white, intent, with vertical slits for irises, one might think. "Add me to that lawsuit? You amaze me, Mahler. You can't possibly know what you're doing."

Mahler looked shocked. "Did I say that? I only mentioned a possibility. I'd give it thought, Doctor, as to your own role in this case." The suggestion of menace lingered. "Why didn't you say you were present?"

She was silent a long moment. "Well, it's no secret," she said cautiously. "Of course I was there. But only to observe. Manya was a service patient. Tatum's patient, not mine. And I opposed the operation, as I keep telling you."

"As I understand you say so."

"That is correct." She looked up, somewhat green. "How did you know I was present?"

"I didn't, until just now," Mahler said. "But now I do, don't I?" He smoked thoughtfully, staring at the disconcerted woman. "Did you help the surgeons in any way? Offer a suggestion? Make a comment? Touch an instrument? Take a specimen to pathology?"

"No! And I don't like that insinuation that I did! I didn't even scrub for it! And I left early before the pathologist's report was telephoned in."

69

"Okay! Then there's nothing to worry about. Good. I'm relieved to hear it—because I'd rather have your friendly help." He blew a plume of smoke, feeling the pleasure of a familiar situation. "I'm trying to be fair, Doctor," he said, addressing a generation of reluctant witnesses past. "Well, let me know how you feel about it. On reflection, I'm sure you'd want to cooperate." He glanced at a cabinet of small vials. "By the way, you haven't by chance got a pickled specimen of the pathology on hand?"

"No! Why would I?"

"I thought, maybe as a souvenir?"

"Certainly not! And you're being insolent!"

"Not a bit. It'd help not to have to depend on the version of a hospital pathologist. But I stand reproved." He put out the cigar and went to the door. "Oh, and I should tell you I plan to call Dr. Herlihy tomorrow morning. A prior call to him by you might be helpful. Eh?" A hard smile brought no response. "Well, good night."

The outer door slammed. A moment later the nurse entered. "How'd we do, Doctor?" she said.

"Damn!" said Dr. Gates. Her hands were shaking.

Mahler returned to the warm hotel lobby, wearing a look of satisfaction. No messages, but the noisy barroom got his attention. He entered and found a booth.

"Bill, I think you never come. You got time now for Jeannot?" A bald, squat man slid into the booth with a conspiratorial look. Jean Baptiste Beaupré, investigator, had arrived, ready to go to work.

"By Gar!" Mahler said with pleasure. "By Gar! Let's go someplace where we can eat."

After two days of scouting, Beaupré had found a certain marvelous French-Canadian restaurant with a quiet bar and fine whiskey to suggest to the good friend of James Curtayne. There one could talk. Pâté, clear soup, salad, coq au vin, petits fours, Turkish coffee were promised. It was a happy coincidence that the *patron* had the same meat supplier as the hospital in question who could be a mine of information. And what did one think of that?

It was midnight when Mahler returned to the hotel—cheerful

70

enough and drunk. A message from Dr. Gates asking a meeting was in his box. Let her wait! he thought.

He fell into bed and into troubled garlicky slumber.

The telephone was ringing. He groped for the receiver. "Uh?" The call was entirely unexpected.

The voice was a soft whisper. "It's me, Manya."

"Oh? Oh, yes? What's up?"

"I'm in the parlor downstairs," Manya said. "I don't want to wake Frank. He took a pill so I can call without his hearing."

"People take pills. Can I help you?"

"Did you see Jane? What did she say?"

"A lot of things. Why?"

"Did she say how Frank and I get on? You know, in bed?"

Mahler struggled to an easier position. "Mrs. Shroeder, is there anything that can't wait till another time?"

"I'm sorry. Excuse me. I didn't mean to wake you," she said in a small voice, and hung up.

Mahler sat up and lit a cigarette. It was dawn before sleep returned. He could not get the sick woman out of his thoughts.

6

The blizzard with its disruption of traffic put all systems to the test. Shortly before dawn, Mrs. Emma Scudder, dietitian, was personally on hand to greet Uncle Archie's Meat and Poultry Store van with a load of boxed meats and poultry for the awakening kitchens. Archie Philipowski leaped into the packed snow, flailing his arms, pleased to arrive on the dot.

"Saved you the gizzards, Emma," he boomed.

"Just get it in and get it over," she replied. An affair was going on between town and gown, so to speak, but that was reserved for the bedroom over the store three times a week. Meanwhile people had to be fed. This day the van carried an extra helper— a squat French Canadian who leaped with a will to the unloading job. Three men—Philipowski, his regular helper, and the new man —were in white coats, respectful of antisepsis in the highest. "Let's go, let's go," Philipowski grunted, slapping his mittened hands. The crew worked fast, carrying boxes into the receiving shed of the kitchens. Warm steamy smells of soap and rendering fats wafted into the freezing air and condensed in wisps of fog. The vast building was coming to life. Without those supplies, it would grind to a halt, come to the end of its purpose. The van departed without the new helper.

Beaupré turned a corner into an underground maze of corridors. He smoothed his white coat, affixed a pince-nez, stuck a stethoscope into his pocket, put a red ribbon in his lapel, and hurried at a trot to the noisy cafeteria. He got on line and studied the chart.

"Very good," he said to the attendant. "Reasonable prices. I like that." He took a loaded tray to a table of doctors and sat.

"Sorry, Doctor," a doctor said. "We're holding that seat."

Beaupré smiled. "In my country," he said in thick gutturals. "*Oui. Bien.* First day."

"Oh? You're new?"

"Very new."

Beaupré beamed and tackled the morning specialty—boiled cod and saltless, watery mashed potatoes—and looked about with interest. Several scores of tables were occupied by all the hospital hierarchy from doctors to filing clerks—buzzing, whispering, bitching about promotions, appointments, fringe benefits, mutual funds, and other matters of medical concern. A doctor who was staring at his red ribbon said, "Oh, Doctor? What service are you on?"

Beaupré frowned. "Service?"

"Yes, service. You're not wearing your tag."

"Fantini," Beaupré said, bowing his head. "Emanuele Fantini. *Dottore.* Top class." He consulted a watch and exclaimed at the time. "Now you excuse?" He gulped his coffee and hurried off.

Dr. Komoflorenzahl exchanged a suffering glance with Dr. Hradliko. The influx of foreign doctors into the system was getting much.

Beaupré took the elevator to the first floor. He picked up the telephone at the reception desk. "Miss, please! Call Dr. Fantini! *Vous comprend?* F-A-N-T-I-N-I? This is Dr. Sinibaldi."

"Wait a minute, I don't have the extension number."

"Try Medical Records."

A long pause. A slurred voice came on. "Medical Records." Beaupré made his request distinct. "He's not here, Doctor," the voice said.

"He must be there. I have said it so," Beaupré said severely. "Look again, imbecile."

"Up yours, Doctor." An abrupt click.

Beaupré chuckled. Minutes later he called Records again and asked for Dr. Emanuele Fantini of the École Supérieure de Médicine de la Corse.

"Dr. Fantini! Dr. Fantini!" the system said.

Ten minutes later Beaupré approached a guard. "Attention, my boy. Where are the medical records?"

"Ah, yes." He nodded. Information in hand, he followed an arrow to Medical Records. A student nurse in the hall was railing to an older woman against death-oriented nurses who, superb when faced with death, were utterly cold and sadistic to living patients. Beaupré interrupted. "Mam'selle," he said, tapping his watch. "Frightfully important. First day. You comprehend?"

The young nurse was freshly graduated from school and daunted by nothing human in the hospital setting. "What do you want?" she said slowly and distinctly. "Dr. Fantini! Dr. Fantini! Call Medical Records!" the system blatted. "Ah!" Beaupré presented a card with his credentials. The card had been printed the previous day. "First day? You see?" he said with earnest conviction.

"This way," the young nurse said, and strode off, followed by Beaupré. She glanced at his red ribbon. "Legion of Honor?" she asked.

"*Non.* Gare des Invalides. With truffles," he replied with a wink. "Pfft!"

"How nice," she murmured.

A pimpled girl was sorting cards, moving her lips.

The young nurse said, "Oh, Molly, Dr. Fantini wants to see some files. Will you take care of him? It's important."

"I'm not Molly. I'm Kim." The girl held back a yawn. "Okay, Doctor. Sign here. Oh, and call the board. They've been trying to reach you all morning."

It was Kim's first day too.

Earlier that same morning Mahler had been awakened by the inexorable telephone.

Landowski was on the line. Mahler's presence was now known everywhere. Father Zator had called to express concern that the lawyer from New York act with vigor in the interests of his parishioners. "You ought to see him, Bill," Landowski said in his complaining voice. "He can line up the whole parish to testify to Manya's change of personality. He'd be a hell of a witness himself. He saw one or two spells too before the surgery, and since then too. No one'd dare cross-examine him. We can call on him anytime. This afternoon, if you like."

Mahler gave this thought. Father Zator loomed large in the headlines. One could not escape this. "No, that's not good," he said slowly. "We'll need agreement, a jury consensus, and he's controversial. I'll see him, but let him come to the office like any other citizen. Okay?" He yawned sourly, wondering at the taste in his mouth. What in hell had they been drinking besides snail juice? "If you want Father Zator, get Father Zator." He yawned again. "What else?"

"Well, what do you think?" Landowski said, exasperated. "You've met the clients. You talked to Jane Gates. Have we got anything?"

"Maybe," Mahler said.

"Only maybe?"

"It's better than it was," Mahler said. "Look, Gene, I've got an impression we're onto something. Something that's funny. Gates is too anxious to keep out of the picture to be kosher, but I may be wrong. Let's see what today brings. Okay?"

"I'll be waiting," Landowski said.

Mahler called for breakfast in his room. "Lots of coffee," he croaked. A hot shower was a blessing, after which he sat to a compulsive morning ritual. The *Chronicle* was not *The New York Times*, but, like methadone, it eased the withdrawal symptoms of the addict. He skimmed the world news—staring with incredulity at statements emanating from the Middle East—and passed to an equally mad local scene. The urban crisis was in full blast. A headline was devoted to a turbulent community whose rival leaders were vituperating each other as misleaders of their people and tools of the Negro elite—a pejoratively intended term. Deplorable! he thought. Why could not those chaps get along and set an example?

By nine he was dressed and off for the Shooler Building, where Landowski was waiting with mounting impatience.

Some few hours later, Beaupré arrived at the Shooler Building, an old red brick structure erected in Lewiston's classical days of glory of the canal and four competing railroads. After studying the directory, he entered a busy law office on the top floor and went to the reception desk. A spare Yankee spinster looked up pleasantly.

"My card," he said.

"Oh. Fifth door down," she said, grinding her rr's. "Knock before you enter."

Beaupré trotted past a series of doors with frosted glass panels, each lettered in gilt with a lawyer's name. A sprinkler system overhead was reassuring. He knocked and entered a large sunny office with modern furnishings. Mahler was at the telephone. Landowski at a side table was scribbling notes.

"Okay to come in?" Beaupré asked.

A hearty precise voice booming over a telephone amplifier was Dr. Paulus Herlihy summarizing his observation of Manya Shroeder at the Luzzatto Institute. He was speaking in guarded terms. Mahler beckoned and made quick introductions in pantomime.

"I'm honored," Beaupré mouthed.

Landowski touched his lips for silence. The boom went on. Beaupré affixed his spectacles and listened with a learned air. "What's the son of a bitch saying?" he asked aside.

"What's that, sir?" Herlihy boomed.

Mahler said, "One of my associates just came in the room. Mr. Beaupré, Dr. Herlihy. Dr. Herlihy, Mr. Beaupré."

"How d'ye do?" the voice boomed.

Beaupré stared beadily at the device. "Dr. Herlihy, eh? Tell me, sir, you lecture one time at the Sorbonne?"

"Why, no, sir. Sorry."

"Bologna University?"

"I'm afraid not."

"Okay, as long as that's clear," Beaupré said severely.

"What's that?" Herlihy was puzzled.

Mahler broke in hastily, "Could you repeat your summary for my associate's benefit, Doctor? It would be helpful if he could hear that directly from you." He glanced up and motioned Beaupré to a chair. A yellow pad held an occasional note, but it was hardly necessary. The notes were mere guides. "What happened to the medical file?"

"It went back to Lewiston Central Hospital," the booming voice said. "I must say, it was like pulling teeth to get that file.

We put in a dozen calls and finally sent a messenger. Never saw a hospital so unwilling to part with its records. Unfortunately that's not uncommon."

"What would you ascribe that to?"

"Lack of messengers."

"Could they have another reason?"

"You're free to speculate, sir. I'm merely stating our difficulties. I'll go this far, Mr. Mahler. I saw no convincing evidence to establish any diagnosis of the seizure problem beyond hysterical seizures."

Mahler said slowly, "Now, Doctor, this is important. Is it conceivable that the seizures were caused by a tumor?"

"Yes. It's conceivable."

"But not likely?"

"Not in my opinion."

"Can you say it's not possible?"

"No. All things are possible—and more so in this field. That's its charm. But I saw no evidence of it." A chuckle was self-appreciative. "Excuse me." A cough interrupted, followed by orders to someone named Ethel to have the bags ready. "If you don't mind advice?"

"Please?"

"Your best claim to large damages would rest on her extreme emotional suffering—"

"The depression?"

"Yes, that. If I were you, I'd take it that the pain, anguish—the cancerphobia, if you will—the emotional suffering outweighs all the rest combined. Although she denies making an attempt to kill herself—she insists it was an accident—my impression here was psychosis, depressive type."

Mahler glanced at Landowski. "Psychosis?" he echoed.

"Oh, yes, oh, yes." Herlihy chuckled. "Aside from seizures, which are well controlled—real enough but influenced mainly by psychiatric considerations—the neurologicals are not too severe. The main impression was a schizophrenic reaction combined with a chronic brain disorder. The problem is the combined effect of one on the other."

"What? What?" Beaupré declared.

"Beg pardon?" Herlihy boomed.

Mahler said, "Can you put that simply, Doctor?"

"I just did," Herlihy said. "The main disorder is this phobic disturbance, cancerphobia, in a schizoid woman. She's flat, inappropriate, the smile is all wrong. She feels sinful, unworthy, and conflicted by sex, yet promiscuous impulses torment her. She's too passive. She's not even resentful or hostile to the surgeons even though she now knows that their diagnosis was absurd—"

"How does she know that?" Mahler interrupted.

"I told her so," the voice boomed. "She has no sign of malignancy. Never had. I made it quite clear to her." A distant throat was cleared. "The family relationship has broken down under those combined effects. Her personality has been altered resulting in a distorted emotional state and depressive psychosis. That doesn't mean she can't be maintained, but it does mean she's gone dull emotionally. She's apathetic and tends to withdraw. There is no serious intellectual impairment. On the contrary. Now, if—"

"One moment." Mahler made a note. "Doctor, help me out. Did the surgery cause this psychiatric condition?"

The voice went cautious. "Well, she had no prior psychotic episode that we know of. For your purposes I'll suggest the hypothesis that the unwarranted treatment imposed on a weakened emotional condition might well have produced that effect. Not easy to prove, but worth the try. Now if that's all . . ."

Mahler said, "One last point, Doctor."

"Yes? I have to leave. . . ."

"I won't take long." Mahler mopped his neck, glancing with meaning at the others in the room. He sat forward to the amplifier. "I appreciate the difficulties of sorting out all these elements. My problem is legal. In your opinion, could the other side argue that her psychiatric condition is simply the deterioration of a prior long-standing psychiatric disorder?"

"Ye-es, they can—and will no doubt—but why suggest it yourself?" A chuckle. "I'd let sleeping dogs lie. You're better off with the present record without raising that specter yourself. Now if that's all . . ."

Mahler said hastily, "Before you hang up—"

"Look here, sir, if you want my opinion, this woman was treated with the grossest degree of incompetency to reflect a level of care below accepted standards anywhere at any time. Your concern as to malpractice would seem to have a sound basis, if that's what you want to hear. We'd certainly never permit an exploratory on the history I read. Eye-ther we know where we're going, or we let the patient alone. Any operation is risky at best, especially in the hands of incompetent surgeons."

"Were these surgeons incompetent?" Mahler said.

The voice went cautious. "I'd never say that. I can only characterize their work by our own standards. I assume all this is still off the record?"

Mahler went stolid. "Of course."

A pause. "If you quote me, you're in breach of confidence, sir. I have no intention to get mixed up in your lawsuit. Call my secretary for an appointment if you wish to chat further. But I will not be a witness."

Mahler's voice had an edge. "Do you think that's fair to this woman, Doctor?"

"Sorry, it's a matter of principle," the voice said. "I won't help you against another doctor—"

Beaupré said nastily, "We can summon you, Doctor!"

"Yes, you can," the voice boomed. "You can also summon spirits from the vasty deep, but will they come?"

A click was a rifle shot.

"Pfft!" Beaupré said. His wink was broad.

Landowski's sigh of relief filled the air. "That's it! Incompetency! Just what I said we'd find." He paused. "Something's wrong?"

Mahler shrugged without enthusiasm. "No, this worked out fine," he said. "But it's only a lead. You heard him. He told us something, but he won't back it up. It's the old story. Oh, Christ, I'm stiff!" He stretched painful muscles and stared at Beaupré. The last question had really not been answered. "What was that last crack about a summons? I'm walking on eggs with this prima donna and you put a feather up his ass. Why?"

"I might have reasons," Beaupré said silkily. "Shook him up a bit, eh? Why not? A doctor can help and he gives you that? For true he can be summoned. Once in court ask him what the damn hell you like. You comprehend?"

Mahler sat back with an unlit cigar. He measured Beaupré with cold eyes. "Did you find something this morning?"

"Yes, for sure. I see the Shroeder file in the hospital. First to last. Beginning to end. The son of a bitch is definitely not out of the picture." Beaupré jerked a thumb at Landowski. "Can I trust this guy?" he asked. Enlightened, he lit a cigarette and studied the office appointments with an air of leisure. "Nice layout, sir," he said appreciatively. He strolled to a plaster model of the human brain, enjoying the moment, and studied the artifact. "Where'd they operate on the lady?"

"Left parietal lobe. Very important area. It's marked," Mahler said.

Beaupré puffed thoughtfully. "You know, Bill? Blanched, sliced, salt, and lemon—*au beurre noir,* you know?—and that could be delicious. The trick is to make the butter sauce separately." A Barlow color illustration of the brain with explanatory medical terms was pinned to the wall. "Fabulous with mushroom caps," he said, dropping ashes.

"What's this about?" Landowski complained.

Beaupré touched his nose. "I see where this so-called Herlihy write a note that the surgery was wrong. So like it or not, he could be dragged in front of the judge and be confronted. He must respond. No?"

"Well, of course," Landowski said, light dawning. "That's right, Bill. That way we can get Herlihy's opinion as an expert. . . ." He halted. "Something wrong with that?"

"Not a bit," Mahler said. "Willing or not, we can summon any doctor on both sides of the case. But would it be wise?" He turned to Beaupré. "What else is in that file?"

A grin showed carious, splintered teeth. "Listen to Jeannot. We got to assume that this lazarette, this hospital, must keep records. So first to last every step must go down in writing—what she eat, how she sleep, how much she pee? No? From this you cross-examine what they thought they were doing?"

"So?"

"Bellinger is supposed to be top man? He is supposed to say who operates? When? What? Where? So it should be an order in writing—no?"

Landowski said, "That's right. How else could they get the

operating room? There had to be an order signed by Bellinger. Wasn't there one?"

"Oh, sure, there is an order," Beaupré said with contempt. "I copy it out." He handed over a copy of a medical order. Mahler laid it flat, put his elbows forward, and studied the document. Beaupré's handwriting was an illiterate scrawl but clear enough.

"What does it say?" Landowski said.

Mahler said, "It says they decided to open the skull and explore the brain to prove the nature of the pathology with the hope of instituting specific therapy. They suspected a scar or a slow-growing glioma." He held Beaupré in a steady gaze. "It looks all right to me."

Beaupré was savoring the moment as though a dish of cooking meats, rare herbs, and fine ingredients were bubbling before him. "Oh, sure, it *looks* all right, but who signed it? This guy—Bellinger—or one certain *crapule* named Tatum?"

Mahler stirred. "How do we know this?"

Beaupré was now serious and professional. He did not think the order was written by Bellinger because Bellinger's fist—his handwriting—appeared nowhere in the records. Other handwritings appeared. Entries dealt with sleepless nights. So much of this. So much of that. The patient complained, screamed, refused food. Everyone had a hand in writing up the charts. Where was Bellinger? A waggling motion was suggestive. "What we do see, Bill, is Tatum. Tatum is all over the chart, but never in his own name. It's always Bellinger. 'Dr. Bellinger and I agree.' 'Dr. Bellinger and I think.' 'We prescribe so and so be done.' And so forth. Bellinger? Never. Like a ghost."

The cold eyes did not waver. "Stick to this specific point. How do we know Bellinger didn't authorize the order?"

Beaupré was enjoying a crafty effect. "First, he never sign it. Here is the signature as it appears." He placed a paper on the desk:

J. H. BELLINGER, M.D.
By *P. Tatum, M.D.*

"It could have been authorized orally," Mahler said slowly. "It's not conclusive."

"Sure. But then it would have to be explained. No? Not like

81

the guy's own true signature? Once they show up in front of the judge you could tear their head off like a chicken, Bill. No?" A baggy eyelid was reflexed. "So what kind of doctors are they? I wouldn't let those people cut my hair. Hey?"

Mahler said, "What's your second point?"

Beaupré glanced at Landowski. "This is in legal confidence? Totally off the record?"

"Come on, come on, for Christ's sake!" Mahler said. "What have you got to show?"

Beaupré dipped into his pocket and placed a handful of small black cylinders on the desk. His smile was one of deepest professional satisfaction.

Mahler considered the display. They formed a pattern, those tiny black cartridges, he thought. Imbedded in emulsion, photon-drunk, miraculous films of frozen truth. Beaupré's splintered teeth were a piranha grin.

"Isn't this illegal?" Landowski said.

He might not have spoken.

"You son of a bitch," Mahler said with respect.

Beaupré bowed from the waist. He exclaimed at the time and slipped into his coat. A full report on the morning's work was promised, but first things first. Certain confidential Kodak people in Rochester would process the films. No problems. A distinct pleasure. Where would he send his bill? He bowed and left for his special world and a problem of tracing certain stolen corporate funds to Swiss bank accounts in Geneva.

Landowski mopped his neck. "I don't trust him," he said.

Mahler said, "He wouldn't trust you, but he did."

"Why?"

"Because you're with me, and I vouch for you," Mahler said. "On some levels reputation still means something." He swiveled about, drumming the armchair. A voice was whispering, desperate eyes were on his own, he felt the unpleasant pressure of a woman's too-soft breasts against his hands. He turned away and asked for a telephone number. Jane Gates was instantly on the line. The grandfather's clock was reverberating. One long solemn stroke.

"Yes?" she said cautiously.

"Herlihy took my call. Very informative. Thanks for the assist," Mahler said.

"Oh, well, that's nothing. What did he say?" she asked. There was a trace of anxiety.

Mahler said, "More or less he agrees with what you said, but in more detail. I'd like to see you again, Doctor."

A sigh was heavy. "Let me know when you're ready. Oh, and, Mahler?"

"Yes."

"I hope . . ."

"Yes?"

"Never mind."

Two clicks in a neutral zone.

Mahler felt his scalp and head suddenly wet in the release of tension. He felt gloomy, fated, oppressed. Along a dark tunnel all exits but one were blocked. A tunnel to infinity with a distant light flickering. He glanced up. "Where do the lawyers eat in this town?"

"There is only one place. Everybody goes there," Landowski said, smiling.

Traffic was moving in front of the Shooler Building. Mahler drew a deep lungful of cold air and felt better. White snow and a bright sun in a clear winter sky were welcome beyond words.

7

"Someone you know?" Sabbattino said.

Sarah van Loon turned and glanced about the room. Flynn's Chop House was an old restaurant off the Genesee Post Road patronized by everyone with good income from the County Courthouse and Municipal Building at the Civic Center a short distance away. A photograph of Jack Dempsey in a fighting pose decorated the dark oak paneling. Mahler was seated almost directly across the room, studying the bill of fare. Landowski was talking with animation. "Yes, it's that chap, Mahler," she said. "He seems to be hitting it off with Gene."

Philip Sabbattino, chief assistant city attorney in charge of the trial bureau, was on cigars and whiskey sours in a routine that had not varied in years. The table had a mixed bag of lawyers —a group to whom attendance was deemed almost obligatory. Everything was discussed—political advancements, sexual gossip, corruption, city contracts, who was up, who down. Occasionally strangers joined, but then the talk faltered, the silence became uncomfortable, the knot broke up. It was an inner group and recognized as such. Sabbattino was a cold man in his forties with a blunt, sallow face out of a Florentine painting.

Ordinarily he was afraid of Sarah—her sharp tongue, decisive manner, and social superiority were intimidating elements— but the hard drinking carried him along. "So that's Mahler," he said. "I thought he'd be seven feet high. Why not call him over?"

"If he looks this way again," Sarah said. She had indeed been overtalking the encounter with Mahler on the plane, but then

84

Sabbattino had a way of worming things out of one. If he was not Florentine, he had the proverbial malice, the biting tongue of that remarkable people. She felt a mocking gaze on her neck. A slowly rising flush had no business there in a woman of her age and situation.

Sabbattino twisted an Hercule Poirot moustache and leaned over. "He's looking this way," he said in an insinuating whisper.

She met Mahler's eye. Mahler rose and came over. Landowski followed.

"Mrs. van Loon? Nice to meet you again," Mahler said.

She smiled formally. "Yes, how nice. I hoped you'd join us. Hello, Gene." A handshake was firm. Landowski smiled broadly. Mahler's appearance at Flynn's was a feather in his cap. Sarah said, "I'd like you to meet Mr. Sabbattino. This is Mr. Mahler."

"Oh, yes. The Shroeder claim." Sabbattino showed his teeth. "We were talking about it."

"So were we," Mahler said.

Sabbattino put out a hand. "Call me Phil," he said.

"Mr. Sabbattino's our chief assistant," Sarah said.

"Yes, I know," Mahler said.

"You do? How?" Sabbattino asked.

"It's in the phone book. It's a good place to look for missing people."

"Why? Were you looking for me?"

"Actually, no. I was looking to call on Mrs. van Loon to discuss that matter." Mahler turned to Sarah. "Would late afternoon be a good time?"

Sarah seemed surprised by the direct request. "Well, ye-es. Five would do, I suppose. If I'm not at my desk, ask for Detective O'Dwyer. He'll find me."

There was an awkward moment.

"Well, have a drink," Sabbattino said. "Maybe we can help you. That's why we're here—to help. It's our city motto. Mike! Two chairs!"

"I'd like you to meet some of our associates," Sarah said quickly. Two dogs were sniffing each other out, but there was nothing amusing in the guarded antagonisms that instinctively sprang up. A half-dozen lawyers were introduced, several from the city attorney's office—Dan Otto, a humorous baggy-eyed trial assistant, James McAdoo, zoning-law variances, Oswald Vallee, condemnations, and others. Mahler had an impression of heavy drinkers, crushing grips, upstate chaffer. They were friendly enough but wary. He was the outsider. They were the home team. Provincials, he thought, but competent. Sabbattino, who seemed to dominate, had a familiar suave cruelty, a cheerful ruthlessness he could only measure against his own.

"So how's litigation in the big city?" Sabbattino asked. "Are the calendars crowded?"

"Depends how you view it," Mahler said with good humor. "The courts say they are being plagued by the tremendous volume of highway negligence claims that are choking the calendars. Some of our judges were recently heard to complain that those long liquid lunches are harder than ever to manage. But it's improving."

"Oh, how? I'd be interested," Sabbattino said.

Mahler smiled. "It just takes firm policy. They're calling crash calendars to get rid of this unconscionable burden on the system. Ready or not, claimants are being forced to settle at any price or go to trial—or it's out the window with that busted spine, that silver plate, that shortened life. The insurance companies are laughing like hell. I'd be laughing too—if I owned some of their stock. What it's doing to the people is a tale best told by a company-minded administrative judge."

Sabbattino looked thoughtful. "Crash calendars? I like that. Are they effective?"

"I can report progress. In just one year they tossed out fifty thousand claims. It's clearing the courts of people like a breath of fresh air. One day they'll sweep 'em clean and never come back from lunch. I dream of that. We'll sit around and contemplate the judicial process in pristine purity. I wonder if we'll enjoy it." He gazed at a vision in space. "We might even abolish the very concept of lawsuits for personal injuries except that maybe—tragically—we'd have to get rid of courts and insurance companies too."

"And lawyers?" Otto suggested.

"That too," Mahler agreed. The vision faded. "It's nice to think about, but it won't happen in our day." He sighed.

The restaurant was getting noisier, more crowded with fresh

arrivals. "Everything all right, folks?" Flynn asked genially, rubbing his hands.

"Just keep 'em coming," someone said.

"It's not a simple highway case that brings you here, Mr. Mahler, but this medical claim," Sarah said pleasantly. "Quite different, wouldn't you say—when you consider what it means to the doctors?" She placed her elbows forward, twirling her glass. It was a cool, not unfriendly but firm throw from left field. She was smiling slightly. A trace of mockery was there.

Mahler said, "I'm not against the doctor, Mrs. van Loon. Just against the careless doctor."

She sipped the cold drink with enjoyment. "That's easy to claim, but who knows that?"

"But we do know—" Landowski felt a pressure against his knee and halted.

Sabbattino said, "You've got a point, Bill. What's worse than the careless doctor? If you find one around, let me know. Frankly, I think you're performing a useful social function to call this to our attention."

Otto broke in lugubriously. "Mahler, good or bad, we need doctors. What worries us isn't one doubtful nuisance-value claim like yours. It's the future. This trend to insane malpractice verdicts is wild and dangerous. Hundreds of thousands of dollars—even million-dollar verdicts—at a clip. It's driving doctors out of the profession. My personal doctor tells me he can't stand the rising premiums. He's thinking of pulling out of private practice because of those terrible premiums and settling in Florida. What's to happen if they all pull out? Who'll keep medicine going?"

Mahler said, "How old is your personal doctor?"

"Seventy-nine," Otto replied, "but spry."

"Maybe it's time he left for Florida." Mahler swallowed his drink and went on with a hard smile. "I wouldn't worry about those premiums. I'd worry about their causes. Claims don't come out of thin air. They come out of serious medical situations and the breakdown of relationships. If doctors are being sued, it's because they're doing something wrong. It's the impersonal way medical services get delivered between the broker's office and the golf course. Medicine's big business now—an extension of government and industry. It's gotten to be routine with laboratories, blood banks, therapy offices, pharmacies and appliances and the rest. The heart has gone out of our doctors. They've forgotten to look, hear, tap, smell, touch. They spend more time on bookies than on books while the analyzers do multiple tests on random samples of bladder juice and whatnot. So if the common man strikes back? Why not? It's not patient ingratitude. It's the customer shaking the coin box when it's got your dime." Amused chuckles were encouragement to go on. "I think well of doctors as a class. I think so well of them that I want to keep them to the highest standards imaginable—like the dedicated humanitarian doctors and warmhearted nurses we see on television."

He held his glass to the light and squinted. "I'm trying hard to see what's wrong with a million-dollar verdict. And honestly I can't."

Sabbattino had listened with cold eyes and an ironic grin. He rolled some crumbs on the tablecloth. "Bill, it's not the case with merit we resist. It's the faking we can't stand. A doctor cuts a hangnail and gets charged with miscarriage, total blindness, general paralysis, and assault. I mean, really."

Mahler said, "I know the case. *124 Alabama Reports* at page 260."

Everyone laughed.

"And what happens if there's merit?" Mahler said.

"We try to settle those on the best possible terms," Sabbattino replied. "Especially if we're convinced we'll get hit by a verdict anyhow. Why not?" he said with aplomb. "I see your point, Bill, but remember you have only one case. We have thousands. We have to take the larger view." He pointed a breadstick at Otto. "Dan, you remember that plumber's helper who sued for loss of sexual function? And mutilation? And won?"

"The penectomy?"

"The very one."

Otto looked sad. "The one whose girl hit him later with a paternity suit—and won that too? I thought that was a happy ending. Both verdicts were upheld on appeal."

Mahler said, "Somebody's got to pay. Why not plumbers'

helpers?" He turned back to Sabbattino. "So! How's the trial calendar in these parts?"

"Very bad here too," Sabbattino said with satisfaction. "We have a special city calendar too. Also years behind. Everybody hates us," he said cheerfully.

"Who controls the city calendar?"

"You might say I do."

"How does one get a preference?"

"On what grounds?"

"Imagine some grounds. Hardship. Influence. Any sound legal reason. What are the chances?"

Sabbattino closed his eyes in thought. "Weak cases seem to move fast. Strong cases?" He squinted nicely. "That's up to me too."

"Or up to the court?"

"Of course the court," Sabbattino said with a cruel, quiet smile of ultimate power. "Say! I hope you don't think we'd use our powers like some bunch of bureaucrats—you know, drag cases out—wear people down—discourage them into settlements? Sarah wouldn't let us. High-minded. Liberal. Den mother."

"You're undermining me, Phil," Sarah said reproachfully. "Mr. Mahler might not realize you're joking. And you are, aren't you?"

Sabbattino turned back to Mahler. "Of course if you'd waive the jury and submit to one of our more responsible judges—one who for example understands the city's fiscal perils, who sees how wrong it is to mulct the public treasury to enrich the random phony—I'd be glad to help you get an early trial. You'd be in and out before you could say traumatic shock and extensive hematomas. I have one especially in mind. What say?"

Mahler pondered the proposal. "I don't *quite* see the advantage to that," he said nicely, "not over twelve soft-hearted slobby jurors. But I'll think about it. Those choked-up calendars are food for thought and I'm far from home."

Sabbattino glanced at his watch. "Bill, actually—in spite of what we're saying—we don't get too many malpractice cases here. Nothing like the situation in the big cities. And we don't like to see, or encourage them, of course. But if you or Gene have any problems with your case, you'll find us pretty easygoing about practice up here. Informal, you know? Country lawyers. We keep our doors open. Drop in anytime."

"I'd like to do that," Mahler said. He had been dismissed, he realized with a lick of annoyance. "Phil," he added.

Sarah made a flirting gesture. "Phil's such a tease," she said cheerfully. "Actually I run the trial division with a fairly free hand up to a point. But any settlement over ten thousand is reviewed by Phil." She smiled fondly. "And he's such a bastard!"

Mahler said, "What's Phil's limit?"

"Twenty-five thousand. Above that, the city attorney reviews Phil. He's worse."

Mahler said, "What message am I getting about Phil?"

Sarah said, "Watch him. He'll pull every comma on you he knows. And he knows them all."

Sabbattino said, "Commas, no. Periods, yes."

Everyone laughed including the waiter who was bringing another round.

Sarah said, "So my advice is to lower your sights if you ever want to settle. Phil wouldn't give his mother a dime—doesn't, in fact—but happily I like to pay claims. I feel like a better human being. That's why they've got a ceiling on me." All laughed with her.

Mahler said, "Who mentioned settlement?"

"Oh, dear! And I thought I was getting vibrations. Ooh, it's not the gin, it's the olive." She blew her breath. "If we see malpractice, we'll pay out on a fair basis. But we won't settle without liability. Real liability. We'd rather go to trial." She finished the drink and smiled less pleasantly. "And we haven't lost one yet."

Dan Otto turned a mournful face. "Hard as nails, Mahler," he said in sepulchral tones. "Watch the knee."

"Flattery, Danny boy?" Sarah drawled.

Otto brought her cigarette to his mouth. "Sweetheart, this is the closest I hope to come."

"Be sure of that, darling." Sarah laughed reproachfully. She turned back to Mahler, now serious. "We'd have to be convinced of malpractice before we'd even discuss it. And we have to think of our doctors too. They're our clients too if they want us to represent them. Their contracts required that we defend

90

them against these claims. And that's what they'll get—a defense."

"But if you conclude they were guilty?"

"I'd never let that thought enter my mind, not unless and until it's proved." She hesitated under a fixed stare. "I'm sorry about the patient's difficulties, but what can I say? We're always dealing with tragedies. And I'm not purblind—in fact we looked into this when we heard of the matter. I telephoned the administrator—Dr. Grimes—who told me there was nothing in it. The hospital doesn't guarantee cures. Only good treatment. Which she got."

"According to Dr. Grimes?"

"Well, of course."

"Did you review the record yourself?"

"What would it mean if I had?"

"You might be enlightened," Mahler said. He turned to Sabbattino. "Which brings me to something. I'd like to see those records this afternoon, if possible. Do I need a clearance from your office?"

"Oh?" Sabbattino was noncommittal.

"It might be to your advantage. If I don't see malpractice, I might even be inclined to withdraw from the matter."

"Would Gene withdraw?" Sabbattino asked pointedly.

"That'd be up to him," Mahler said.

"Well, I don't know," Landowski said uneasily. "I'd have to make up my own mind. I don't understand all this."

Mahler went on. "Unless you're afraid of what I'll find, Phil?"

"I'm not afraid of anything." Sabbattino glanced at the other lawyers. "Am I?"

The circle went silent. Mahler studied a cigar ash with growing anger. "What makes you so uptight about those records?"

Otto broke in. "It's an uptight situation, Mahler. You're here to accuse our fine black physicians of wrongdoing and you expect smiles and a red carpet? Oh, Mahler, Mahler." He shook his head. "We walk a tightrope in this city. Any hint of sellout might bring on black unrest. Militants, you know. And any smell of black favoritism brings out the ethnic vote. What do you want us to do? Lose elections? Encourage riots? I mean, what—what?"

"Well, that's frank," Mahler said.

He drew a careful line in the cloth. "Does it add up to this—

that I can't get consent to see those records—even informally—for collateral political reasons?"

Sabbattino smiled sweetly. "I'd love to help, but I couldn't get myself to do it—emotionally. On the other hand, a guest is entitled to something." He examined his fingernails. "You're in charge, Sarah. You decide."

Sarah flushed. "Mr. Mahler, on second thought, I think you'd better apply to the court in the regular way—and we'll see what happens."

Mahler's face darkened. "On second thought," he said coldly, emphasizing the phrase, "you might be right. Gene, let's get back to our table." He stood in an odd, formal pose. "I'll try to explain this to the sick woman we represent. Waiter, bring those checks over." With a curt nod, he returned to his table. Landowski mumbled an apology and followed.

Sarah bent an elegant wrist. "Oh, you lawyers," she complained. "Can't you talk of anything better than law? Did anyone see the news last night? What right have police to fire back at students . . . ?"

At the next table, a group of judges resumed an interrupted conversation.

Mahler picked up a menu. So much the better, he thought angrily. If that was how it was to be. To his surprise, he was breathing hard, a pulse was beating at his throat.

Landowski took the seat opposite, much worried. "Bill, was it wise to antagonize Sabbattino like that? Practically saying you didn't trust the records . . . ?"

The stare was baleful. "Would it be wise not to? Do you expect a fair shake from that guy? He was wiping his feet on us. Fake malpractice claims! How long have you known Manya now?"

"Her and Frank? About ten years, I suppose. Actually I closed title for them when they bought their little house. Charged twenty-five dollars, I remember, and they were grateful. Why?"

"You think she's a fake?"

"Oh, no, no! You know I don't."

"Then what let you take that crap from Pal Phil? I thought you'd have generated more heat yourself—she's your client, not mine. If you don't feel that, say so—because you won't last this out. You don't seem to understand what kind of fight we're in."

Landowski looked up. "We are?"

"That guy was brushing us off like flies while you sat with that silly grin enjoying the jokes. Well, they weren't jokes." Mahler looked across the room. Sarah van Loon was laughing heartily. He caught Landowski's eye and made a gesture of dismissal. "Okay, that's for later," he grunted. "Let's finish and get to that hospital while the day is still young. So far we have two doctors who think the seizures were hysterical. That's where we'll prove it out." He returned to the menu, wondering at the swing of mood from pleasantries to anger and gloom. He looked up with a frown. "What I don't like here is that woman lawyer. If she gets a fix on this case, she'll dig in and then God help us! We'll never settle anything."

Landowski studied the problem of London broil. If there was a small grin of satisfaction, it was hidden by the bill of fare.

8

City Detective Emmet O'Dwyer was cheerful, towhaired, quite young, baby-faced, and jaunty. He wore cheap suits, flashy ties, and frayed shirts. He had three children and an energetic young wife who ran a taut home. He had served the city five years as patrolman, two as detective, and was now assigned to the City Attorney's Office as special investigator to Mrs. van Loon. He ran her errands and shared her office at the Municipal Building. It was an ancient structure built by corrupt contractors, and it stinted not the ugly, the heavy, the uncomfortable. The flooring was oak on concrete, the walls were plaster on brick, the lighting system appalling. Air ducts ran everywhere but gave no air.

A rail divided the office. On one side Sarah had installed a burled walnut desk—that desk had been her husband's. O'Dwyer had inherited its predecessor. An oversized rolltop sat on the other side. It was a good place to slouch away the days and hard to leave at night.

From behind his desk, O'Dwyer could watch his elegant chief. She mothered him and he adored her. She never ceased to fascinate him. She was a good tough lawyer, she drank like a man, and looked sexier than his wife. He knew her every indication of mood from the bored withdrawn look at the heavy flirting approaches of her colleagues to the delicate wrist gesture of amusement, the ringing laughter that masked discernment of fraud, the drawl that coaxed the truth from witnesses. This day something was on her mind, he saw. She had returned from lunch ebullient as ever. She had settled several minor claims of injuries resulting from icy sidewalks, open manholes, and rat bites in a low-rent city-housing project with unusual generosity and had dealt with a claim based on alleged police brutality with skill and vigor. But her heart was not in it. She had been watching the clock all afternoon. She had combed her hair and had fixed her face more often than was normal. She was now arching her spine with a satisfying opulence of figure. She was in a bored and restless mood.

O'Dwyer was on the telephone dealing with a reluctant witness to a claim of misbehavior by a city bus driver. "Listen, wise guy," he rasped, stubbing a cigarette, "you think you got problems? That liquor license of yours could be problems. So why not tell the truth?" The earpiece rattled.

Sarah stifled a yawn. "Emmet, dear?"

O'Dwyer covered the mouthpiece. "Yes, Chief?"

"Were there any messages while I was gone?"

"No, Chief. I don't hide messages."

"Don't you want to go home? It's late."

"Not before you do."

"I hate to keep you late."

"No trouble. It's a lousy night for driving."

"Do you want Marilyn to worry?"

"No. Why should she? When I'm ready, she's ready."

"What are you working on?"

"This Hogan claim. This guy knows more than he's saying. Look, don't you want to powder your nose or something? It's past five. Time for lawyers to go home."

"I'll stick around. I have this tentative appointment. Something may happen."

O'Dwyer knew every appointment in the book. He said, "If he were showing up, he'd have called."

"We'll see," she replied, and resumed doodling.

O'Dwyer returned to the telephone. "Okay, mister, but isn't this what *really* happened? The lady swung *first* and *then* the bus driver called her that dirty name? And he didn't close the door on her deliberately? She tripped on a shoelace—right?"

The afternoon was far gone.

Dan Otto entered and paused at the doorway, a hand upraised as though to declaim. Sarah looked up. "Not now, Dan," she said.

Otto sighed. "I came to ask if you'll join the boys at Fisher's Tavern?"

The telephone cut off an answer. O'Dwyer took the call. "For you, Chief. Dr. Grimes."

"Have a seat, Dan," Sarah said with a suffering glance. She picked up the telephone. "Yes, Doctor?" The line went silent. "I could murder people who do this," she said. She lit a fresh cigarette and waited. Staff people passed the open door, waved good night, and went on.

Finally a cautious syrupy voice got on the line. "Sorry to hold you up," Dr. Grimes said through a lozenge. "I only have a minute. Now about this nonsense . . ."

Sarah frowned. She did not like Grimes's report on the state of the pending Shroeder matter.

"Well, it's done," she said. "Thanks for letting me know." She dropped the telephone in the cradle and made a note in a large red buckram diary, Property of the City of Lewiston, that ruled her professional life.

Otto said, "So what happened?"

"Doctors!" she said witheringly. It appeared that Mahler had arrived with Landowski at the hospital offensively determined. Absolutely incredible! Of course lawyers were free to roam a public building, but instead of referring questions back to the City Attorney's Office as instructed, that fruity ass, Dr. Andrew Grimes, had given the lawyers sanction to visit and pry without restriction. So much for discipline. A slender toe was tapping.

Otto said, "So why didn't you pass the word to give Mahler the polite freeze? The quick shuffle? The heave-ho?"

"I'm not amused," Sarah said shortly. She glanced at O'Dwyer. "Em? What do you think?"

"When I know what you think," O'Dwyer said, "I'll know what I think."

"That helps me," she said.

Otto clucked. "It's the younger generation, Sarah. Thinking's become a group thing. Command him and he'll think anything."

Sarah contemplated an array of filing cabinets. Those cabinets cluttered the building everywhere. Since they had never been indexed—were in fact beyond indexing—they stood universally undisturbed except for those against the far wall of her office.

In a few short years she had closed thousands of files, quickly, efficiently and to the city's advantage. She had nothing official yet on the Shroeder claim, not even an index number. The feeling was one of vacancy—and anticipation. She shivered and drew a wool coat about her shoulders—the heating plant, as usual erratic and inefficient, had been banked by a distant hostile janitor with a dwindling coal pile. "I'm annoyed with Mahler. I thought he'd call me first," she said slowly, "and try to talk me into an accommodation. He could have gotten a crack at those records informally—if he hadn't made such a public point of it." She stared at Otto. "The next table and those judges getting an earful, Dan, while you were bleating about race riots—including Judge Parrish, who's got a thing about black issues. Did you realize that?"

"Oh, sure," Otto said. "But Judge Doyle was also listening. And Judge Urquart. So?"

"So you could have lowered your voice," Sarah said sharply. "Everybody took positions and we blew it. Instead of Mahler's coming here, he's in that hospital talking to people and we have no idea of what they're telling him." She continued to smoke. "You're a dilapidated old war-horse, Dan. What's his point?"

"First slap and tickle, sweetie," Otto said affectionately. There were things between them as lawyers and human beings including a common interest in dirty limericks and string quartets. That sort of interest in music was unique in the building and perhaps in Lewiston. He went on placidly. "I don't believe Mahler wanted or expected your consent to see the records. He deliberately got under your skin."

"Why would he want to do that?"

"Why, indeed?" Otto shrugged. "I think you did exactly what he wanted you to do—you refused."

"You thought so then?"

"Sure."

"Did Phil think so too?"

"Naturally. That's why he threw it to you and made you the villain. Didn't you see that too?"

Sarah went thoughtful. "Seems awfully elaborate, doesn't it? But Mahler came on so strong, what else could we do?"

Otto smiled sadly. "This isn't *Kinderspiel*, my darling. Juries are funny. Anything below the neck—heart, liver, bones—and they're not impressed. Small verdicts. Peanuts. Above the clavicle—facial scars, the eyes, skull fractures—they'll give away the keys to Fort Knox. Be careful. You're dealing with the brain, sweetie. The uncanny, gruesome brain!"

Sarah's glance was speculative. "And you sat there without a mumbling word?"

Otto bleated. "You are my bureau chief, Sarah, my leader. I adore you. Who am I to come between a beautiful woman and a mature American lawyer with fire and lust in his eyes? Frankly, I enjoyed it. Didn't you?"

"I am besieged by infants," Sarah observed, patting a yawn. A faint flush appeared. "And you think Mahler's that subtle?"

"Who says that's subtle?"

"In that case we'd better go by the book from now on with Mr. Mahler," she said grimly. "It's like everything I've ever heard about him—the Mahler special. He'll be working this to embarrass us—to put the city and the hospital in the role of oppressors. People already think it's a house of body-snatching pathologists and dangerous interns. On top of that we'll have the racial issue for salad dressing. Well, I'm not playing that game. The brain is just another part of the body."

A secretary looked in. "Night, Mrs. van Loon." She glanced at the glum faces, grimaced, and skipped on.

Otto stared at Sarah keenly. "You're looking worried. Why?"

"I hate these doctor cases," she replied.

O'Dwyer yawned luxuriously, wondering. His chief prided herself on certain qualities, he knew. She was an experienced lawyer, a cool practitioner of clear purpose and lucid thought. The amount of feeling was unusual. He said, "Chief? I could call the security people up there and get him locked up next time for something—like loitering? No?"

"Emmet!" Sarah was annoyed.

Otto said, "So what did Grimes tell him?"

"Oh, that! Well, apparently he got around to saying nothing. He claims he diverted Mahler with talk about investment opportunities in Montego Bay in Jamaica. Some hotel condominium project that returns twenty percent with a free vacation in the bargain."

"It's natural to talk about one's investments," Otto said.

"Yes, but Grimes doesn't invest his own money. He gets options. He talks it up. Other doctors invest and he sells the option at a profit." Sarah frowned. "But why in Montego Bay?"

"Why not?"

"Because last year he was touting hotel shares in the Virgin Islands."

O'Dwyer reminded himself that his chief was a sharp corporation lawyer with a year of S.E.C. background in the not far past. "What about the medical records?"

"That's funny too. He didn't ask for them. But he should have asked if only to scream when he makes his motion to inspect and photograph. Now why?"

Otto stood. "On this I leave for Fisher's Tavern and its rollicking brotherhood of the bar. Coming, sweetheart?"

"Thanks, but I've got a boring dinner affair tonight. Ghastly business at the Simpsons'. It'll start with sweet sherry. I'm expected to meet a rich widower as usual—I don't know why. I'm so happy in my work, I couldn't bear to leave all this. Run along while I wash my hands."

Otto clumped off, grinning. A rich basso mockingly went down the hall:

> "But along came Bill,
> Who's not the type at all . . ."

Sarah finished her cigarette. "Em?"

"Chief?"

She hesitated. "Maybe I'm jumping the gun—I should wait for a claim letter, I suppose—but I want to know what else is going on at that hospital. Off the record, I want to know what the case is really about." She picked up soap and a towel and made her wishes clear. "So get busy like the nice cop I know you essentially are. Can you start in the morning?"

"Oh, sure."

"And you won't be obvious, eh?" She shivered and strode down a deserted hall, suddenly oppressed. She was not easily affected by aggressive lawyers, but the remembered thrust of Mahler's jaw was disconcerting. She had no relish for the growing sense of uneasiness at the task ahead. It was simply too annoying that he had not called.

The next day was a working day. Sarah was restless and undecided in her work. She settled several claims and put a trial over for a week. Her mind was on the Shroeder matter, and without O'Dwyer about she felt lost. When he failed to call, she left early, leaving word that she had gone to Fisher's Tavern. She kept watching the clock and drinking with the crowd. There was a blast of icy air.

"Hey, close that door!"

O'Dwyer was at the door, stamping in the cold. Everyone was reasonably drunk, reasonably orderly, but the noise was much. Sarah saw his signal and finished a stiff Scotch. She put down a bill as a lawyer among lawyers and followed O'Dwyer to the street.

"Where's your car?" he said.

"Transmission trouble," she said. "You'll have to drive me home."

They got into a battered Chevelle and started off.

"I thought I'd never hear from you," she said with irritation. "You didn't call once. What happened?"

"Chief, don't mess with me. I had a hard day. Okay?"

She was not inclined to press him. The car was skidding alarmingly on the icy pavement. Every possible accident was only too clear to her experienced eye. She was not drunk, but she was fairly high. They drove along icy streets from downtown Lewiston to the entrance to the Freeway.

O'Dwyer peered into a swirl of snowflakes in the headlights. "Smooth guy, Grimes," he remarked. "Breeds tropical fish. Cheeks like jelly. Smiles like a comic strip. Grabs-your-knee type. Watch that hot clutch at the joy stick."

"I know Grimes," Sarah said shortly. That a vital and energetic widow in a small city attracted proposals without number or encouragement was not wisdom she cared to share. "What'd you learn?"

"I learned that nobody loves a cop."

"What else did you learn?"

"Basically, that we're in good shape," O'Dwyer said. "Mahler got no place really. He's wasting his time."

"Oh?"

"I wouldn't put you on." O'Dwyer turned into the Freeway. The Freeway was a six-lane highway rumbling with trucks that led past shopping centers and filling stations. It would lead to the lakefront area where Sarah lived. "What's a Bárány test?"

"How do you spell it?"

"I forgot to ask. It's a test for brain tumors. They spin the patient and watch the eyes. If the eyes don't zigzag—or do zigzag, I'm not sure which—it's a definite sign. It's called 'night' something. . . ."

"Nystagmus?"

"Yeah. That. Involuntary eye movements. Supposedly infallible. It'd be on the chart, if it was done, Grimes said." A pregnant moment passed. "He told Mahler he might look for it. Now why would he want to put that notion in Mahler's head?"

"Pretentious ass parading knowledge, that's why," she said. "Why, do you think?"

O'Dwyer shrugged. "I'm no genius in these things, but I'd say Grimesy was only going through motions. It's no skin off his budget. Those two doctors are on their own. And that's the unofficial report."

A moment passed in silence. The rumble of ice and cinders in the frozen roadway was suddenly loud.

O'Dwyer said, "Or am I just being a cop?"

"Em, dear, I prefer you as a cop," Sarah said with sudden savagery, then contained herself, conscious that her rich contralto had gone unpleasant and harsh. "I can't stand you sometimes, but you have a gross instinct for dragging things out. Yes. Now let's have a real report."

O'Dwyer described the lawyers' visit to Lewiston Central Hospital as gleaned from the staff. Mahler had gone through half-a-dozen departments, had talked briefly to personnel, had asked trifling questions, and had left apparently with little to show. One nice thing about the hospital was its turnover, O'Dwyer said with satisfaction. Everyone was new. They could not talk if they wanted to.

Sarah sank deeper in the seat, smoothing her cheek against a fur collar. The jocularity was not convincing. "Em, you're being a nuisance. Did you get to talk seriously to Grimes?"

"No problems. Aside from that chitchat about investments, he told Mahler that Bellinger had come with great credentials. Outstanding neurosurgeon and so forth. Tatum too. Useful roles in the community. Grateful for their contributions. Every confidence in them and no doubt everything would be worked out. All that crap." O'Dwyer grinned and dropped the fruity imitation. "He also told Mahler he was so very, very sorry he couldn't help him out—that Administration wouldn't know what went on in the services, let alone in neurosurgery. And anyway that Bellinger would have sole knowledge of the matter. He stressed that."

Sarah reached for a cigarette. "What else did he stress?"

"Nothing much." O'Dwyer noted an edge of irritation. "Except that each department has its own independent procedures." The imitation resumed. "We administer the hospital as a whole with respect to central functions, payroll, things like that. Medical board makes rules with respect to matters of general medical policy, but each department chief runs his own show. Each suh-vice has its own rules of practice. Chiefs of suh-vice make standards in med'cine, surg'ry, and so forth. General committees—utilization, medical records, tiss-yew—will follow up periodically." He paused. "What's an acceptable level of mortality?"

"A level of mortality that's acceptable," she said, annoyed.

"I thought so," O'Dwyer said, "but I didn't want to ask. Anyway, the hospital stands behind the doctors and their work. Grimes told Mahler he was sorry for the patient but he didn't expect to see the hospital pay a dime. That's the official report."

Sarah brought the dashboard lighter to the cigarette. The glowing coil threw a soft light to the clear features. "How did Mahler take it?"

"That's funny. Didn't seem to care one way or the other. Does it matter?"

"No, no, of course not," Sarah said. "What else did Grimes tell him?"

O'Dwyer let a moment pass. "Actually Grimes did mention a few routine tests to check out besides the Bárány test. Also said he wasn't satisfied with the tissue and audit committees and a few tidbits on that order. I wonder what he had in mind."

"Em, stop the nonsense. I'm sure you know Grimes has an ax out for Bellinger. They were feuding for years about community control of medical services. Everybody knows Bellinger was pressuring the city to hand over the hospital for his own programs. Ghetto medicine, all that. If you'd watch something besides hockey and football, you'd recall that all that was aired on television about five years ago—in a polite professional way, of course. Grimes is a pompous puffing officious bore. Bellinger was charming—just charming. He wiped the floor with Grimes. Which explains why Grimes was so helpful to Mahler." She pressed her mouth to a tight line. "And, damn it, that's not the first time he's sabotaged us. We'll have to see about that man." She was considering something unpleasant. "Well, the hospital's loyalty and cooperation are important, but we're in danger of a lawsuit, not of a popularity contest. In the last analysis, the claim will depend on the medical evidence. Did you get up to neurology?"

"Naturally. Well, it was the same story. They got a new acting chief there—taco eater, accent, elevator shoes, excited, answers to Dr. Anibal Almadovar. Complete turnover there down to a new secretary. A Senorita Ramirez who *no habla da inglés*. Never heard of Manya Shroeder. Got annoyed. He told Mahler to respect the dignity of his department and to subpoena the records through the front office—and threw him out." O'Dwyer smiled widely. "He also threw me out, then marched off to surgery honing a gravity knife to do a spinal something on a victim. A beautiful little man. *Muy guapo,* as they say in the islands. I liked heem."

"Sounds charming."

"Small enough to sit on your lap."

"Oh, get on with it, Em. What else did you get?" she said, laughing reluctantly.

O'Dwyer grinned in turn. "Nothing official but I trailed him and got to something good—the head nurse in the operating room—a tough old Irish battleax named Rosie Kernochan. Father was a cop, so she was ready to open up to me. Real old-time terror, riding the nurses, working around the clock, screaming for supplies. Built like a pyramid. Nobody knows surgeons like

103

these old-time nurses—so her opinion is important, I'd say. And she swears by Bellinger."

"I am relieved. I didn't know what was coming."

"Oh, sure! Well, she told Mahler that Bellinger was the most brilliant surgeon she ever scrubbed with. Scrubbed with! Funny word. If she didn't have a face like Paddy's pig, I'd have to wonder what that meant." Sarah smiled faintly. "The operation went on schedule, she says, and Bellinger supervised. This resident, a guy named Tatum, handled the knife. Dr. Ling, a good anesthetist, back in Korea now, handled the gas works. Two interns assisted, one from Pakistan, another from Chile. Two O.R. nurses, circulating and scrub, plus a student kid who ran errands. Everything was in order. No complications. She claims it was a nice clean job and the patient was lucky to be in and out so quick. Less than three hours from first to last. Everybody's gone home, or scattered, but if you need a solid witness, Rosie Kernochan is your girl. Let her know what you want and she'll testify for you like a bazooka—and there you are. How's that for a plan?"

Sarah turned a cold eye. "Depend solely on a nurse? That's nonsense and you know it."

"If it's nonsense, why am I saying it?"

She was exasperated by the indirection, and somewhat alarmed. "I don't know why you have these childish instincts. We'll find the doctors, of course. Bellinger can handle it, I'm sure. He's very persuasive. We'll get Tatum too, if necessary."

The stocky shoulders lifted and fell. "You're a lawyer. I'm a cop. Okay, if you want to get into areas."

"What does that mean? What areas?"

O'Dwyer touched his nose. "Emergency, for one."

Sarah frowned. "Emergency? What made you go there?"

"You asked me to nose around. Get background. Atmosphere. And that's where it started." O'Dwyer was aggrieved. "So there's a Mrs. Ponsonby. Big six-foot woman. British West Indies. Mrs. Ponsonby's a sharp letter-writing type who complains to the governor about everything, mainly the horrible conditions in the ambulance and emergency services—delays, no oxygen, untrained drivers, too much stopping for red lights, patients arriving with syncope, heart arrest, exhaustion, crowded conditions, that kind of stuff—so it took lots of listening to get down to our case. . . ."

"Please, Em." Sarah touched her temples. "What's this got to do with anything?"

"I'm trying, I'm trying," O'Dwyer said imperturbably. "Mrs. Ponsonby's got it in for Bellinger and Tatum. She told Mahler they were both too arrogant to practice in a hospital setting— that they ran roughshod over the other services. She told Mahler that Dr. Goldfarb, this fiery little surgeon in charge of Emergency, bawled the hell out of Tatum in front of the staff for grabbing this case without his consent or authorization—a case that wasn't surgical at all in his opinion. She told him Tatum was fighting with everybody. She's black too—so it's not one of these race things—it's the suspicions of an old-time nurse with plenty savvy. Something funny was going on, she said."

"Funny?"

"Well, she told him Bellinger had posted a private standing order—never passed by the medical board—to send every patient with possible neurological complications to neurology for a work-up." O'Dwyer smiled mystifyingly.

"What's funny about that?"

"Well, it sounds all right. But every highway-accident victim can have a neurological problem—concussion, whiplash, whatnot. He also always has a lawsuit." O'Dwyer grinned. *"Capish?* So for years Bellinger was a witness in almost every one of those cases and cleaning up. That's what had Goldfarb screaming— that neurology was grabbing people from Emergency even if they had nothing but crushed toes—just to get Bellinger that witness business. Charming guy, Bellinger? Sure. But if he gets on the stand, you can just hear Mahler howling from here to the Court of Appeals on cross-examination. Maybe Bellinger won't be so charming then."

A mile later, Sarah said slowly, "But this was not a highway accident, Em."

"I'm not saying it was, but then the procedure at least would be according to rule. But why was Manya waltzed upstairs? All she had was her normal fits." O'Dwyer was driving cautiously, thinking aloud more than making a report. "Mrs. Ponsonby thinks Tatum saw an interesting case for himself—he's got to rack up so many operations to qualify for his specialty—and grabbed the case with an operation in mind. That thought is bound to come up in this case. So now you know what you might expect from Mahler if Bellinger or Tatum take the stand—a lot of questions about snatching patients when most hospital services complain they got no beds and take cases only when absolutely necessary. With a frozen-faced British West Indian nurse to make it stick."

Sarah sank deeper into the seat, conscious of the blowing heater and its discomfort. She knitted her brows, considering the implications with unexpected dismay. "Motive is always imputed in these cases. It's irrelevant. The decision would depend on tests and diagnosis."

"Sure, but was the diagnosis influenced by what that guy had in mind for himself? Look how we're trying to justify these guys ourselves. I mean, everybody's got an angle. You haven't seen the tests."

She glanced up. "Did you?"

"No. All sealed by the time I got there."

"Then what's that funny look for?"

"I got an idea what you'll get from the pathologist." A smile was grim. "I got this from one of the security men. It seems a student nurse, this kid named Gertrude Longfellow, brought down a hunk of brain to Dr. Cassidy, the chief of pathology, for slides and for a frozen-section report. This Cassidy is a squinty old-timer who got his training in the old Harlem Hospital in New York so he's not taking crap. About a week later, Tatum came slamming into the pathology office like a wild man. He demanded Cassidy rewrite the report or see his head torn off. The whole floor heard the uproar. Tatum said he'd bring charges for incompetence and whatnot. That's why Tatum *really* was dropped —his contract wasn't renewed and he left after completing the year—disruptive conduct and reckless charges against a senior staff doctor." O'Dwyer smiled thinly. "Figure out what Cassidy will likely say in court."

"Oh, dear," Sarah said. A long silence passed. Tires were crunching through packed snow. "Nice encouraging picture," Sarah said grimly, "but I won't believe there was malpractice on one or two items of inconclusive hospital nonsense. Not until I know what our doctors have to say. This was extremely serious surgery. A fully qualified chief of neurology was in charge of the service. I've got to assume that every medical standard of good practice was met."

"I guess you're right," O'Dwyer said.

Sarah frowned. "Don't play with me, Em. You've had something on your mind since we started. Spit it out."

"Chief, look. Right now, as I said, you're in good shape—or as good as you can be. Good or bad, the records speak for themselves. So let's dig up some expert, or our own staff guys, to swear from those records that this was outstanding—the best brain job since Cain and Abel. Experts are no problem. They'll explain a bullet through your heart. Do you really want to bring Bellinger and Tatum into court and rake up all that stuff —fights, threats, rackets, motives, whatnot? Aren't you better off with the records?"

Sarah was silent. "Nonsense," she said after a moment. "Doctors always quarrel, but that's no proof at all of malpractice. I'll want them both in court, certainly Bellinger. They'll have to justify the surgery as an exercise of their best judgment. Who else would we produce?"

"Rosie Kernochan."

"If that's a joke, I'm not amused."

"Who said it was a joke? Let Mahler cross-question her. She'll handle him. If not . . ."

"Then what?"

"See if you can settle your case," O'Dwyer said with a hard smile.

"You're maddening," she said. She stared at the swirl of dry snowflakes falling in the headlights. "I never saw anything like this," she muttered. "Mahler's ten steps ahead. Even before we start, he's got every witness pinned down. What's he getting at?" She paused. "Em? Whose instincts would you trust—yours or mine?"

"I'd trust yours, Chief," O'Dwyer said loyally.

"So would I," she said. "I think Mahler knows what's in those records. Maybe he's even got them. Is that possible?"

"All it takes is twenty bucks. Ten on the night shift."

"It's an unpleasant thought," she said. "And what else has he got? Em? You remember that little girl who had the fractured arm where the intern rotated it three hundred and sixty degrees? A page of progress reports was pulled from the records. And the medical historian added some embellishments that cropped up. It's obvious we'll need a carefully written-up history of this case, and I don't want anything funny over there. I'm not going into court this time with rotten medical records. Not with Mahler. If there's anything missing, phony, inserted, improved, torn out, or deleted, I'll crucify somebody. And if you're not serious about this, I'll get a replacement. I mean that."

O'Dwyer slackened speed at the exit to take a wide curve. Ahead lay Point Berlove and the frozen lake, tormented by hummocks of ice and snow, the open water black in the distance. The road ran along the shoreline, passing residence after residence in which families were gathering for dinner. It was an area of wide lawns, towering old trees, rich homes. It was now under snow. He drew up at a large Georgian-style mansion with lighted windows. "Whatever you say, Chief," he said. "We'll go in and beat Mahler's brains out, if that's what you want. I don't mind at all."

"Good. Is there anything else?"

O'Dwyer set his brakes. "Well, just one little thing more. We know where Bellinger's holed up if you really want to find him."

"Emmet, where?" Her voice was strained.

"Montego Bay. Where else?" O'Dwyer grinned. He handed over a prospectus for the sale of shares in a hotel called Flamingo Arms picked up at Grimes's office. Among the local sponsors the most eminent was John Howard Bellinger, M.D.

Sarah's voice was strangled. "Very well! I'll want to see everyone in the morning from Dr. Almadovar to Nurse Kernochan and down. After which I'll want a heart-to-heart talk about your tenuous future in this business. Good night, *Officer!*"

"Good night, *Ma'am*," O'Dwyer said sweetly.

He waited for Sarah to pick her way through the feathery drifts and disappear. Ma'am, he chuckled. Nothing irritated his chief more than the insolence of studied respect.

9

Mahler was tired. The trail through the hospital with its drafty halls and overheated offices had drained his energies and yet he could not sleep. It was past midnight before he put aside a magazine article on recent developments in diagnostic techniques for the location of brain tumors—radioactive tracers and scintillation photography coupled with computer technology were the latest marvels in the field—and turned off the light.

"Yes?" he said suddenly.

The street lamp threw a dappled light on the ceiling. He picked up the telephone.

"Did you just ring this room?"

"Mister, do you *know* what time it is?"

"Just answer the question."

"Ring? No, sir."

Mahler dropped the telephone and lay back, wondering what had awakened him from deep sleep.

By eight next morning he was at work at Landowski's office arranging his notes on the investigation. A pro-and-con session on all angles of the case followed. Landowski was buoyant, optimistic, brushing difficulties aside in a sense of achievement. His office associates dropped in to discuss his matter, pleased at the progress. It was a real case, moving forward with purpose. Parts were falling into place. At three Mahler asked the operator to make a call. The ringing was interminable before a click brought emptiness at the other end.

"Mrs. Shroeder?" he said.

There was silence, then a whisper. "Is that you, Mr. Mahler?"

"Yes, I'm going back to New York tonight on the eight o'clock plane. I wanted you to know."

Passivity. Nothingness. "Oh?"

"I'll be back, of course."

"Are you going ahead with my case?"

"It looks hopeful. We'll soon know."

"Oh. Can I see you before you go? Just for a minute. I'd feel reassured."

"I have nothing definite to tell you."

"Oh, please?"

He hesitated. "I have an appointment at my hotel first. I'll be over at five."

"Thank you," she whispered.

He heard nothing and hung up. He was not sure he wanted to visit the shabby little house at all. He filled a satchel with notes and papers and left. A cold brisk wind was blowing. The sky had cleared. Every bone was aching as he walked the distance along Front Street back to Lewiston House. The tall black youth with the Afro hairdo came to attention.

"Hi!" Mahler said.

Chaka folded his arms with the hauteur of kings and glared. So it was already out! Mahler thought wearily. He entered the barroom and found a booth. Jukebox rock music was blaring painfully. A thin smiling man came from the bar and joined him. "Mr. Mahler?"

"Yes?"

"I'm Horace Baldwin," the stranger said, fingering a business card with yellow stained fingers.

"Sure, Baldwin," Mahler said. "So?"

Baldwin wondered whether he might buy a distinguished visitor in town a drink. Mahler shook his head with a foreboding sense that was not disappointed. The stranger had heard about the poor woman's case. Terrible situation. He'd like to help, if possible, he said. The card, bearing the legend Insurance Claims was handed over.

"An adjuster? Already?" Mahler said.

Baldwin smiled. "Let's say special consultant in situations. The lawyer, especially the outsider, can go just so far with his claim before he hits a stone wall. There comes a time."

Mahler finished the thought. "When the man shows up who knows his way around?"

"Exactly!" Baldwin said, not losing his good humor.

The heavy shoulders rose and fell. "What are we talking about? There's no case that I know about."

"Ah, but there's talk, sir, talk," Baldwin said wisely, glancing about the darkened barroom. "I don't presume you're here on a wild-goose chase." He lowered his voice and advised that he had settled hundreds of claims against the city—all legitimate, but tough—after leading firms had given up in despair, and asked ten points of gross recovery. Very reasonable. He knew all the judges and could show references. His eyes were wary.

Mahler returned the card. "I can't hear with all this noise, but you could do me a favor," he said. "Get somebody to turn down that jukebox? I'm sensitive to noise."

"Look here, sir—" Baldwin began angrily, then paused. Jane Gates had entered meanwhile, breathless with cold, and was waiting at the booth. "Wa-al, another time," he said. "Funny, but you don't look simple—" The rest was lost in the blare.

Jane opened a mink coat and sat. "You look annoyed," she said.

"One of the local gentry. Paralegal," Mahler grunted. "Nothing to trouble your pretty little head."

She stared. "At least you sound human," she said, "not just the cold bastard I think you are."

Mahler shrugged. "I can be aroused, but not by sweet nothings."

She pulled off her gloves, shivering with the chill. "How did you make out with Grimes?"

"I'm developing a case," he said and called for drinks. "You have something to tell me?"

She dabbed her mouth. "Yes, that. Well, I'm not impressed by threats, but . . ." She sighed.

"Threats?"

"It's not me. It's the clinic. If it gets out that I'm helping you against those two doctors, my community people would resent it. As it is, some of them want to throw me out. And I built that clinic." She smiled bitterly. "Well, the depths of ingratitude in storefront medicine have yet to be plumbed." She rolled the glass in her hands, then looked up. "If I should be helpful, can you leave me out?"

"I'm not sure," Mahler said. The woman looked haggard, he thought. The rings under her eyes were darker than he recalled. She was smoking nervously and gulping her drink. It was not an unfamiliar situation. He said reasonably, "Tell me why I should."

"Because it would not be a good idea to call me." A glance of understanding passed.

Mahler said, "I'll try. But I want to know more precisely why you objected to the surgery." She failed to answer. "We're wasting time, Doctor. . . ."

She said abruptly, "Well, let's say I had seen the X rays. I discussed them with Tatum." She again dabbed her mouth with a tissue.

Mahler felt something queer shift within. At last! he thought. It was one of those moments that come in every investigation. He put a question carefully. "When was that?"

"The day before the surgery."

"Who showed you those X rays?"

"Nobody. I went down to radiology to pull those films myself from Feke. Dr. Feke's our radiologist. Ordinarily he'd be reluctant to discuss them, but I wasn't taking that nonsense. . . ."

"One minute. What made you do that?"

Jane paused, thinking back with anger. "I was upset at what was going on behind my back. But the X rays were already upstairs. I went up to neurology to find those films and have it out. . . ."

"Where'd you go?"

"To Bellinger's office, of course. I wanted to know what the hell they thought they were doing to my patient—"

"One minute. Was anyone present besides Bellinger?"

"I didn't see Bellinger. As usual, he'd left Tatum in charge while he was off to New York on business of some sort." She frowned, thinking back. "I forget the day, Tuesday or Wednesday. Anyway, Lurene, that's Lurene Storrs, Bellinger's personal secretary —insolent piece, really—swished off to the john when I came in—"

"One moment. Did she witness what was said?"

"Only at the start, perhaps."

"Oh. Do you know how to reach her?"

"No-o. She got another hospital job in New York, I heard. But to get back, Tatum was on the telephone, arguing with one of the other residents. There was an atmosphere, I recall, but that wasn't unusual. Everyone knew they were constantly fighting there like cats and dogs. Meanwhile I looked at the X rays. Tatum said he had noticed a mass pressing on the left lateral ventricle here." She touched the side of her skull. "He said something about the inexorable law of growth of tumors of the brain and the immediate need to explore and so forth. He told me Bellinger agreed with his evaluation and had authorized the operation. I told him I'd talk to Bellinger myself."

"Is that when you were threatened?" Mahler asked innocently.

She paused, and laughed harshly. "Who told you that? I wouldn't make too much of it."

"What did he actually say?"

"That he'd have me thrown out of the hospital if I interfered. Nonsense, of course. Empty threats. I wasn't impressed. Just doctor talk, you know."

"Go on." It was surprising how useful empty threats and doctor talk might prove in court. "Then what happened?"

"I told him he was full of shit."

"Did he care for that?" Mahler said dryly.

She frowned. "No, but I must say I was sorry I said it. I simply meant that he was wrong. I hadn't allowed for his sensitivity and arrogance. His reaction was too ridiculous. He screamed that he was working his fingers to the bone, that the rigidity and red tape were intolerable, that no one let him give his God-given talents to the poor, the sick, all that nonsense. It was not my field, he reminded me. I said I saw nothing to justify the brutality of the treatment. I urged him to let me take Manya home, to watch her progress with medication and so forth. It was talking to the wall. The silly ass began ranting at my rudeness, reminded me he too was a doctor, unbelievable stuff, and I left. When I got there the next day the operation was in progress. There was nothing I could do." She folded her arms. "So you see where that leaves you, so far as making your own kind of threats. Eh?"

The jukebox wailed to a halt.

Mahler said, "If it's not your field, how can you be sure what the X rays showed?"

"That's what Tatum said," she replied. "But Dr. Feke had agreed with me. Tatum was furious with Feke. He snatched those films before Feke could put his findings in the record and stalked off. Ostensibly to take them to Bellinger for review."

"Well, *was* there a tumor?"

She said cautiously, "I know Tatum said he'd found a tumor and removed it. He may have removed something. But what was it? We really have no way to know." She ran a hand through the short graying hair. Her mouth took on a dogged cast. "Well, that's it. Stick to the lack of physical proof. I wouldn't go into the rest too deeply."

Mahler considered the matter. Was there a warning? A hint of danger? He glanced at the clock. "You've been a big help, Doctor. Oh, one thing more. What's your real impression of Bellinger? As a woman?"

"Thank you for that." She smiled faintly. "Plausible. Unscrupulous. Handsome. If I were a man, I wouldn't give him five minutes with my wife."

"And Tatum?"

She hesitated. "The stuff that martyrs are made of—whatever that is. Rigid. Impossible man. Totally sincere. I'd concentrate on him. You can destroy him like *that*—if you like." She snapped her fingers. "And you will, I'm sure. I can't stop you because you won't listen and because I certainly can't hurt Manya's chances either." A grimace twisted the heavy features. "Christ knows I've tried."

Mahler threw up his hands, disconcerted. Nothing was a surprise, but all this matter, reluctantly given, had a ring of conviction. "Doctor, you're a doll," he said with a tired grin. "Don't worry about a thing. I haven't lost a witness yet. Are we friends?"

To his surprise, she laughed.

The canned music returned, light and winsome now—the music of an older generation and still good to hear. It was of all things a polka.

After they had parted, Mahler went up to his room and put through a call to New York. A dulcet voice responded.

"Why, honey!" Cinabelle Webster cooed with pleasure. A pause while newspaper clatter filled the background. "Any special reason for this call?"

"Yes, there is." Mahler added Lurene Storrs to his prior list. Could she be located? he asked.

"No sweat. I'll ask around the bars," Cinabelle drawled. "Take care now, honey. Your giant medical claim is getting to be the chitchat of uptown medical circles."

He replied in kind. Honors exchanged, he packed his bag and called for a taxi. It was almost five.

Shroeder had dressed for the occasion. He sat in a working-man's pose, stiff, formal. His worn hands rested on his knees. The man was gray, beaten, destroyed—and angry, Mahler thought.

"So what does it add up to?" Shroeder demanded.

Mahler had patiently summarized the position. He was now ready to leave. It was an odd empty moment in the small room—received with apathy. "You don't have and never had cancer, Manya," he said. "Isn't that good news?"

She was staring at a watercolor. "In a way," she replied in a dull voice. "If I could believe it. What good does it do me?"

"All right, in that sense," Shroeder said. "So where does it leave us? When do we start the action? I mean, when?"

Mahler said, "I can't tell you anything for sure until we get the records reviewed by an expert. But it looks hopeful."

Manya interrupted. "I smell gas, Frank."

"Forget it," Shroeder said.

"Will you look?"

"I did look. You don't smell gas."

Manya was seated on the parlor sofa, propped on a pillow. She turned inquiringly.

"There's no gas," Mahler said.

"I smell it though." She turned back. "Frank. Turn it off? To satisfy me?"

"Jesus! What I mean," Shroeder exploded in exasperation. He went to the kitchen, wincing as a muscle cramped, and closed the door.

Manya gave the lawyer a queer glance. "It gives him some-thing to do," she said. A pale tongue went out provocatively. "And it gives us a moment alone."

"What does that mean?"

"I only mean it's easier to talk without him." She was smiling oddly.

"Do you smell gas or not?"

"How do I know?" she giggled, then frowned. An expression of intense suffering gathered. She closed her eyes and went silent, touching her temples. "Don't pay attention," she whispered.

A moment passed.

"It's gone now," she said with a sigh.

Mahler said, "I'd better go."

"Must you?"

"I have a plane to catch. I'll be back in a week or so."

"I'll show you out." She stood and swayed. "Oh, I'm weak. Help me." Mahler took her arm. The loose robe fell open showing the swell of overfull breasts. She was a weight against his hand. "You know what's really wrong with him, Bill?" she said confidentially. "Frank misses it."

"It?"

The coarse expression of amusement was unexpected.

"Oh, sure. He's too old maybe, but he does. Not that I don't try." There was an odd intimacy in holding her arm, Mahler thought. Evidently she thought so. "I tried everything but it's no good," she went on with a sly look. "So he won't let me try anything now and then he blames me. Me—when he's the fizzler. Maybe he's afraid I'll go into a tailspin if he ever really gives it to me. Jane tells me it's my fault." Her tongue was teasing. "What do you think, Bill? Is that part of the problem?"

"It may be. Let the doctors handle it."

She shrugged him off, petulantly. "I don't like you like this, Bill. I have feelings. Maybe I have more itch than you think. I'm not the one that's old." There was a rising note of excitement.

Jesus! Mahler thought. It was not the first such verbal assault in his years in law, but this out-of-character vulgarity was uncomfortable. "Come on, Manya. I'll see you again next week," he said. A medicinal smell was strong.

The look of expectancy faded. "Okay." They walked out to the tiny foyer. She shivered and stood close. "I'll tell you something else," she said. Her face was a white triangle of urgency. "You and I could be lovers," she whispered. "We could, you know.

I could come any place you say. I wouldn't care about anything —not Frank, not the baby—if you'd have me. Would you?"

Her clutch tightened, her breasts rose, her breath was noisy. In the dim light her large green eyes were desperate. It was unexpected, and yet not entirely so. He found himself thinking how vulnerable her plump neck was. "Manya . . ." he began uncomfortably.

"Ssh!" She came close to his ear and whispered almost too faint to be heard, but the meaning was clear.

He said, "You don't mean this. It doesn't make sense."

She saw his expression and stood back in horror. "Oh, God! What's wrong with me that I do these things?" She buried her face in her hands. "What is it? What is it?"

He touched her hair. "Manya . . ."

"Oh, no! No!" She turned about, stricken, and ran back to the ill-smelling parlor.

What the hell was that about? he wondered. It was unappetizing, part of the pathology. Was it something to show the jury? Would a jury understand?

The flight back to New York was uneventful. Then suddenly in midflight he knew why he had awakened the night before. He had neglected to keep his appointment at the offices of the Honorable Mrs. Sarah van Loon. Or even to call to apologize for the lapse of protocol. His notes lay in his lap, unread.

Mahler was at his desk in shirt sleeves when Curtayne entered, pink-cheeked and pleased to report a lead. There was a top-flight neurosurgeon at Featherstone Memorial Hospital, Dr. Joseph Yarberry, who was a likely prospect.

"He's never testified before," the old lawyer said, beaming, "but he might be persuaded. Outstanding man. Marvelous, if he would."

"It sounds good," Mahler agreed. "When can I see him?"

"A week from Tuesday. They start at seven sharp. You're invited to see brain surgery by the master. You ought to know what it looks like. Can you make it?"

"I'll sure try. Where'd you get the lead?"

Curtayne chuckled. "I dropped in on Charlie Seidman with

the problem. He was glad to help. This case couldn't happen to a more deserving guy, he said. And laughed."

"Charlie's not exactly an admirer of mine. He turned it down himself," Mahler said. "Tuesday, at seven. Thanks, Jim."

"Don't thank me," Curtayne said. "Just don't spend all your time mooning in Lewiston. One case doesn't make a law practice. Now what about lunch?"

The following day a call from Cinabelle Webster brought Mahler to a busy restaurant in Harlem. Cinabelle, buxom and bursting in a white knit dress, threw out her arms. "Welcome to Frank's," she cried, triumphant. "And to the finest sauerbraten in town."

Mahler looked about with pleasure. Frank's Restaurant was an anachronism, a throwback to an older Harlem when its cuisine matched its Central European patrons' tastes. It was the best eating place in the area. "It hasn't changed much since this was my stamping ground," he said. "Now, what have you got?"

"This way, honey." Cinabelle led him through a babble, greeting everyone in soul talk as she went. "You two beautiful people should know each other," she announced.

A sulky young woman was drinking at a rear table. "I hear you're the busy little man," Lurene Storrs said with a resentful look. "Are you really going after Bellinger?"

Mahler ordered drinks. "It depends. Do you remember the case we're talking about?"

"That exploratory craniotomy? Sure. Real mess. No wonder lawyers get rich."

"Some do, some don't." Mahler said. The girl was drunk, he thought. "How do you feel about Bellinger?"

Lurene removed a flake of tobacco from her mouth, considered the matter. "John Bellinger is a chinch," she said with precision. "What else?"

"Were you on duty when that surgery was done?" he asked.

"I was there that day," she said.

Mahler studied a latter day Queen Nefertiti, the straight nose, olive skin, high forehead, and lambent brown eyes, all topped by an enormous halo of finely spun hair. She had not answered the question, he observed. "I know the operation began after five. Wasn't that late to begin?"

Lurene shrugged. "It could happen. Bellinger was late getting back from New York. Percy Tatum waited till the last minute. I know because he sent a stinking memo on it the next morning. Percy could be a real pain in the ass. Okay?"

Mahler waited a moment. "At what point did Bellinger show up—if you know?"

The girl looked up with calculation. "I'm not sure I like this. . . . Fritz? Hit me again," she said, calling the waiter. She came back to Mahler. The searching eyes, a strong humorous smile seemed to put her off. "Well, mister. My answer is crystal-clear. I am in a state of confusion about those events."

Cinabelle rose and left diplomatically to see a man, as she put it, about a dog. When she returned, Lurene was giving the discursive story of an unhappy episode in her life to a somewhat baffled member of the bar. Mahler's manner was one of dogged patience.

10

Featherstone Memorial Hospital in New York overlooking the East River was a quiet institution of chrome and indirect lighting and low voices. On the sixth-floor corridor a dozen neurological patients lay on tables, pale, immobile—more like corpses, Mahler thought, than living beings. He was directed to a locker room where he was given shoe covers and operating-room garb—white coverall shirt and trousers, a cap, and mask. He stripped and changed. A Chinese doctor was changing into working gear and filling the air with dull, filthy jokes. A beaky, handsome blond young doctor with serious eyes introduced himself as Fred Eckstein, chief resident and assistant to Dr. Joseph Yarberry. "Follow me," Eckstein said. "Setting up is like a religious ritual. You might as well see it. We're starting an hour later than usual. The nurses had a seminar or lecture in something. That sort of thing is always fouling up our schedules."

"Thank you, Doctor," Mahler said. He closed the locker and followed Eckstein down a long wide corridor lit by fluorescent lamps. Eckstein's quiet manner bred confidence. Mahler felt like a new schoolboy, but then in a way he was new in a strange school.

Eckstein halted. "Here we are. Just do what I do," he said and entered an operating room.

Mahler put on his mask and followed. The operating room was being set up by a team of nurses. A slender young scrub nurse was preparing the operating theater assisted by an even younger circulating nurse. Two black student nurses were assisting. It was an ordinary square room equipped with surrealistic monitoring equipment and anesthetic gear. It was almost eight.

Eckstein said, "Where would you like to stand?"

"Anywhere you say," Mahler replied.

Eckstein looked about. "When we begin, I'll show you where you can watch. Meanwhile, just take a chair."

Mahler sat, feeling totally inadequate.

The circulating nurse smiled. "Having fun?"

"Fun's not the word," Mahler said.

A sound like cups rattling brought a patient in from the hall—an old Jewish-looking man with defeated eyes swimming with sedation was wheeled in. Eckstein leaned over the old man. "What about those headaches, Papa?" he asked.

The old man gestured feebly. "Not too bad now."

The door flew open. "Ready? Ready? Ready?" The Chinese doctor whose scatology had filled the locker room strode in. Dr. Chou, introduced as Dr. Fu Manchu, smiled and turned to inspect his equipment.

Mahler said, "I see a Sanborn Oscilloscope and Monitor. What does it do?"

Eckstein said, "We can monitor respiratory and other functions on tape and review it later. Tape is kept in the computer room. It can be set to signal when vital functions fall below a certain rate or level."

Chou said heartily, "Anything you want, Mahler. Heart rate. Venous pressure. Temperature. Spinal pressure. Anything. Excuse me now?" He wheeled over a table with a container of pink pebbles and tanks marked N_2O and O and got busy.

Eckstein said, "We're going to do a small cut down on the wrist. We'll insert a catheter into the artery to get a continuous blood-pressure reading on the scope. By visualizing you get an idea as to the regularity of those functions. Just watch the nurses and you'll get an idea how they work. The scrub nurses pass over the instruments and that stuff. One nurse circulates—that is, she finds anything the other girls aren't prepared for and things like that."

A nurse walked in and apologized for lateness. The train had been thirty minutes late.

"Okay, okay," Eckstein said. "Scrub up."

"Don't eat me, Fred," the nurse replied. She joined the others in preparing swabs and bottles and piling up sterile sheets and bandages.

"Here's how you insert the catheter," the first scrub nurse said to the student nurses. The second scrub nurse began to lay out a tray of instruments, counting with earnest attention. Eckstein turned to the patient. "How are we doing, Papa?" he said.

"Okay," the patient said.

The first scrub nurse said, "Doris, did you get that requisition from the storeroom? Oh, God, why don't people remember? Get that stuff over, will you?"

The second scrub nurse was smearing conductive paste on a metal plate. "In a minute," she said. Circular reflecting lights over the patient were lowered. Floor lights blazed.

"Where's my tape, Fred?" the first nurse said.

"Right there," Eckstein replied.

"Oh, sure," the nurse said. To the patient: "This won't be tight." She wound the tape on a limp wrist.

"Are you sterile?" a nurse said.

"I'm sterile," the other replied.

"Is Fred sterile?" the first one asked.

"I don't feel sterile," Fred joked.

Disinfectant was poured freely onto a swab. It dripped on the floor. "Let me get finished with this," the first nurse said. The skull was daubed and swabbed. She put on sterile clothes. "Where are those sterile forceps?" she asked.

Eckstein waited for attention. "I'll start the cut-down," he said. Chou meanwhile had inserted an ankle catheter.

A bleary young doctor entered, yawning. "Sorry, I'm late," he said.

Eckstein said, "Yeah, sure. Oh, I'd like you to meet Mr.—What's your name again?"

"Mahler."

"Yeah. This is Bob Ross. He's observing. You can ask him questions." Eckstein returned to the cut-down. "Oh, Bob, can you run down meanwhile and get the X rays? They didn't send them up yet, I don't know why."

Ross nodded and left.

Chou hung a bottle on a hook and bent to the patient. "How are you doing, Mr. Stein? Getting sleepy?"

"Not yet," the old man said.

Mahler crossed over and examined the monitoring devices. A dot was dancing on an oscilloscope in steady rhythm. The work went on.

Eckstein said, "You're getting a little sleepy now?"

"So I'm getting sleepy," the patient said.

Chou said, "Relax now. Try to sleep. Take it easy. Relax. This is oxygen so don't worry about it." He put a mask over the patient and straightened the tube from the dripping bottle to the ankle catheter. The patient's clenched fists fell limp. Chou vigorously squeezed a black bag to force a mixture of gasses into the patient's lungs.

Ross entered. "Here are the X rays," he said. He clamped a half-dozen films into the viewer at the wall and came over to Mahler with a friendly smile. "Can I help you?"

Mahler returned the smile. "What's this canister of pink pebbles?"

"Anesthetic," Ross said.

"Halothane?" Mahler said. "Is that good?"

Chou looked up. "It's a good anesthetic if nothing goes wrong. He's out now." He directed a pencil-shaped flashlight at the patient's tongue and wedged open the mouth. With Eckstein's help, the oxygen mask was replaced by a tube leading to the black bag. Chou gave the patient a kindly pat and sat to a monitoring post and began to write up a record. The circulating nurse swept soiled cloths into a hamper. The second scrub nurse began mixing ketchup-red paste in a steel bowl.

Eckstein said, "Bob, come here. We need you for this. We've got to get the head exactly in place this time. We're turning him to the right. This hand goes under him." The doctors and the circulating nurse took positions at the table. The old man lay prone and naked, genitalia and gray hair visible. While the doctors on a signal from Eckstein moved the patient with critical precision, the nurse placed the genitalia in a comfortable position. Mahler began to take notes.

Nurse: Where's the extension for this?

Chou: Connect that, please.

Eckstein: We need a doughnut.

Nurse: It's there under the shelf.

Eckstein: Bob, get a towel under his head. We've got to pull him up on the table more.

Chou: All lines okay. Pull him up.

Another doctor introduced as Paul Keating entered the room. Eckstein said, "Paul, we're both scrubbing for Yarberry. Okay?" Keating nodded. The nice business of placing the patient's head in position went on.

Nurse: Paul, give me a hand. We'll need a pillow.

Eckstein: Let's move the whole body.

Nurse: Gloria, wait. I'll show you how those straps go on later.

Mahler joined the doctors who were studying the X rays on the wall. Eckstein touched the film. "This is where it is," he said. He went back to the patient and outlined the area for operation. The naked skull had been cleaned with strong soap and painted with yellow antiseptic solution. Ross was examining the X rays. Mahler said, "Can you explain what's happening here?"

Ross explained the matter pleasantly while keeping his eye on Eckstein. "This patient came here from another hospital with a history showing brain tumor. The symptoms began four weeks ago with visual defects and field cuts—"

"Field cuts?"

"Field of vision gets cut off left or right like holes in the field of vision. Loss of part of the field of vision means pressure and destruction of the optic nerve. Pressure shows the mass is growing." Ross went on. "Then he had energy loss with writing and speech defects. He had trouble in finding words. There was remote and recent memory loss. . . ."

"I have that trouble too," Mahler joked.

"Yeah," Ross said. "But we use Latin terms when it's significant. The old man lost interest in daily work and activities. A few days ago he began to have seizures and entered this other hospital. Severe headaches began from the top region here"—he touched the top of his skull—"with nausea and vomiting. These are all pretty much signs of brain tumor. Jet vomiting when pressure gets past the critical point is especially significant. It's the sudden onset and abrupt severity that tells that something dramatic has built up."

Mahler lowered his voice. "What if the seizures are long-standing and other symptoms have been chronic over a period of time? Would that necessarily show a tumor?"

Ross shook his head. "Not necessarily. It'd take precise tests to establish the tumor. What I've just described are breakdowns of functions located in specific areas of the cortex of the brain, especially here in the speech and motor areas." He touched a point above and slightly back of the left ear. "Temporal and parietal areas—so-called from the names of the temporal and parietal bones. Visual area is occipital. Back here." He touched the back of his skull. "Funny. The optic nerve runs back to the base of the brain, which shows what our fish ancestors began with—smell and sight. But pressure from a growing mass isn't limited to the point of origin. It's exerted on the entire brain. That's why we look for papilledema. That means swelling and inflammation of the eye grounds—that is, the optic nerve which you can see on inspection where it enters the eyeball."

Mahler made a mental note. "Can that effect always be seen?"

"Only if the pressure's there. Now that's the general picture. The problem is to get specific." Ross went on in an undertone. "In this patient's case the verbal losses are up front. The tumor is in the back. Here, I'll show you." He made a quick sketch on the blackboard. "It's all very well to know there's a tumor, but we can't operate on the entire brain. We've got to pinpoint the location and that takes these tests—X rays. If they were doubtful, we've got fancier tests now—scan-imaging in which radioactive elements are converted in a photomultiplier tube, electronically processed, and data recorded and displayed in color photographs —scintiphotos, you know?"

"I've read about that," Mahler said. "Did you take scintiphotos?"

"Not needed. This is clear enough." Ross snapped on the viewer lights. Ghostly visualizations of the arterial tree sprang into view. "Front views. Side views. You can see what's happening in this arteriogram. The dye which was injected into the carotid artery outlines the arterial tree."

"I don't see anything wrong," Mahler said.

"If you knew more, you would. You'd see that these arteries

are being pushed aside by something. Did you ever see that old movie, *The Invisible Man?*"

"The one with Claude Rains?"

"Yeah. Invisible, but if you dusted him, you'd see his outlines. With this air pollution, he'd be a walking bubble in New York."

"Or a tumor?"

"Right. The tumor itself is invisible because the density is identical with normal tissue. Tumor and normal tissue in fact are virtually alike. It's the function, the wild growth, that makes it malignant. All you can see then are its effects like here. . . ." Ross moved to another film. "This is a pneumoencephalogram. The brain has four empty spaces, ventricles, connected by small aqueducts through which fluid circulates. If a tumor, even a tiny tumor, blocks one of the aqueducts, the pressure can build up suddenly with catastrophic effects. If the brain stem, which controls breathing, is jammed into the spine, it's curtains." Ross snapped his fingers to illustrate. "It's possible to drain that fluid and fill the ventricles with air through the spine. Since air has a different density, those spaces stand out on the X ray. Provided, of course, you can get them properly filled with air. If the air space is distorted, a mass is indicated. This shows a mass here at the left lateral ventricle."

Mahler peered closely. "Is that pressing the parietal lobe?"

"Yes, why?"

"Just interested. What kind of mass is it? Can you tell?"

"It's probably a glioma. Tumor of the supportive cells and fibers of the nervous system. It may be a variety called astrocytoma, named for the star-shaped nerve cells, astrocytes, from which they originate. This variety of tumor tends to infiltrate deeply into the brain tissue so that it must be removed together with the surrounding tissue to be effective. At this point, of course, that is difficult because the speech area is involved." Ross paused. "The speech area is the seat of the soul, so to speak."

"Seat of the soul? That's a funny phrase."

"I mean, the speech center is the center of cognitive thinking. In right-handed people, it lies in the left brain, as you probably know."

"I know," Mahler said.

Ross smiled. "We do have two brains, you see, and while one

dominates, they function together. The two sides exchange information through connective fiber bridges, blend and keep in balance. If those bridges are cut for surgical or experimental purposes, you've got two independent thinking centers, two brains—almost two persons—in one individual. Literally one hand doesn't know what the other is doing."

"Sounds like city government at work," Mahler said. He peered closely. "These shadows mean nothing to me. Can you be wrong here about the interpretation?"

"No, because this displacement from the midline is gross. Finer cases can be disputed. Yarberry recently had a hell of a time trying to get Fred to see a kink in the aqueduct of Sylvius. That's located here." Ross touched the film. "Fred refused. Wouldn't let Yarberry browbeat him either. He said, 'Joe, you want to see a kink? So see a kink. Just let me alone.'"

"What did Yarberry say?"

"He got sore, then laughed. He's king of kinks around here. He's arbitrary as hell, but good-natured too. And he's good, of course. But you have these stuffed shirts who'd kill you for talking back. Brown-nosing goes a long way in this business." Ross grimaced cynically. "There's a fallback procedure when you can't get those ventricles to fill with air through the spine—the ventriculogram. In such case, you stick a needle directly into the ventricle to drain the fluid and to introduce air, but that's rough. You will always destroy some brain tissue and might hit a blood vessel and cause bleeding. It's safe but it has a given percentage of mortality too. About two percent, I believe."

"I don't call that safe," Mahler said.

"If you suspect a tumor, you might like those odds."

"It's a game of odds?"

"It's not an insurance policy, for sure."

A monitor began to click.

The circulating nurse said, "Fred, stand still." Eckstein held out his arms while the nurse put a smock on him. The nurses were small, lithe girls with squirrel faces, Mahler thought, very energetic and muscular. The patient was now enclosed in a tent over which a tray of instruments had been swung into place. A scrub nurse, poised and ready, peered down over her mask. Her eyes seemed to snap with intelligence. Nothing of the patient showed but a small patch of brown skull marked with red lines.

Eckstein said, "Electricity checked? Suction?"

A suction device growled.

Eckstein looked up at Mahler. "We think it's probably a glioma, but there's an outside chance of a clot. Some tumors are highly vascularized and show up as part of the arterial tree. Some not. They show up as an emptiness. Okay?"

"Okay," Mahler said.

He noted a sign that required that all neurological specimens be promptly placed in formalin solution.

Eckstein looked up. "Request permission to start."

"Go, man," Chou said.

The scrub nurse standing over the instrument tray handed down a knife and the operation began. Eckstein sliced into the scalp and reflexed a flap from the skull. Bright arterial blood was being sucked by Keating, whose nimble hands followed Eckstein's.

"These are called Dandy clamps," Eckstein said.

Perhaps thirty Dandy clamps were going into the cuts, clamping bleeding vessels. A matching array of clips held the bleeding on the opposite side of the flap in control. "We leave enough vessels attached to keep it vitalized till closing," Eckstein said. "We call this a reverse Frazier flap."

The operation went on. The scrub nurse was handing down instruments without instructions. A cautery controlled by foot pedals was sending up a burning smell. Eckstein looked up at one point inquiringly. "Well?"

A sponge was handed down.

"Can someone get me a towel?" a nurse said.

The scalp flap, now fully reflexed, was no longer bleeding. A tough layer of fibrous tissue capped the naked bone.

"Let's get rid of this," Eckstein said. "Periosteal, please." He began to scrape with vigor. Except for a center island, the fibrous tissue, called the pericranium, was scraped to the bone. He looked at Mahler. "We leave that portion intact to nourish the bone and also to anchor it back later. Right?"

"Sounds right to me," Mahler said.

"Bring that bucket over, Gloria?" the second scrub nurse said, then followed the student nurse's glance. The oscilloscope of the

128

arterial pressure monitor had stopped. All eyes went to Chou. Chou turned a valve and the signals resumed as before. Ross said in an undertone, "We watch Chou. When he gets worried, we get worried. Otherwise it's his container of chow mein." Chou smiled and made a note. He was keeping records and time schedules correlated with the surgical and other procedures, he explained. Vital signs were going onto tape for future study. A student nurse brought a bucket into which bloodied towels were flung.

"Perforator," Eckstein said.

An instrument like a carpenter's drill was handed down.

Eckstein said, "Starting perforation. Doris, will you move that table back? I haven't got room."

Eckstein went on to drill the skull methodically by hand. Shavings of skull emerged from each drill hole—like wood shavings, Mahler thought. "I'm going to make three burr holes," Eckstein said, "and then take off a skull flap. You can watch it over my shoulder if you like. Bob will explain." Keating squirted cooling saline solution to keep down heat.

Mahler had once seen wildcatters drilling for oil in West Texas. Except for scale, the burr was not unlike the drill head he recalled—a blunt head that gouged more than it cut. Eckstein's burr, which was three-quarters of an inch across, was a No. 2 burr, which meant it had been used twice and could be used only once more before being discarded.

"How does he know when to stop?" Mahler said.

"By the feel," Ross said.

"Is it that delicate and precise?"

"Nothing better."

"And if he misses?"

"Fred doesn't miss," Ross said. He was watching intently as the burr ground through bone. A mash of particles was wetted by the cooling saline solution.

"Good God, he's got pressure," Eckstein remarked to Mahler. "Take a look, if you like? That's the dura—the outer skin of the brain."

The burr hole was an inverted cone sunk into raw bleeding bone. A taut skin filled with blue veins was bulging at the bottom of the cone. "See, look, you can palpate," Eckstein said. "That's pressure. Lots of pressure."

"I see that." Mahler stared at the opening.

Keating touched a finger to the dura mater. "The gentleman has pressure," he agreed.

"Let's widen that," Eckstein said. He applied a crunching instrument to enlarge the hole.

The second burr hole was easier. A third was harder. Evidently the skull had varying thicknesses. Keating followed with the sucker and helped with the burr as Eckstein tired. The holes were crunched wider in methodical fashion. It was hard work. Metal guides were inserted from hole to hole to detach the dura from the skull.

"Ready for that craniotome," Eckstein said. The craniotome was a saw activated by compressed nitrogen. Following the guides, it was passed along the skull from hole to hole. A high whistling note sounded as the expanding gas chilled the air. Keating squirted cooling solution on the heated path of the saw. Eckstein said, "Bob, notice we always do the midline last because the sagittal sign lies beneath it. If we have trouble, we can always go back." He leaned forward intently, guiding the saw along the bone. "Ah!" He grunted and lifted off a section of skull about four inches in diameter. The inner surface looked like fibrous white coconut meat dotted with beads of red exudate. "There it is," he said.

The taut dura was the outer velum covered with a network of blue veins. Beneath, the brain pressed for release. It was alive, a sensate thing, it struggled. Mahler felt a sweet taste of horror; he was not sure what he felt. Eckstein said, "I'd like to open it, but I should wait for Yarberry. It might herniate. Where is he, by the way? He's late."

A nurse said, "I heard he was at a meeting."

"No, he's in his office." Eckstein began to apply bone wax to raw bleeding bone. Keating swabbed the open wound. The outer membrane, the dura mater, bulged.

Mahler whispered, "What happens if it herniates?"

Ross said, "It could spurt. Right now Fred could open the dura and expose the brain to decompression. The effect of that is to relieve headache and nausea and some deficits. Some deficits are irreversible, of course, where the tumor's encroached. Nerve tissue can't regenerate. Too highly organized. Not like skin or liver, of course."

"What happens if Yarberry doesn't show up?" Mahler said. "Can he go ahead alone?"

"Fred can do it," Ross replied.

The operation came to a standstill. The operating theater was being cleaned. The brain was covered with wet gauze. The circulating nurse crossed to the autoclave and fiddled with its controls. Mahler stepped over to Chou's console. Chou was seated at his table studying vital signs on the instruments. A dot on a small oscilloscope was darting up and down like a rocket, flickering its life signals. Mahler said, "I see you're making notes. Is that standard procedure?"

"Oh, yes," Chou said.

"Doesn't this get you jumpy?"

"Sure. A ruptured aneurysm took five years off my life last week."

Eckstein looked up. "I hate to admit it but Chou's the best man on the job," he said. "Will somebody call Yarberry? I'm waiting but the dura is very tight. . . ."

A nasal Midwestern voice in the hall said, ". . . hyperventilate? Okay. I'll be in to see about that. . . ." A red-haired energetic doctor strode in, putting on a mask. A spangle of freckles on a weather-beaten face and a jaunty grin could have been worn by an oversized jockey. "What kind of woodpecker surgery's going on here, Fred?" Dr. Yarberry demanded. "Is that a cyst?"

"Can't tell," Eckstein said.

"I told you it's not a cyst," Yarberry said. "Tap for that cyst, if you think it's there."

Smiles, if any, were hidden by the masks. Mahler was introduced. "Fine. Good. Glad to have you. Watch Fred," Yarberry said. He stepped to the patient. "Okay, open the dura and get in, Fred."

The room had been energized.

Eckstein put up his hand for scissors, then quickly cut and folded back the white membrane, leaving it attached to a network of blood vessels to keep it alive. "For Christ's sake, Fred, don't cut the brain," Yarberry said. He turned to Mahler. "These particular malignancies, gliomas, are never really cured by surgery when they've gone this far, you know. You take out what you can and treat what's left with radiation and experimental drugs. Ultimately it fails."

"Always?" Mahler said.

"Yes. At least it will in this case. In this area, there's just so much surrounding tissue we can take out without destroying the man himself. This is an infiltrating bitch at the wrong place."

"But as a type are they curable?"

"In a small percent of the cases only. Possibly."

"It sounds so statistical."

"It's a statistical game." Yarberry grinned. "We try to make life bearable here—what's left. The old man had a run for it. He can't pay for this high-class doctoring, of course."

"Why are you doing it then?"

"The old man kept the cigar store near my house. Why not?" Yarberry said. The brain was now exposed. He said with excitement, "See the tumor? See that red area? That's the tumor. On the surface, so that's good. Take a look. Dead center."

The convolutions of the brain were shot with angry purple blood vessels. The red area was the size of a quarter. "Look at that. Look at that," Yarberry said. The arteries were beating visibly.

"I see it," Mahler said. A universe as remote as the galaxies of space lay before him.

Yarberry touched the spot. "Feel that, Fred?" Eckstein placed a finger on the red spot. "Feels soft," Yarberry said. "I'll take it now. Okay, get that sucker going. Cautery?" A scrub nurse handed over a cautery. Eckstein stood opposite holding the sucking device. The two surgeons continued the procedure, alternately cauterizing and sucking soft edematous tissue. The cautery buzzed like an angry bluebottle on a windowpane. The burning smell returned. The student nurses were standing aside, discussing personal matters.

"Patties. Patties," Yarberry said sharply.

The scrub nurse handed over a dozen paper strips.

Mahler said, "What are patties?"

Ross said in an undertone, "Those paper strips. That brain tissue is too soft to fool with and hard to handle. Like Jell-O. You can't apply the sucker directly or you'll suck the brain itself.

Watch him." Mahler and Ross mounted stools to view the operating area over Yarberry's shoulders. Strips of tissue were laid delicately to protect the brain. The device sucked fluid oozing through the strips.

"More cottenoids, for Christ's sake. Come on, Doris. A trained seal would move faster," Yarberry said intently. "This brain is abnormally soft. And full. See that soft stuff, Fred?" He glanced up. "Get closer. There, there, there. Come on, come on." The sucking sound was high-pitched, angry. After an interval Yarberry said, "Feel it, Fred, feel it. This is what tumor is. Don't squash that tissue. Gently with that thumb. What are you, a lumberjack?" The remonstrances went on, sharply but not unkindly. Cautery and sucker alternated. It was close work. The wound had become an open hole.

Mahler felt a wave of boredom, disengagement suddenly. He said to Ross, "How do they keep the wound sterile with everybody breathing on it?"

Ross said, "What can you do about it?"

Yarberry stood back to clean a cautery tip of coagulated gook and called for a light. An elaborate arrangement like a miner's headlight was put over his forehead. The circulating nurse ran a line down the back of the smock into an electrical connection. He focused the light and returned to the deepening hole. Chou's oscilloscope was rising and diving like a mad firefly.

Yarberry kept up a running fire. "Light, please? Hold it. You wiggle. Hold it now. There's tumor there plus brain. See? Give it to Bob to find." An interval. "See the difference? The gray? That's brain. Edematous brain. Soft brain, see it? The other gray material there, see it? That's tumor arising from the brain." He looked up at Mahler. "Step here. I'll show you something. That's hemorrhage of the tumor. Now you see the reason for the rapid onset of the problem. Bend down and look."

The excavation seemed endlessly deep, a cleft between walls of bloodied gray matter. Deep under the skull, a blackberry jelly seemed to infiltrate farther. "You see that black stuff?" Yarberry said. "That's old blood. Okay? So now you have tumor plus hemorrhage. Fred wouldn't believe it but there it is. See it, Paul?"

Mahler was staring into the endless recesses of the cavity. Down caverns measureless to man, down to a sunless sea, he thought. Yarberry was saying, "We're going to take out more brain. Okay, come on, Fred. Hold it there."

A girl in a blue smock entered. "Doctor, Larry wants to know if you can spare a piece of specimen now?"

Yarberry looked up. "What's the boy friend studying now? Meat cutting?"

The girl giggled. "Histopathology. He's doing frozen sections and making slides."

Yarberry nodded. "Come back later. I'll see you get a good piece." He picked up the cautery and returned to the work. Eckstein followed with the suction device. Yarberry said impatiently, "I've told you, Fred, when you're making a noise, it isn't sucking. Put it into the tissue, then it'll suck up. You're too slow." A moment passed. "You've got it all gummed up. Wipe it off on the surface. See? Scissors, please?" A moment passed. "Put your finger there. Don't you see it? Ah, ah. Bring that light down. That's better. Let's change over now."

The surgeons changed places. The sucking growl went on.

Yarberry said tensely, "You're beginning to see a big lump of tumor. You're frying. Don't fry it. You had it in too far. It's what I told you, Fred. This is an occipital glioma. . . ." A burly doctor entered and stood at the table, waiting to be noticed. Yarberry looked up from the working area. "Hi, Walt. I was able to get those tickets." The doctor nodded and left.

A moment later Yarberry said, "You're shorting and you're all fouled up. You're all dirtied up in there. Let me do it awhile." He took over. "Okay. Now I can get in there and get some of this cortex out. Watch. See what I do . . . ?" He broke off. "Can I have my headlight now?" He looked at Chou. "You're not hyperventilating him anymore?"

Chou said, "No. Doesn't need it now, you know. Keep it up fast."

Almost a half-hour later, Yarberry said, "This cortex we're taking out now is the visual cortex. He already has a visual-field defect because the tumor was interrupting the pathways between the visual cortex and the visual center. So we can safely sacrifice this and not give him any extra deficit. At least now he has more room. . . . Oh. We're going to have to take out more of this. Lots of hemorrhage . . . there it's pretty firm. Come on, Fred," he said sharply. "You didn't hold it right. No, you can't do that. Cautery, please! Get that hand out of the way. That's fine."

Eckstein said, "Am I supposed to hold this on the left side?"

The conversation went on. Yarberry scolded, reprimanded, laughed, got sharp, but, full of purpose, went deeper into the cavity, cauterizing, sucking as he went. "Watch that retractor, Fred. That way you mash him on the whole hemisphere instead of trying to lift it, see? See that clear fluid coming out? See it? That must be the ventricle we perforated. Whole big vein was thrombosed like you see in pathology. See it, Fred?" he demanded.

"I see it," Eckstein said.

Yarberry laughed. "Okay, I'm just talking to myself. Bender wouldn't have done that. Well, that's why we have different authorities. Terrible mess. Look at that brain rot. Ah, here. Tumor."

The piece of tumor held in a forceps was small, a silver half-dollar in size, vaguely menacing. It was critically studied and placed in a container. "See that it gets to pathology, somebody?" Yarberry said. "Now let's get as much of the rest out as we can."

A student nurse took the container and left.

It seemed to take forever. An hour later Ross said in a whisper, "He wants to stop the bleeding and get out of the area." Yarberry simultaneously said, "I want to get out slowly. Leave the cavity open and make a long drain. Okay, Fred. Finish it." He stood back at last and stretched. The work went on. The circulating nurse began to remove the smock and headlight. Yarberry seemed to be grinning behind the mask. "Are you smarter for the late start this morning, boys and girls?"

The nurse said, "No, it was an awful bad lecture this morning."

Yarberry said, "Who lectured?"

The nurse said, "I wasn't sure. Some man from that instrument company."

"One day they'll invent something as useful as a finger." Yarberry grinned engagingly at the lawyer. "Now you know what this is about, Mahler," he said, stuffing the shapeless shirt into the trousers. "Could they do anything like this at that hospital of yours up there in the hills? Look at the help I've got—Fred, Bob, Paul, real good boys, and these terrific girls. And that equipment in there? Computers, tapes, whatever we need. I could have anything, continual blood chemistries all along, if I asked for it—and all that to make an old man comfortable for another six months maybe. You can take off that mask."

The masks came off. "Did you learn anything?" Yarberry asked, rubbing the fatigue from his eyes.

Mahler looked back at the huddle of workers. "I'm not sure. I think something extraordinary just took place. I felt privileged to watch." He hesitated. "Thank you, Doctor."

Yarberry laughed. "Let's get dressed."

Eckstein waved and went on working. Chou made a progress note. The watchful eyes of the nurses followed them out.

"Where'd you get this summary?" Yarberry said.

Mahler had explained the case and had handed over a summary of Manya Shroeder's medical history including a copy of Herlihy's opinion attached at the Luzzatto Institute. "A good friend was helpful," Mahler said obliquely. "Is it enough for your purposes?"

"Oh, yes," Yarberry said. They were down to shorts, dressing in the smells and messiness of the locker room. With the mask gone, he was grinning like a gnome, "It's enough to form an opinion, if that's your point. What's your question?"

"Assuming that medical history, the tests and all that, should they have operated on Mrs. Shroeder?"

Yarberry glanced through the few pages with quick intelligence. "What was their background, those doctors?"

"Gorham Medical College."

Yarberry frowned. "Wasn't that one of those small freedmen's schools set up in the South after the Civil War? Gorham?" He shrugged. "Okay, the school doesn't matter, I suppose. But you've got a tumor in the left parietal lobe of a right-handed woman? In the same area I just operated on?" He handed back the summary. "Hell, no!"

He pulled up his trousers. "For those doctors to have gone in on this showing was outlandish. We wouldn't feel justified here at Featherstone and we practice real medicine—not that cockamamie kind they commit in places like Lewiston." He tucked in a gaudy shirt of crimson stripes and began on a startling necktie. "We'd regard those tests as wholly inadequate and the clinical history even less persuasive. I haven't time for all the reasons now, but it's clear enough. What did Paul Herlihy say this was?"

"Butchery," Mahler said.

"The other fellow's work always is," Yarberry said, grinning, "but I agree. Those doctors were crazy even to try a craniotomy, much less an exploratory craniotomy, whatever that means. Okay?"

Mahler felt a gush of satisfaction. He buttoned his shirt and said carefully, "Might anything have justified this surgery?"

Yarberry said, "Yeah. Sure. A life-endangering situation would be such a case. Sudden headache, jet vomiting, papilledema, a steep increase of pressure that could drive the brain stem into the spine and destroy vital centers—you might as well operate because it's a last chance. Egyptians trephined. Incas too. But that wasn't the case here," he said with a friendly blink. "How will you prove it?"

Mahler hesitated. "Frankly, I had hoped you'd be willing to testify as an expert. It'd be so helpful. They've heard of Featherstone Memorial even in Lewiston."

Yarberry zipped his fly. "Even if not of Yarberry?"

"Neurosurgeons aren't basketball centers," Mahler said. He waited with apprehension, not daring to breathe.

Yarberry scratched his chin. "Well, it could be fun," he said. "Hey, Chou? What do you think of this?"

Chou, who had entered wearily, got down to bare skin. He listened to the matter with an amused smile. "You're an eccentric, Joe," he said. "I can't buy your views on sex, politics, or anything. If you want to charge up hills, charge up hills. Don't ask my sanction."

Yarberry was now dressed. "I don't agree with all this cover-up of bad medicine, Mahler. It gives us all a bad image. Tell you what: don't count on me but send me the full record. If it stands up, I'm inclined to help. Okay?" He looked up quizzically. "What are you thinking?"

Mahler said somberly, "Simply that I'm grateful to have a final medical authority to be sure of what I'm doing."

Yarberry laughed. "I can be wrong too. Fred's always correcting me and he's right two percent of the time—which isn't bad. I make mistakes, you know."

Mahler said, "What happens if you do?"

A grin spread. "Nothing at all. I'm allowed mistakes. It goes with the fees I charge." Yarberry squeezed Mahler's arm reassuringly. "Stop worrying. On what you've told me, I'll have to agree with Paul Herlihy. Herlihy's a fatuous old windbag but a good man. It was butchery. Good enough?"

It was a brisk day, New York weather at its best. Mahler walked the distance to the United Nations Plaza, skirted a demonstration, then turned west and arrived at his office, buoyant but drained.

"What are you thinking?" Curtayne said.

Mahler settled to the comfort of his deep leather chair and started a cigar. He was between secretaries. He would have to write or dictate into a tape, but those were hardly problems. He described the operation in detail, drawing out the moment. "I expected it to be grisly," he mused, "like one of those Nazi human experiments, an assault on the man's life, but it wasn't. Maybe because the patient was hidden by the drapes. Maybe because everyone was casual, gentle, trying to help. The old man was so sick, and they were trying so hard for him—even though he was hopeless, just meat on a slab. I dunno, Jim." He looked up oddly. "There's something to medicine, I guess."

"Good medicine, yes," Curtayne said. He frowned anxiously. What was this about? he wondered. "So where do we stand?"

Mahler took a moment to draw on the cigar. "Well, for the first time since we got this matter, I believe we've got a real case," he said with a tired smile. He pressed aching eyes, seeking to retain the vision of the operating room at Featherstone Memorial, to keep the medicinal smell, to hear the whine of the saw, the growl of the device sucking the watery brain tissue of the man under the silent drapes. "You know something, Jim? I find brain surgery hard work. It takes strong legs and a peculiar frame of mind. Let's notify the clients and then let's get to the Old Timers' and tie one on."

Carefully, feeling her way in the dark, she got out of bed and walked downstairs in bare feet. Surreptitiously she whispered a number to the long-distance telephone operator. The ring was answered by a deep voice.

"Yes?" the voice said.

"Did I wake you, Bill?" she whispered.

"No. I was up."

A giggle. "Doing what?"

"What do you want, Manya?"

"When will I see you again?"

"You'll see more than enough of me when the time comes to prepare."

"Do you mind if I call like this?"

"Call any time you want. What is it?"

"I just wanted to talk. What are you doing?"

"Manya, what's on your mind?"

A pause. "Will I have to be examined by the other side? More tests? Things like that?"

"Well, they'd have that right."

"I couldn't stand any more of that, Bill."

"I see. Well, maybe not, considering your condition. We'd need a court order to protect you. Is that all right?"

"I feel relieved." The same giggle. "Sorry if I'm out of line. I really called to say I'm grateful you took the case."

"That's not necessary, Manya. It's just part of the job. Look, if you're going to call like this, you'd better reverse charges next time."

"That's thoughtful." A long silence. "Well, just thanks. I'm thinking of you."

After a wait, the telephone clicked. She went back to her bed and turned to the wall.

11

He had hung up twice before he let the call to Lewiston go through.

"Wait a minute," O'Dwyer said.

Sarah got on the line at once. "Oh, yes, Will?" The cool voice with its flat accent was pleasantly inviting. She said, "Lunch is fine. What about meeting at Flynn's? The usual time."

"Could we make it dinner instead?" Mahler said.

After a moment, to his intense relief, she said, "I'll be delighted. I'm free Thursday night. Eight o'clock at my home?"

"I'll pick you up," he said.

Well, he thought. That wasn't so hard after all. A week later in Lewiston, he hired a car and drove out in the snapping cold to Point Berlove. He arrived with a box of chocolates.

"Come in and get warm," Sarah said. "Throw your coat anywhere. What do you drink? Or would you like a chocolate first?"

"I thought of flowers, but your only store was closed," Mahler said. "I seem out of practice. Can we start this all over?" He was tired, but smiling.

"I have no quarrel with chocolates," she said solemnly. "Let's get comfortable, eh? The maid left some canapés. And I am pleased with the thought. Nougat or caramel?"

"I'll take that drink," he said wryly. "And the canapés."

An old Bavarian piano heaped with music was dominated by a portrait of Judge Schuyler van Loon in full robes. Van Loon was silver-haired and scholarly in looks—somewhat vaguely familiar. "Looks like a good painting," Mahler said, rubbing his hands at a purring fire.

"I suppose it is," she said. "Martini?"

"Oh, good."

She sat and studied the portrait in a first awkward moment. "Strict judge, you know. His strong point was procedure. Did you ever see his book on civil procedure? It absorbed him completely. That sort of thing does." She smiled pleasantly and smoothed her hair. "He was a bit older than me," she added.

"Oh. Yes. Great book. Must have taken years to assemble." In fact he had never heard of van Loon on New York civil procedure.

Sarah was gracious and amused and full-breasted in a claret-red velvet dress of striking cleavage, but the conversation, hardly sparkling, seemed constrained. She sat back with smiling lidded eyes. "Um. Will, what do you generally do with yourself aside from work? Hunt? Fish? Ski? What about your summers, say?"

"I've had a house in Fire Island for years," he said. "It's my release hatch—and don't raise your brows. Ocean Beach, where I stay, is full of families with kids. Can't even go around without a shirt. All that wild stuff has moved to Cherry Grove and the Hamptons. Some sleeping around goes on, of course, but no more than here at Lewiston, I'm sure." Sarah looked thoughtful. It was a definite pass. Or was it?

Mahler smiled. It was an enjoyable and promising line of table talk he had no thought to divert. "And your summers?" he asked.

"I've got a place in Vermont." She went on with the halting talk. Sports. Books. Theater. Growing up in Brooklyn—an exotic world of Oriental color and splendor she had never imagined. It was slow going. And finally she finished the canapés, licking her fingers, and suggested they move on. She slipped into a fur coat and waited in the hall. "I'll tell you, Will," she said quizzically. "Your call was a surprise. I never expected it." Her breath was aromatic.

"Neither did I," he said. He took a slender arm and escorted her to the car.

Two lawyers dining out should not have drawn attention, but it did. Every eye in Northland Inn's Top of the Hill turned as they were shown to a corner table in the rear overlooking a parking lot. Sarah shrugged off her coat and glanced at a familiar scene. The music was sedate.

"We're getting looks," she said. She noted a party of doctors and their wives across the room. The doctors gazed curiously at Mahler. The women pointedly turned their backs. Sarah settled down to the moment's luxury. "Is something wrong?"

"I feel uncomfortable," Mahler said. "Lawyers, you know. Opposite sides. I didn't realize this'd be so public."

"Don't be an ass," she said. "I'm sure you didn't get me here for an assignation; I'd be thrown out of the country club." Her tone was light, mocking. "Or did you?"

"Not this time," he said.

"Oh, dear," she said after a moment. "Well, I think I'd like another drink. Do you mind?"

The moment passed in silence. She looked off to the distance. "Lewiston's a fishbowl, Willie, and there's a strong convention here. We do not meet at the public room of the Northland Inn for fun and games. We meet elsewhere. Chicago. Detroit. Paris. London. New York."

"What would bring you to New York?"

"Music. Opera. I come in often enough. Sometimes for business. Are you interested in music?"

Mahler faced a frank, bold stare. "Not my bag, really. Would you come in for a refresher course in trial tactics? I do some of that, you know."

"I'm not sure, but let me know. It might be possible," she replied brightly. "Ah! Here we are."

The martinis were cold and dry.

"Good-o," she said. "I'm enjoying this, Will. Let's not talk shop. Eh?"

"Right."

"Good. Now then! Are you going ahead with your case?"

"Seems so."

"Pity," she said, making a sucking sound. She took in the dark room, the tables lit by guttering candles. "Candlelight. Smorgasbord. Piped music—and a bloody lawsuit? You were so mysterious when you called. I hoped you'd have better news than that."

"I've got a pretty strong case," he said.

"I pretty much know your case." She smiled. "I'm not sure it's strong. Am I?"

"No, but it is."

"Then I'll have to watch myself, won't I?" she said pleasantly.

He sat forward, hesitating, aware that a scarlet-faced man with bushy eyebrows was staring with intensity. He lowered his voice. "I wanted you to hear this first. We'll serve our notice of claim in a day or two. Once that starts, it may not be easy to meet at all. I want to know if you'll resist late filing."

"Oh." She was taken aback.

He lit her cigarette. Their glances met. "Is this leading to a contract?" she asked.

"No. I simply wanted to know what to expect."

"Ah. I see. Well, I'm flattered. This is more attention than I ordinarily get. The locals just telephone and ask." She sat back, blowing smoke, resolving a point. "Look here," she said with an edge, "I'm paid to defend the city and I will. I won't give up any advantage simply to be friendly. Would you?"

"That's different. My clients are people. The city isn't. The city's here to pay just claims and not raise technical rules. That's what the law is for—or should be for."

"Oh, Will! Not that, please! The city's here to carry on city business, not to play Lady Bountiful. And it's not just the city we defend. It's the doctors and their families. Have you ever defended a doctor in an action?"

"No. I've only prosecuted them."

"Did you enjoy it?"

"One or two, yes. A case of septic abortion on a woman six months gone was a pleasure. Others broke my heart. Okay?"

Her eyes dropped. "Sorry. I've only defended them against these claims. Not all serious, of course—hot-water-bottle burns, chipped teeth, that sort of thing—but I know the anxiety of the ordeal. Doctors are sheltered people, easily shattered by threats, not used to fighting in court. They have a stake in the outcome—and they're people too," she said with feeling.

"Maybe they are," Mahler said. The ringing voice was attracting attention, and she had of course touched a vital element of the case. "Since the city has unlimited capacity to pay, the doctors here don't even face a money judgment—unless we sue them independently. I'm not sure I shouldn't go after them in the first instance. I might get more cooperation. So might you."

She resumed smoking. "And you think I might waive a possible defense that might cost these doctors, not to mention the city, a lawsuit?"

Mahler shrugged. "I'm simply trying to reach an understanding. You worry about the hospital and the doctors. I'll worry about the patient. I see no reason for soft feelings or sympathy—especially when the profession makes it so hard to prove a case. It's bad enough when insurance companies are involved—but when that mantle extends to a city hospital I have to look the other way." There he was again, raising his voice. He thought, Well, let it be so!

"You seem to have something against hospitals? Or is it just city hospitals?" she said, breaking the silence.

Mahler frowned. "Nothing personal. It's just the conditions I've seen. I once had to investigate an incident in a psychiatric hospital—a patient strangled to death by attendants who were trying to pacify him. I turned the place upside down to find out why that happens. All I got from the medical staff was excuses, lies, and evasions—and dumping blame on the underpaid slobs left in charge when they took off. They blamed everything but the lack of good solid medical practices and standards. I wrote a two-hundred-page report to the governor and that's where it's buried—in some file in Albany and up here. It hasn't been forgotten up here." He tapped his forehead. "I still see ignorance, carelessness, patient exploitation, neglect. Maybe, just maybe, it should be ventilated—" He broke off. "Well, I'm sure you know the conditions too. I'm entitled to think strictly of the patient's side, don't you agree?"

"Of course you must, but it doesn't follow from the general condition that in this case this city or these doctors are guilty of anything at all. You keep hinting so but I don't know that. It remains to be proved." She paused. "And you might do more harm than good. There's a public interest here. It's hard enough for the city to run its hospitals—to attract interns, to hire staff, to start a teaching program, to get budget through city council—and . . ."

"Yes?"

"Well—the real need to bring in more black doctors to satisfy the black community, without having someone blow up a stupid scandal to give ammunition to the really nasty elements in the city. We had plenty of flack to get these black doctors on staff in the first place—and we were lucky to get them at that. We're a reform administration, you know?"

"Yes, I know," he said without enthusiasm.

"Well, we are!" she said sharply.

"Is that why Bellinger got appointed?"

She paused. "What makes you ask that?"

"To hear an answer," he replied. He sat forward. "I've been trying to find out about Dr. John Howard Bellinger," he said. "I find very little. Everybody swears he was outstanding in neurology, but I don't find much to support that. I find even less for Tatum—from what few traces of him remain. I'm not quite clear how Tatum managed to get a chief residency from Bellinger. Personnel was strangely silent when asked. I must wonder, mustn't I? What were their credentials? How good were they actually? Good enough for anyone? Or only for city hospital poor? If we're to take a broad, social, compassionate view, those are good issues to raise too, I'd think."

Sarah stared. "I don't know what you're talking about. Bellinger was appointed with everything in mind—experience and ability included. It's curious you raise these points when you consider the miserable record of the exclusion of doctors by hospitals for racial reasons—and religious too. I don't see why you would." It was a direct personal thrust. "The fact that they're black is no reason to insinuate they were less competent than anyone else."

Mahler stared through a gathering fog. "You said that. I wouldn't dream of it. We're not comparing races, but doctors and their behavior. If you're satisfied, fine! But I've had information that Tatum, who was only a resident, did the actual surgery himself without—" He broke off. "Was that the standard set in that hospital?"

She bit her mouth. "Residents need training too. Where will we get our next crop if they couldn't do this work?"

Mahler changed the position of a goblet. "I can see why you'd say that. I agree, in fact. But if it comes to trial"—the candle flame cast odd shadows upward—"it might appear that this country has two medical standards—real doctors for the rich, residents still in training for the poor. The thought that anyone with less than full qualifications would dare to tamper with the brain strikes me as sacrilege. I wonder if a jury wouldn't agree. Eh?"

"You're full of surprises," she said with an uncertain laugh. "But you're barking up the wrong tree—"

A hoarse voice interrupted. "Mr. Mahler? You Manya's lawyer?"

Mahler looked up. "Ye-es?"

The heavyset man who had been staring put out a horny hand. "Cass Wrebolski, mister," he said angrily. "Plumbing supplies on Front Street. About time somebody's helping the poor woman. We appreciate it."

"Thanks," Mahler said.

Wrebolski grunted. "You show 'em, mister. They been getting away with murder."

"I'll try," Mahler said.

Wrebolski nodded coldly to Sarah, pointedly hostile, and returned to his table. Disapproval of Sarah, admiration for Mahler were registered by a birthday party of elderly celebrants. "Hold hands, Papa," someone said gaily as a birthday cake with a candle was brought in.

"You see?" Mahler said. "There's the other side of the coin—the feeling against these doctors. You've got to figure on it. Sure, a public trial may be harmful, I know that, but what's my choice? Abandon this woman? Walk away from her real problems because some historic injustices took place in this country before she was born? I know all about the public interest. I served it for twenty years. . . ." A gesture put this aside. "I don't know and I don't care about that. I've got a narrow interest to follow—a money judgment for a sick woman. And if the hospital which hired the negligent doctors isn't responsible—who is? Especially where the birds have flown the coop. Have you been in touch with them?" he asked abruptly.

She blinked at the unexpected thrust. "I don't see why you'd ask me that."

"Because it'll come down to them in the end. Do you really

know them? What kind of doctors they are? Did you ever meet them yourself?"

"Yes, I met Bellinger at some civic and political affairs, of course. Everybody knows everybody in this city. I thought he was . . ." She stopped. "Well, he does have charm," she said slowly. "Why?"

"It might pay you to know something about them." Mahler drew a line on the tablecloth. "I hear Tatum's a very troubled man. Emotional. Quarrelsome. Didn't get on with other doctors. A bully. Nurses and orderlies had no use for him. Neither did the rest of the staff. He seemed always to be under great pressure. Hard worker. In fact, too hard."

"Maybe. What of it?"

"Nothing really, except that he seemed very anxious to operate in this case." Mahler was silent. "And now he's dropped from sight. No forwarding address. None at the hospital. I thought you might know how to find him?" The suggestion was delicate.

"Tatum? No, I don't."

"But you might find out?"

"Yes, I might. So far I haven't."

He drew a second line, cross-hatched it slowly, reluctant to come to the point. "Bellinger's out of the country, I learn. Do you know where?"

"I don't think I should say anything," she said coolly, "until I know why you ask. I'd like another drink. Do you mind?"

The wait was silent and uncomfortable. The mood of pleasantries had vanished.

"What do you have in mind?" Sarah said.

"I have this suggestion," Mahler said after a moment. I think this case should be disposed of now, if possible." He went on carefully, studying the cold, chiseled features. "If you produce medical records and the doctors for voluntary examination and disclosure, I'll negotiate the matter in good faith—but I do want to examine those two doctors first and then talk. Maybe we can avoid a trial."

The cigarette had gone out. She lit another, studying an implied threat. "Why must you examine our doctors first? Why not talk settlement now?"

He shook his head. "I think you might agree to that, but will

Sabbattino? I doubt it. Not unless I show that he has no choice. He has a no-pay mentality. He'll delay, try to wear us down, hope for suicide or death. Anything to beat the case. He'll drag it out to the last moment to settle, and then not till the damage is done. Yet there may be aspects of the case he doesn't know yet. I want all that down in the record in black and white. Then we can talk."

Sarah faced the cold, level eyes. "Why not tell him what you have in mind?"

"Because he doesn't tell me." The heavy mouth was pressed tight.

"I see."

"It's going to get dirty," he said uncomfortably. "I've been getting stuff on your doctors—and it's not good copy. This case can't stay friendly, or professional, or even decent. Once I walk into court with my file—which I've got to do—Sabbattino will be out to kill me. And I'll have to kill him. You too. And we'll wind up enemies. And I'd rather not. I want you to know that. Maybe that's why I asked you to dinner." He paused and felt a hot tide of blood rush to his head.

So that's it! she thought. She had no intention of helping him out.

He went on. "I've been stalling this for weeks. I was afraid to ask you here, afraid you'd refuse. I suppose I made a mistake. But I can't fight by day and get serious at night. I never could."

She continued to smoke, surprised at the show of feeling. "I wish you'd thought of it earlier," she said slowly. "You must know I can't decide this alone. I'll put it to Sabbattino." Too ridiculous, she thought with resentment. How clumsy could the man be? She felt moved and repelled by the confusion of purpose. Against her better judgment, she asked curiously, "How much will you claim?"

"It may go past six figures."

"That much?" She laughed uncertainly. "Well, it sounds ominous. I can't imagine what you think you've got on our doctors."

"Didn't your man O'Dwyer give you any idea?"

"Not the foggiest," she said with a face of stone. "And I'm not sure all this isn't a crude ploy of some sort. We'll have our doctors

148

on hand." A pause. "Can you tell me what you're driving at?"

"If we go to trial, we'll both know, won't we?" His heart was beating unpleasantly. He had not expected that feeling. "Then let me suggest something—I'd like nothing better than to have your doctors show up in court."

"Let's order before I float away. I'm starved." She paused. "Did you expect any other answer than to tell you to go ahead and prove your case—if you can?"

Mahler slowly shook his head.

What an ass! she thought angrily, and went on to make talk in a strong voice.

They left early and drove back in silence. The night was frozen and beautiful. The sky was hung with enormous, brilliant stars. The aurora borealis was weaving patterns over the black lake. The mood of anger drained off. She said, "Can I tell you something, Will, then put it aside? I've practiced law in this city ever since my husband died. I try to enjoy it. Let's not mix things up?"

"I'm sorry about tonight," he said. Their breaths, like smoke, mingled in the cold. "I'd like to make up for it. Can't we meet again? I promise not to talk about the case."

She hesitated. "Let's see how it goes," she said, relenting. She pressed his hand and went into the house. What rotten luck! she thought.

It was a ruined evening.

Two weeks later, Tom Rorke, clerk of Special Term, Part II, called Sabbattino to advise that Maria Shroeder had filed a motion for permission to file late notice of claim against the City of Lewiston for damages in the sum of one million dollars. It would be the largest such claim ever brought in the county.

With the papers was a formal notice to inspect and copy the medical records in the case.

Mahler's telephone was ringing again as it would through the nights and days yet to come.

It was Manya with a question.

12

Judge Abram Urquart, an old man with a seamed granite face and a thicket of inky brows, glanced at the plaintiff's table. "Mr. Mahler? This is your first appearance in this court?"

Mahler rose. "Yes, it is, Your Honor. And I hope to get to enjoy a trial experience. *If* the motion is granted to allow late filing of this claim."

"Will counsel step to the bench?" The judge studied the array of hard faces, thinking of the informal and often warm ties of kinship possible between bench and bar. The longer he sat on the bench, the warmer and mellower he felt toward the lawyers before him, and hoped for their warm feelings in turn. A judge soured by age could well lose the respect and deference that otherwise he might earn—and this he meant to avoid. How he would fare with that fellow from New York City he had no idea —but the strong jaw held little hope for an early disposition of the bruited claim before him. Settlement talk would be put off for another day, so much was clear.

Judge Urquart closed his eyes. The parties were worlds apart. He was a methodical judge who had presided over trial and motion parts for twenty years after a good but undistinguished career as a trial lawyer for insurance companies in upstate New York for many years before that. He had been appointed by a Republican governor, reappointed by a Democratic governor, and elected twice by both parties. He was slow in speech, deliberate in manner, judicial of temperament, and devoted to the dignity of the court. He was not comfortable with the motion on the calendar. But there it was. He said, "Thank you, gentlemen. Are there briefs?" Briefs and motion papers were handed up. "Mr. Mahler, I see that your notice of claim was not filed in time?"

"That's why we're making this motion," Mahler said.

Judge Urquart sat back. Someone had sent him an article from *Modern Medicine,* a periodical which specialized in learned topics like the value to the doctor of automated letters, calculation of fiscal net worth, profit-patient ratios, fee setting, and of course how to avoid medical malpractice suits—the critical problem of the day second only to tax avoidance and inflation. Most disturbing article, he thought. "I'll be glad to hear argument, but it hardly seems fair to wait so long. The private insurance companies seem to find it impossible to manage. A lot of them are going out of the business, they say."

Mahler polished his spectacles. The statement had been put in all seriousness. "Your Honor, this claim will be paid out of general city revenues, so that problem doesn't apply."

"It seems to me it's the same thing," Judge Urquart said stiffly. "If people are going to sue doctors, they should file at once. It puts the defense at a great disadvantage not to."

"I suppose it does," Mahler said. "And I can't tell you how concerned I feel about their problem."

Judge Urquart saw nothing in the lawyer's face but gelid concern. His voice dropped. "How much are you *really* looking for here, sir?"

"The figure in the complaint," Mahler said.

Judge Urquart considered this. "I see what you mean. Proceed."

Mahler bowed and returned to place. Something cold had settled in him. He began in a low tone. "Louder, please!" Sabbattino interrupted, cupping his ear. "You'll hear me soon enough," Mahler said.

"Oh, good!" Sabbattino replied. "Sorry, I didn't mean to interrupt. Go on."

"When counsel is ready," Mahler said.

"Counsel is ready," Sabbattino replied.

"Can we get on?" Judge Urquart said. "Really, Mr. Mahler, you were inaudible."

"Perhaps so," Mahler said. "I'm not sure it warranted the bellow I just got."

Sabbattino stood. "I never bellow. I try to be distinct."

"I heard a bellow," Mahler said.

Judge Urquart tapped. "Mr. Mahler, you're entitled to courtesy. You'll have it. Mr. Sabbattino, you'll give it. Proceed."

Mahler glanced at Sarah, whose clear and tranquil face showed no interest in the matter. He placed a paper aside and launched into a recital of the hospital's concealment of records and the wretched flight of the doctors—all of which was tantamount to a conspiracy of silence to obstruct the claim of a poor sick woman to her day in court and a chance to prove her case. He spoke calmly and slowly in a strong, clear voice with rising effect. It was a model argument of its kind. But if an impression had been made, it could not be read from the rugged features on the bench.

"Mr. Sabbattino?" Judge Urquart said.

Sabbattino began with a clever diatribe against the curse of malpractice claims and their instigators. The unbridled attack outside permissible limits brought a sputter of protest from Landowski. "Won't you do something?" he whispered to Mahler.

Mahler shook his head. "I don't much mind," he whispered in turn. "It gives me latitude for myself and it doesn't mean a thing. This judge's mind is made up."

"I don't like it," Landowski grumbled, and drew a warning glance from the bench.

Sabbattino ended in emotional silence, trembling and perspiring. He bowed to the bench and returned to his seat. As he passed, he bent to Mahler's ear. "Good kick in the belly, Bill? Hey?" he whispered genially. He sat, twisting his moustache with a fine display of civic outrage.

"I'll reserve decision," Judge Urquart said.

Six weeks later, the motion was denied and the notice of claim dismissed. In due course the decision was reversed without opinion by the higher court on appeal and the action formally launched.

PART TWO

13

The summer was endless.

Mahler managed the stifling New York weather with stolen weekends at the seashore, but the politics and small talk of a summer community were tiresome. The cool weather and the return to Lewiston came as a relief. His visits became more frequent. He talked to reporters and taxi drivers and opinion makers of all sorts. He contributed to the Torch Fund and other local causes. He met Sarah at lunch with her entourage and turned up on some occasions at Fisher's. They were friendly, casual, and aware of each other—and kept away from law and politics. But of course nothing could stop the wise looks and innuendos about them. On one occasion Landowski brought him to the country club, where they met by chance.

"How are things in New York?" she asked.

"Pretty good," he said. In fact the practice was growing. Several dozen new files had been opened—a good omen, perhaps—and he was considering hiring a clerk. "Trouble is, it takes me away from you," he said. "It kills me."

"Come on, Will," she said.

"It's true," he said. "I'm getting chewed out for it by Curtayne. He's helping me, you know. . . ."

"You told me about him."

"Did I? Well, he is. He thinks I spend too much time here. Maybe so, but it has its rewards—even if I'm caught between a fight and a frolic. Sarah . . . ?"

"Ye-es?"

"Well, nothing now," he said, and broke off. But it was at least a reminder that she had promised a visit to New York.

The exhausting procedural struggle in court went on. Each step was marked by fierce courtroom clashes within and outward geniality in the halls. The struggle was to compel the production of medical records, to examine witnesses before trial, to frame the issues, to force an early trial at the head of a crowded calendar. As the resistance mounted, the attacks sharpened. Mahler grew brusque in court, his impatience and outrage offensive to every judge in the county. He walked about in a thundercloud.

At the same time he went on to build his case. It was surprising how freely tongues would wag. Nurses gossiped and secretaries chattered. Strangers stopped him with tales of medical horrors. The neighbors were friendly, sympathetic members of the parish, more than ready to swear to the family's sufferings and to Manya's deterioration from a lovely young woman to the wraith with haunted eyes they now knew. Hints arose that Manya was no longer the pious matron they remembered, although there was nothing one could place a finger on. She had gotten careless, some thought, dressing in strange ways, and the vacant moments were now more frequent. Father Zator described a typical brief spell before the brain surgery—really nothing, he observed, a momentary daze; in contrast he described recent, more violent seizures. Sister Joseph of Arimathea who taught Betsy at the School of Our Lady of Victory spoke of the child's disabling fears.

His visits to the Shroeder home were painful. Manya no longer dressed for him. She lay on the small sofa propped on a pillow with translucent hands crossed on her breast. A quilted robe would be loose and parted to show a swell of white breasts. Deep rings circled her eyes. She spoke painfully and in a hesitant whisper, striving to pierce an uncertain veil of memory. It was unsatisfactory more often than not—loss of names of things and people, confusion of dates, confusion of concepts. She was suffering and showed with an apologetic manner her embarrassment at the recurrent theme that haunted her life—the conviction that her time had come.

. . .

The telephone rang in the clinic hubbub. Tatum patted the boy on the examining table and left for the crowded little office inside.

He was tired—more than he liked to admit—and the pressures and humiliations of his position were more than he could bear. Queenshaven was an inglorious end of ambition, he thought. It was a small city on Chesapeake Bay in Maryland, to which he had retreated after the humiliating fiasco in Lewiston. It had some small metal industries, a cannery, a dwindling fishing fleet, and a plant to reduce oyster shells to useful size.

Queenshaven had a general clinic—which he ran—and a plan of group medicine—which ran him. Its members were black. At least those who sought him out were black. He had joined the county and state medical societies, but referrals failed to come. His return to private practice with a specialty in neurosurgery had not worked out at all.

He had thought to join the organization of black doctors, the National Medical Association, but the attacks of activist students on the black doctor for false middle-class values put him off. A proposal to abolish written medical examinations as culturally weighted and unfair to black aspirants to medicine was the last straw. He had passed stiff examinations himself and had no mind to see that license go cheap. A reply to student barbarism at a county meeting in Baltimore brought him hooting and threats. He declined to apply for membership. His isolation was complete.

He gave three days a week as paid assistant to Dr. Milton Kaplowitz, an elderly cosmetic-surgery specialist in Baltimore, and spent that salary on the clinic, where he saw an impossible caseload of patients. He lived alone now—his wife had left him after the quarrelsome years of marriage—in unkept, dusty solitude in a leaking, swaybacked frame house. He walked the streets, gaunt and hollow-eyed, abstracted to a pitch. He worried about his clinic and followed the Shroeder case in the daily newspaper sent from Lewiston.

It was to Kaplowitz that he looked for professional respect and occasional family dinners and a change of mood at a dinner table of wide-ranging interests not otherwise found in Queenshaven. He felt like a different man—good-humored, conversational, relaxed, human, himself. But he was not often a good

157

guest. The race question, real enough perhaps, exasperated him. All very well for others to pursue, but he was a doctor, trapped in restraints he refused to recognize. He had no intention to fall back for support on black organizations. He'd practice his specialty freely or not at all. Kaplowitz, who was active in Jewish organizational life, found this incomprehensible.

"You're in a dream world, Percy," Kaplowitz had said often enough. "Medicine isn't above society. It reflects it. And if it's a racist society—and it must be racist because the kids keep discovering that for us—deal with it in some real way. Build your own institutions, or you'll get no place."

"Black schools? Black hospitals? Black patients?" Tatum retorted. "I can see why a Zionist would say that."

Kaplowitz sat back. "Why bring Zionism into this?"

"Because it annoys you," Tatum said sardonically. "And it tells you how I feel. I'm not giving in to the chauvinism. I'm black but I'm not a black doctor. I'm a doctor of medicine. And my specialty is neurosurgery."

Kaplowitz recognized the obsessive anger and dropped the topic. "Maybe so, and maybe it's changing, but if not for Gorham and the other black medical schools, where would there be even a reasonable number of black doctors today? Zionists have built some pretty good hospitals. So listen to them. Maybe they've got something to tell you." He smiled sourly. The morose sensitivities were too much to handle, and there was, as he knew, that other matter preying on Tatum's mind. "And I'm not convinced by the rationalizations," he said dryly. "You're looking for something in medicine you'll never get. You want the white man's love. How can he love anybody? He doesn't love himself."

Tatum was annoyed, but that was not unusual.

And now Kaplowitz, never polite, was on the telephone from Baltimore with disquieting news. "Hey, Percy. It's caught up with you. That malpractice business. Aren't you listed anywhere at all?"

A mist formed. "What are you talking about?" Tatum said in a choked voice.

"I got a call from a Mrs. van Loon in Lewiston. She got onto me through your ex-wife's lawyer. It was ridiculous to give her a cent. . . . Hello? You all right?"

158

Of course he had known it would come to this. Kaplowitz, who had been more than patient with his endless compulsive rehashing of the matter, knew all about the situation in Lewiston. Still the cheery nonchalance was irritating.

"I'm here," Tatum said.

"She wants you to call her collect. Will you?"

"She can go to hell."

Kaplowitz changed his voice. "Come on, Percy, that's no use. Unless you cooperate, the hospital can ruin you in a cross-action. The woman says she wants to help you."

"I don't need her help."

Kaplowitz in an ancient tongue invoked the Ruler of the Universe. "All right. One question: is your malpractice insurance policy paid up?"

And suddenly Tatum was shouting. "I've told you a hundred times, there was no malpractice!" he cried passionately. "I did exactly what should have been done for that woman. Are you going over to their side too?" The hearing piece was rattling.

"Yes, you've told me, but stop yelling about it," Kaplowitz said.

Tatum lowered his voice. "Sorry, Milton. I shouldn't bark like this, but nobody seems to believe me. I know it's serious. If she wants to come here, I'll see her. But I won't crawl to anyone. Let's drop the subject, eh? I'm unhappy enough as it is."

"You begin to make sense," Kaplowitz said.

"Go to hell," Tatum grumbled.

Kaplowitz laughed. "Tomorrow at seven, Doctor. We're giving a fat, rich widow the breasts of a virgin. I'll expect you scrubbed and ready to assist. 'Bye."

Tatum stared at his skillful hands. Black skin, white palms. That first moment in the emergency room at Lewiston was before him, the stricken woman, the vacant, dazed eyes and the smell of danger. He sighed and opened a cabinet. A folder held a file of pathology reports on the Shroeder brain-tissue slides he had sent to a dozen laboratories around the country. After a moment of bleak contemplation, he closed the file and returned to the practice of poverty medicine.

"Open your mouth, Claude," he said. "How long have you had this cough?"

* * *

Early in fall, one of New York's brisk days brought Mahler to the City Bar Association Building for a panel discussion by three professions—legal, medical, and actuarial—on the topic of medical malpractice. The weekend audience was typically small. The building was a mausoleum, deserted by every lawyer with something better to pass the weekend. The marbled corridors were grown strange indeed.

When he entered the Carter Room—a great and honored name in the profession—the discussion was under way. Doctors whimpered. Lawyers scoffed. Actuaries warned. The economic effects of medical malpractice claims were debated. The audience was apathetic and Mahler's own eyes glazed. It was a drowsy moment.

Before him was the motto calling on the bar to be bold to regain its ancient honor.

A white-haired lawyer, whose specialty it was to defend such claims, denounced the condition of courthouse toilets throughout the state—a condition as disgraceful to the law, he observed learnedly, as that of hospitals to medicine. In the midst of laughter, Mahler heard a whisper.

"Hello," Sarah said cheerfully, sitting beside him. "Sorry I'm late. What's going on?"

Mahler felt his heart leap up. The clear, thin features were a breath of fresh air. "Stupefying stuff," he whispered. "Not a new idea in the house."

"Good. Then we don't have to stay," she replied. "Just let me catch my breath." She sat at attention. An actuary was advancing to the lectern.

"What about the Plaza?" she said after a decent interval. "I used to own the Oak Room before this city went sour. . . ."

"Were you ever married, Will?" she asked.

Mahler said, "Sure, but it didn't last. I wanted to be a lawyer. I lost a wife, but I gained a profession."

"I know, I know," she murmured pleasantly. "Does it make you happy?"

"The profession? Yes, sometimes. Satisfied, I'd say. When I accomplish something. It's the only thing that does, I guess," he said ruefully. "I don't know what happens, but suddenly one day it's the only thing you're living for. I don't like it one bit." It was a warm, hazy moment and not too awkward. The Oak Room was just the place for this, he thought—good ambience, stiff perfect drinks. For the first time in his life, he talked freely of himself and the brief early marriage broken by the discontents and forces of life—for which no one was to blame but himself.

"What about other women?" she said. "You can't have spent a lifetime like that?"

"I suppose not," he said, "but nothing I want to raise at this session. Another time, I hope. What happened to you?" Thrust and counterthrust.

Sarah laughed. "I got a string of A's and married the professor, but there was no correlation."

The afternoon ended in alcoholic euphoria. He put her in a taxi for the airport with a strong handshake. "It's been lovely, Will. Simply lovely," she said soberly, "but maybe we shouldn't do this again. Do you mind?" Nothing had been said, not really, about the strife imminently upon them. But something had been established.

It occurred to him in the middle of the night that she had said not one word about herself.

Fall was brilliant with crimson foliage and winter returned.

14

The great jet circled over the blue waters of the gulf, dropped alarmingly, and touched the runway. With a screech of rubber, it bounced to a halt. An official went down the aisle spraying disinfectant and the passengers were released from bondage. They emerged shakily into the morning haze—a pair of tourists in suffocating winter clothing. A babble of British-colonial speech was their greeting.

Sarah said, "Do you think he'll meet us?"

"I'll be surprised if he does," O'Dwyer said. "I'll get the bags through Customs, Chief. You rustle up a taxi."

"Go ahead. I'm glad to stop reading." Spectacles were put away and she strolled off, rubbing tired eyes. She had been reading medical notes steadily since takeoff at Kennedy.

Jamaica should have been appealing. A hot sun burned in a clear blue sky. A cool breeze blew over the tarmac from the surrounding hills. The colors were pastel—milky blue, dirty yellow, faded pink—interrupted by violent greens. The shade of the airport building was inviting. She strolled about the duty-free areas, noting that Japanese radio and television sets, Swiss watches, and French perfumes were priced no lower than discount prices in the cold, rainy cities of the North. Well, time enough later for that.

Within minutes a cheerful driver had them speeding in a taxi a short distance to the Montego Bay Arms. It was O'Dwyer's first visit to the Caribbean. They passed pink and white buildings shining in the sun. Construction work was going on. Natives were strolling along the road, heads high, arms hanging, going nowhere. The traffic was mad. The laboring taxi ran up a gravel path and stopped. Birds were twittering in a grove of trees.

"Here you are," the driver said, opening the door. "You can swim. Play golf. Take our famous donkey ride to Bleeker House. See our bird sanctuary. Visit plantations. Walk to the Racquet Club. Study the terrible legacy of imperialism, colonialism, capitalism, mismanagement, and overpopulation. Don't touch the bags. A boy will come. Welcome to Jamaica, sir. I hope your mother enjoys her visit," he concluded. A set of strong yellow teeth flashed.

"Yes, I will," Sarah said. She turned to O'Dwyer. "Em, pay the man."

"Yes, Mumsy," O'Dwyer said. "I'll register while you go up and have a nice lie-down."

Nothing could have been more welcome than the airy room on the third tier overlooking the bay. "Oh, lovely," Sarah sighed and threw a sticky wool dress onto the bed. She unpacked summer clothes and stepped into the bathroom. Moments later she was out cursing. The water main was broken and the toilet would not flush. She rattled the telephone.

"Sorry, madam," the clerk said distantly. "I'll send the boy with a bucket. And don't be cross with him. Blame the British."

"You sound British."

"I *am* British!" the clerk snapped. "So I know. If it wasn't us who mucked all this up, who did? Don't try to take that from us. It's no small thing."

It was a footless moment. She stepped onto the balcony. The swimming pool was inviting. O'Dwyer appeared on the next balcony. "The john doesn't work," he announced.

"Neither does mine, but you don't see me fussing."

"Coo, lumme. You sound sharp. What's wrong?"

She turned from the view with reluctance. "As long as we're here, let's enjoy it, but we've got a job to do. Can you get started on Bellinger?"

"Right-o!" O'Dwyer said and disappeared. Sarah changed to a swimming suit. They had left New York in freezing weather, and the heat had her breathless. She went down to the pool, swam several lengths, chatted absent-mindedly with a Philadelphia couple—schoolteachers were swarming—and returned to her room. She barely noticed the tropical life—a din of birds, an uproar of traffic. She was restless to get it over. She picked up a pamphlet describing the latest radioactive scan-imaging techniques to explore for tumors. The pamphlet was vivid with color photographs, but the explanations were technical. She dropped the pamphlet and dozed off, bathed in a humid wind from the Caribbean. A tap woke her.

O'Dwyer entered and sat painfully. Jamaica's sun had fried him to carmine, but he had a report.

"Either he's clean or paying off. I've got his unlisted telephone number. He's not practicing medicine, for sure, just real estate. That hotel condominium proposition is marvelous. They've got a plot of land, a set of plans, subscription blanks, but nothing's started. If they don't build, they apologize. Talented guy."

"Did you manage to telephone him?"

"Sure. He's got a place out toward Ochos Rios. He said he'd see us after the next monsoon. I said, no, there's no monsoon in Jamaica. This and that, and I said we'd meet tonight, or we'll take it up with the tourist bureau. We're due at eight. I'll pick you up." He paused to peel a plantain. "And, Chief? Stop worrying. Just turn on the charm."

"Oh, dear," Sarah said. Water pressure was restored. She ran water over her wrists thoughtfully, considering the development with no special pleasure. She had hoped for a day to explore the shops—she yearned for Wedgwood—to enjoy a respite. Well, no help for it, she decided. She put through a call to Lewiston. Sabbattino came to the telephone, maddeningly unimpressed. "All right, so you're seeing him, but I want him here for the trial. Not there chewing the fat. What's taking so long?" he rasped.

"I can only try, Phil," she replied.

"So try," he retorted, then caught himself. "Sorry, but I'm getting my own filet mignon chewed up too. They're getting nervous here about this case. Take an extra few days. Have fun. But get that quack here or get a medical excuse—something with a notary's red seal. I'm worried too."

She replaced the telephone with a frown. After a moment, she sat at the vanity and examined the tired lines with care. She

164

could not rest. She returned to the balcony and contemplated a listless man working in the garden below.

The rattletrap Cortina skidded wide, bounced, took a long curve around the airfield, and made fair speed along the road to Ochos Rios. They were driving against wild native traffic, but O'Dwyer handled the car with skill and they made fair time. Sarah sat back and drank in beauty. A black sky hung with brilliant stars was luminous and mysterious. An occasional neon sign punctuated the tropical beauty. "Here it is," he said, at a sign marked WHITEHOUSE.

A black man with the girth of a wrestler came forward. He looked suspiciously into the interior. "Mrs. van Loon? I'm Henry." His accent was Brooklynese.

"Yes, Henry?" she said.

"Who's this guy?"

"He's with me."

"You vouch for him?"

"Of course I do."

"Pass, Mrs. van Loon," the guard said, and gave directions. "But stick to the road," he said. "Land mines."

"You're joking."

"Try it and see."

O'Dwyer drove cautiously. A gravel road led through a salt marsh to a large Georgian house on a promontory facing the sea. A tall man in a white jacket, glass in hand, met them. A black German shepherd on a leash was barking wildly.

"Mrs. van Loon, baby! You are welcome, ma'am. Peace and solitude!" Bellinger said with heavy joviality. "Did Henry warn you about the land mines?"

"Yes, he did."

"Oh, that Henry! He discourages *more* people!" Bellinger shook his head, chuckling. "This way and don't mind Wolfgang. That bark is his only form of sexual expression, poor boy. Unfortunately, it's worse than his bite, but in that he's not alone." High-pitched laughter was almost a cackle. "Come along, ma'am baby," he said with a courtly bow. "And stick to the flagstones. I want you to meet Desirée."

A short stroll brought them to the front. The clutch at her arm was not altogether pleasant. "Oh, this is wonderful!" she exclaimed. The sea lay dark below, vast in the night. Long, slow rollers were breaking on a limestone promontory, phosphorescent and ghastly against a black sky. A veranda was hung with paper lanterns. A dazzling young woman in white satin was waiting, holding a julep. Her child's face, all peaches and cream, was petulant.

"Ah, there you are, you brute!" Desirée exclaimed, and burst into torrential French.

Bellinger took the berating in good part, smiling, good-natured, like an indulgent father. "Quiet, baby. *Tais toi,*" he said. "Our guests aren't interested."

"Of course!" Desirée clapped her hands in welcome. "You must call me Desirée. I will call you Sarah and Emmet. We call *him* Doctor. Later I will show you little Cedric and the Cadillac. Persuade him to give me the Cadillac. . . ."

Bellinger chuckled indulgently. "Come on, baby."

"Ah, yes!" Desirée laughed. She turned and called for drinks. She was young and gay and worshipful of the tired man in whose house she lived.

Bellinger presented the drinks with a flourish and hailed Sarah as the Triple Goddess of Huron County—nymph, woman, and lawyer. They sipped cold sweet rum scented with mint. "How do you like Jamaica?" he said lazily.

"Lovely," she said, "but expensive."

"That it is," Bellinger said with feeling.

Jamaica and its tourist industry were discussed before they got down to the topic on all their minds.

"So how stands the watch on the Erie Canal? Trouble with your lawsuit?" Bellinger said sardonically.

Sarah hesitated. "A bit. They're holding out for a lot of money and we're a bit frightened. . . ."

Bellinger smiled. "Don't go on, baby. I read your letter. It's a big claim and everybody's nervous. Perfectly healthy response. One million dollars!" He whistled respectfully. "Almost better than a government grant without strings. What's that bloke Mahler like?"

"Able. Determined. Convinced. Almost obsessive."

"Some kind of shyster?"

"Unfortunately not. We could buy our way out cheap if he were. He's treating it like a criminal case. He has the whole town talking about malpractice—doctors and public alike. In a big city like New York this lawsuit would go unnoticed. But Lewiston hasn't seen anything like this since Chautauqua stopped coming to town. The *Chronicle's* carrying horrendous articles by that emergency-room nurse. . . ."

"Ponsonby?"

"You remember her?"

"Oh, yes, oh, yes," Bellinger said jovially. "Mamalou Ponsonby. Lovely as a barracuda. The dear dead days beyond recall."

Sarah put aside her drink. A barrier was up. "You know there's a nasty tide of rumors going around—that brutal, reckless surgery was done for improper reasons by you and Tatum?"

Bellinger cocked a brow. "On a white patient? Is that the implication?"

Sarah drew a breath. "Doctor, I didn't invent the situation. The rancor is there and I have to face it. We've had intruders, fights, disputes with community people, all sorts of disruptions. This woman has become a symbol for every vindictive activist in town. The black leadership—your old friends—won't believe we're putting up a real defense. It's idiotic. If this case isn't properly disposed of, it'll be a month of Sundays before another black doctor gets appointed to any hospital in that area. On the other side Father Zatur's ethnic element are outraged just because we're resisting this woman's claim. You can imagine the speeches he's making in the neighborhoods. One side wants a sellout—the other a last-ditch fight. Either is ruinous to our hospital system." She halted, overcome with feeling. "Obstinate closed minds," she muttered through clenched teeth. "God knows I've swallowed every fad and cheap slogan in my day, but this is a serious lawsuit. There's a limit. And we need your help. . . ."

"Refill?" Bellinger said.

She frowned. "Well, yes. What's that grin for?"

"Malpractice, baby," Bellinger said jovially. "My, my! To listen to him, the average doctor practices nothing but defensive medicine these days—overtesting, overconservative—haunted to think that every patient is a potential threat of litigation. Well, with all the bleating, it takes three hundred and fifty thousand patient visits to produce one complaint. So I'm wondering what blessed thing was it that caused the hand of God to reach down into the mire to detect and dredge up this one incident to bring us together?" The flirting and arch, heavy compliments that followed were parried with the strained composure of an old hand at parlor games.

Dinner began at ten.

Bellinger had changed. Sarah recalled the bold aquiline nose, flashing white teeth, red lips, the light skin of Mediterranean hue and an aura of buoyant and assertive sexuality, but now those features were blurred. His eyes were bloodshot, one bulged, not quite focused. A wattle hung from his chin. The lustrous hair was still black, but large brown spots covered his hands. He had in a few short years become established in the local society—old British-born plantation owners, a new crowd of political bravos and activists, swarming Americans spoiling the land, and the crop of motion-picture and show-business personalities flocking to the multicolored homeland. Jamaica had a dream of a rainbow society without color consciousness—and a dream of permanent British subsidies for her banana exports; both dreams were equally real, Bellinger thought, or equally unreal. Real estate, that was the thing! Fishing, sailing, tennis, real estate, and poverty were discussed. He talked of himself, his boredom, his investments. It was all random, witless, uncoordinated. He listened indulgently as Desirée expostulated on the difficulties of housekeeping in the islands. The joking was suggestive, if not filthy. Sarah gave as good as she got and kept the talk going.

"Doctor," Desirée said finally. "Sarah and Emmet are here to talk business."

"So much for philosophy," Bellinger announced with a hiccup. "Let's look at the trophies."

The talk went on in the trophy room.

"Okay. Okay," Bellinger said, interrupting. His head fell; he breathed noisily, then looked up with a grin. "Why in bloody hell should I help? What did they do for me?"

Sarah was unimpressed. "Come, Doctor! You were head of neurology for five years. You owe the hospital something."

Bellinger turned to O'Dwyer. "Do I owe it something, baby?" O'Dwyer shrugged. "You're the doctor. You tell me."

Bellinger cackled. "Head of neurology! Sounds grand, but what was it? The title, *if* you please, was *acting* head of service. Not head. *Acting* head. Don't make it grander than it was."

"If you hadn't left, you'd have been head," Sarah said.

The bloodshot eyes were tinged with mockery. "So they said, but the bloody truth was otherwise. When they needed a black doctor, I was hired to parade to the black voters. I gave them a run for their money. Got every damn foundation handout for them and put across every reform, except those I wanted. When it came to getting black people some real say-so in setting up their own institutions—whoo-ee! I was upsetting the man. I had no future and my rank was fixed. I had a dream, baby, an elusive dream—tenure and my own department. But I found out something—a guy can promise you the sky in the Yale Club and deny the nose on his face in the Harvard Club. So!" Bellinger hoisted a glass. "I fought the good fight in a cold and distant land and here I am. Here I am!"

He roused himself. "You expect me to come patty-paws to the rescue of an unjustly accused profession. I'm too old at the game to be impressed. I've seen everything the patient gets, even in the voluntary hospitals. Half the surgery I ever saw was done by untrained or inadequately trained doctors. And the needless surgery was beyond belief. I've seen good authoritative studies recently—in one of those magazines I still get—that one-third of all hysterectomies are totally unjustified. One hundred thousand women are maimed every year in America alone, not to mention what goes on with tonsillectomies and all that. And why? The pocketbook, baby. The Yankee dollar. The almighty buck. When the surgeon profits, the fibroids bloody the O.R. buckets like mad. So if this poor lady is screaming, 'Hey! What went on in there?' why should I worry?" The white teeth flashed in a disarming grin. "I ain't sore at her, baby. She ain't suing me."

Sarah was taken aback. "None of those remarks apply to the city hospital. No fees were charged."

"Then there's no excuse," Bellinger cackled. "But isn't that your defense? Whatever happened that day was medicine, pure and unalloyed. Like the little girl, when American medicine is good, it's very, very good. When it's bad, it's horrid."

Desirée rose to full height, interrupting the rambling talk, and broke into torrential French. Bellinger listened with the same earlier grin of fatherly indulgence. "Now if you don't mind, I shall leave," Desirée announced with indignation, and flounced out. The opulence of the curved haunches was astonishing.

"She's after the Cadillac," Bellinger said with a grin. "She wants something tangible when I leave her flat. She forgets she's got the baby. So how can I leave her flat?"

O'Dwyer hunched forward, cracking his knuckles. He had been watching the interplay with care. "Doc, what's this horsing about? Was Manya's case malpractice?"

"Please, Em," Sarah said.

She put aside her drink and faced the handsome wreck. "Doctor, I'm tired and nervous. I'd like to drop the persiflage, if you don't mind. We've got serious medical and legal questions to resolve. The first main issue is diagnosis, whether surgery was justified. Or if so, whether the Shroeders were told fully the need and danger of the operation. In either case the wrong answer means the hospital may be liable. The question is how much."

"Ah!" Bellinger said.

Sarah went on. "Even if there is liability, which we won't admit, we think we can show that the deficits—sight, hearing, memory, and so forth—are grossly exaggerated. She says she still has headaches and seizures. Perhaps so, but if we can show she hasn't changed for the worse, we can hope to keep the recovery to a reasonable figure. . . ."

Bellinger looked up. "Have you talked settlement?"

"Too far apart," she said grimly. "Mahler's got something up his sleeve. It'd be pointless to go further until we know what it is. We've run an intensive investigation. Some of the sexual aspects, while understandable, may give the jury a bad taste about her—but it might backfire if brought out by us. It'll depend on how she stands up under cross-examination. Of course it's unpleasant. As to damages, the main single claim is the psychiatric problem. . . ."

"No opinion there, baby." Bellinger grinned. "I'm just a humble surgeon. Cancerphobia's not my line, as I wrote. How are you doing in that department?"

Sarah bit her lip. "We'll meet that somehow with psychiatric testimony, I suppose. We hope to show that the psychosis—if that's what she's really got—antedated the surgery. Otherwise the defense . . ." She halted. "They claim, you see, that the dread of cancer plus the damage of surgery precipitated the depression which sent her to the Luzzatto Institute. The problem is that we have no history of any prior psychotic episode—so while we can scoff, the other side has full range to make that claim stick. It's exasperating not to have adequate data to work from. Without a sufficient history, the other side is free to claim anything. It's so vague, so speculative. Still . . ."

She resumed, knitting her brows, thinking through the maddening alternatives. "If the surgery was justified, everything else falls into place. So it's most important that you appear in court to explain how you arrived at the diagnosis. Will you do it?" She waited a heartbeat.

Bellinger squinted. "I could be sued myself if I leave this haven of refuge."

"We'll guarantee you against any verdict. Obviously your absence raises a cloud of suspicion."

"Well, well, well." Bellinger returned to his drink, much amused. "I always listen to beautiful women. What do you want me to say?"

O'Dwyer broke in. "Mrs. van Loon wants you to tell the truth and to say that you studied the tests, reviewed the history, authorized the operation. Then tell the jury why. What else?"

A torrent of music interrupted, great strong chords struck on an old piano keyboard in the next room. Desirée was playing like a master. Bellinger shook his head deploringly. "But, baby, are you sure I authorized it?"

Sarah glanced at O'Dwyer with dismay. "We have a summary to that effect. It says you were consulted at every step—medication, departmental conference. Weren't you consulted?"

"God, yes. Overconsulted," Bellinger said.

Sarah went on. "The summary says you agreed to consider the question of an infiltrating, slow-growing glioma with the hope that if confirmed by biopsy, radiation therapy would be used and all the rest. If a scar, then it'd be excised." She had gone pale. "Didn't that happen?"

"Who made that summary?"

"It was in your name. Typewritten."

"But I didn't sign, did I?"

O'Dwyer interrupted. "You're saying Tatum faked it, for Christ's sake?"

Bellinger shook his head. "Percy Tatum? Bloody well not. Wouldn't *fake* in ten thousand years. Wouldn't know how. But I didn't authorize the operation. It was his own idea. If I were you, I'd let the record stand."

"Emmet, please!" Sarah turned a burning glance to the young detective. She came back to the mask of mockery and insolence. "Will you please explain?"

Bellinger returned to his glass, plucking his wattle. "You seem bound to get an answer. If you want the truth, yes, I'd seen the patient and the tests. I thought the X rays were negative. Percy disagreed and began to make my life miserable. He insisted everyone was wrong—that the damned tumor was there and had to come out to save the woman's life. I had my own operating schedule, other patients, full load of administrative work, bad liver, and"—a glance rolled toward the sound of music—"demanding women. Finally when he called me in New York one inconvenient midnight, I said to stop pestering me and do whatever he damned liked with the wretched woman."

"Oh, brother!" O'Dwyer shook his head. "But X rays? X rays!" he said reverentially. "How can they go wrong?"

Bellinger grimaced. "Lights and shadows, baby, lights and shadows. Who knows what they mean? Percy had his ideas. I had mine. Maybe he *felt* authorized—but was he? Determined man, Percy. When I got back to Lewiston that next afternoon, he was already into his first burr hole."

The music had changed to the clashing dissonance of hot jazz. The mockery was now savage.

"But that doesn't make sense," Sarah protested. "How could he schedule the surgery without your signature?"

"Hospitals, baby," Bellinger retorted. "People work with blinkers. Who would question him? That's why I'd let the record stand."

"But at least you did supervise?"

Bellinger cocked a brow. "Supervise?"

Sarah frowned. "We've found of course that Tatum was licensed to practice medicine in Maryland and elsewhere but not in New York. The rules call for supervision. I'd hate to face that issue." She contemplated something disagreeable. "It'd be helpful if you could say you did."

Bellinger's head fell, then rose with derision. "Let's say I was standing by."

"Where?"

"Not far off."

Sarah returned to her drink, feeling the moment's constriction. "Mahler seems to know you were elsewhere than in the O.R. Where would he get such a notion?"

"Ah. I see. Well, I suppose that long-legged bitch, Lurene—my, ah, secretary—put him onto that. She's the price I pay for a soft heart." Bellinger glanced at O'Dwyer and smiled with innocence. "Lurene won't go to court."

"Dr. Gates will," O'Dwyer said.

"I see. Sorry about that," Bellinger said. "Do you still want me on the stand?"

Sarah stared resentfully. A year of struggle had brought her to the limit of exasperation. "God, Bellinger, I couldn't care less where you're getting it, but I need better answers. You're telling me the operation wasn't authorized, that an unlicensed resident wasn't supervised, maybe in violation of state law and hospital bylaws. Frankly I'm alarmed. How could he possibly be given that latitude?"

Bellinger smiled fondly. "Percy's a problem. Always was, since we met at Gorham Med. When he heard I was at Lewiston, he applied and I appointed him chief resident over others. It made the usual fuss, but it wasn't black nepotism at all—or he'd have refused it. It was personal nepotism, which he accepted. Strange are the ways. Frankly, I'd have been happier with someone a bit easier to live with."

"What were his credentials?" Sarah asked.

Bellinger returned to his drink. "Let's say I didn't examine those too closely. He claimed a year of residency in neurosurgery

173

out West someplace and I reckon he had. Plus surgical experience in the armed services."

"Didn't you check?"

"Old Percy? Why would I? Old classmate, if you please. He was consumed to pass his boards in neurosurgery. At his age and black—if I may say so—it was his last chance to qualify. I damned well meant to see him make it, and if he had some technical defects in his application, I didn't want to know." He turned to O'Dwyer. "Any comment, baby?"

"I didn't say a word," O'Dwyer replied. "If I were Manya Shroeder's husband, I might want to talk it over in a dark alley."

"Em!" Sarah said sharply.

The grin returned. "Percy had the best credentials he could get. If his record was spotty, nobody was asking questions at the time when city hospitals were begging for black doctors. He was hired with full knowledge by Grimes, who wanted to show his open-mindedness and all that. It doesn't mean he didn't have ability. He does. But it's these damned pusillanimous programs of hiring black skins that ruin the black doctor. Nowadays he gets there, not despite but because of the guilty favoritism, and nobody, black brother included, believes in him. Seems no way out of that trap."

Bellinger was breathing noisily. "So if Percy wasn't Nobel Prize material, who is? He was okay. It was his situation that wasn't. And that, Triple Goddess, is the task—to convince a dozen appleknocker jurors that Percy was competent. You all made the problem. You live with it. Not me."

There was a significant pause.

Sarah stirred. "Did he find a tumor?"

A nightingale was singing in the night. Bellinger waited to answer the question. "Yes, he found a tumor."

O'Dwyer grunted with relief.

"That is"—Bellinger went on—"*if!* If you believe Percy Tatum, yes. *If* you believe the pathologist, no. You pays your money and you takes your choice." He stood to full height and stretched, facing a portrait of his younger self. "You must have gotten an outside opinion by now?"

Sarah took a long moment to answer. "Doctor, I want you to appreciate that we've worked harder on this claim than anything

I remember. We've exhausted every resource we can think of. And we came hoping you might bail us out somehow. I'm afraid we'll have to fall back on our staff for expert testimony. In a way I'm relieved—if only because Mahler seems to know that your own credentials were not what everyone thought."

Bellinger smiled. "Weren't they?"

"No. It seems you're not listed as a diplomate or as a fellow in neurology or neurosurgery in the last directory of the state medical society. Your appointment in Montreal was also temporary. So were your many posts along the way. Correct me, but wasn't that *really* why Grimes refused to propose you as head of neurology with tenure and full status?"

The question seemed expected. "Are you putting me on?" The cracked voice went falsetto. "I was more than qualified to run that shop by reason of skill and experience—which Grimes admitted that day at the Harvard Club when he looked me in the eye and told me he'd deny it under oath. My ability didn't mean a thing. All he saw was his job and my skin." He broke off. "How much truth do you want? How much crap? I'll testify if you insist, but that's what you'll get—baby."

The music had stopped.

Sarah turned from the sardonic mask. "Well, it's not an area of cross-examination we can afford to give Mahler. Sorry, but there it is." Her knees were trembling. "One million dollars." She brooded. "It's absurd. Insulting. Just adding zeros. They won't even talk about it. We'll have to keep the damage to a reasonable figure without you or Tatum. How we'll deal with that psychiatric problem, the cancerphobia, I have no idea."

She finished her drink. "You're as mad as Tatum, you know?"

Desirée entered and mixed a drink in the silence that followed. She looked up dizzily. "I interrupt?"

"I'm really tired now. Em, let's leave," Sarah said. Bellinger showed them to their car in silence. She said, "Doctor, we saw Tatum three weeks ago, you know? It wasn't easy to get him to talk to us. He's angry, of course. Did you know he had that job in Maryland?"

"Oh, yes," Bellinger said. "I never stop getting letters, arguments, recriminations, telephone calls. It's been going on for years. How is old Percy?"

"Mortified. He feels betrayed by his patients, by the hospital, by us," Sarah said, "and not one bit cooperative."

"Will you call him as a witness?" Bellinger asked.

"I don't see how," she said.

O'Dwyer finally started the motor. It was cold and took time to catch on. "Doc, it's eating him, sure," he said. "But I'll say this for old Percy. He thinks you're a terrific doctor and a great guy who sticks. But I think he just got screwed by his only friend. I hope you understand the spirit in which I say that."

Bellinger laughed. "Watch out for land mines now. Henry will pass you through."

Twin red dots of light danced off into the black night. The dog was barking furiously. "You poor unhappy son of a bitch," Bellinger murmured. He tousled the animal. Whom he was addressing was not clear even to himself.

Clerk Rorke was on the telephone, surprisingly gentle of voice. He asked for Landowski.

"Gene? Trial Term, Part Three, Monday morning. Be ready to pick a jury. Urquart's sitting." He rang off with a dry chuckle.

15

The street light threw dappled shadows on the wall at night. Shroeder buried his head in the lumpy pillow. He was unstrung and could not sleep. He had not slept since he could remember. He was conscious of the woman's breath whistling in his ear.

Carefully he got out of bed and went to the bathroom. The floor was cold to his bare feet. He paused at the small bedroom and listened to the child. Christ! he thought. He slid back into the cold bed and heard the stirring.

"Frank? I had the dream."

"Yeah?"

"I feel nervous."

"Did you take the medicine?"

"Yes, that. I still have this choking feeling."

"Try not to think about it. You'll have to get up soon and that should help. You don't want anything to happen."

"Thanks for nothing," she said.

An hour later the alarm whirred.

"Get it, Frank?"

"Yeah, sure."

He reached out and the whir stopped. He sat up with a yawn and scratched his head. It was light now in the backyard. Birds were whistling in the early spring. The house had no comfort. "You got to get up," he said.

"Give me five minutes," she said.

"Okay," he said, "but only five." He went off again to the bathroom. When he returned, he saw the strained expression. "Now what?"

"What are you sore about?" she said.

He halted. "Sore?"

"It's getting me upset," she said. "I certainly didn't ask for this. It was as much your idea as mine."

"I'm not blaming you," he said. "It's just that I don't know anymore. I thought, One, two, three! Bang! We'd get some money. We'd knock it off and get down to Florida and so forth." He dressed in gloomy silence, angrily stuffing a shirt into his trousers. "I don't think we'll see a dime."

"Is that what's biting you?"

He tied his laces. "Never mind what's biting me," he muttered. "These lawyers. Somehow, somewhere they'll make it and we'll be left on the beach. I just know it."

She closed her eyes while he continued to dress. There was the fuss and anger she well knew. She said exhaustedly, "Unless we make it, how can they? If we get, they get. If we don't get, neither do they. It's the way these things work. We couldn't pay for what they're doing. I've explained that."

He turned away, goaded. He resented her superiority, as he resented everything. It was too unfair that no one saw what he had to deal with. "Yeah, Manya's smart, Frank's stupid. You explained that too. What about these expenses they laid out? We'll be stuck for that."

"That's not so. They'll forget it."

"What about that dress, this suit? Will they forget that?"

"I don't know. I'm confused."

"Yeah. You don't know!" He stood over the bed glowering. "You think I want them buying clothes for us?" he burst out. "That portable radio we need like a hole in the head? That dentist for the baby? Jesus! What do they think we are?"

She read the haggard lines of suffering in the worn face. "Listen, Frank, sit down," she said. "I can't stand any more of this. If you want to call it quits, I'll go along. But tell them before we go to court. Don't make fools of them. I don't think they deserve that. What's really wrong?"

He sat, nervously clasping his hands. "I was thinking . . ." He looked aside. "I mean, about the sex part. I can't see I'm supposed to tell it out in the open."

It was an effort to talk with the man. "For God's sake, it's another age," she said. "They talk sex on television." She pitied him, but the stupidity was a pain in her heart.

"I'm not on television. I live on Treacy Street. Half the world knows about you and Coxey's Army. You get the shakes when I touch you. . . ." His face contorted. "Jesus Christ," he sighed.

She was silent. "Frank?" Her face was cold, drained of feeling. "I want you to know I'm trying. You believe that?"

"I believe that. Okay, put on a dress before Father Zator comes. It wouldn't hurt meanwhile to straighten up around this house."

She said something in Polish. What was that? he demanded. Nothing, she replied, but she had wished for death. She said, "You're just excited. Make the coffee and I'll be right down."

"Make the coffee, make the coffee," he muttered and went down to the kitchen. The heavy steps were slow and uncertain. She dressed with pain, with effort, thinking of the night. She had her headache—a pain that split her skull from rear to front. It seemed to bore a hole above her eyes. She feared that pain. She never knew when the demon might not seize and shake her like a rat in a giant fist. His presence gave her dread. There was nothing she could do to shake that presence off. He lived with her every minute of the day and night.

Down below, the doorbell rang. The footsteps returned and Frank was there with his depressed, suffering expression. "Father Zator's here. He's driving us himself," he said.

She turned from the mirror, not satisfied. The watching man was a stranger. She said, troubled, "How do I look, Frank?"

"You look fine," he said. "Nobody would think you got a thing wrong. Now get ready, will you? And just pray we're doing the right thing."

Judge Urquart was less than comfortable with the matter on hand. The undercurrents were apparent. Black activists and their white allies were crowded in the rear. Across the aisle Father Zator's group were staring daggers at the city attorney's assistants. But they were quiet and he was determined to keep them so.

It had taken a week to select the jury. Most unusual in a civil case for damages, but then the persistent questioning by both sides into racial attitudes had gone far afield indeed. Mahler and Sabbattino were bulldogs, worrying each other. He was put off by Mahler. The fellow was getting all he wanted into the record and the case had not yet begun. The jury—well, the jury was a mixed pack: Irish, Italians, Slavs, one Jew, one Puerto Rican, one Yankee, one black on whom attention was subtly focused. Five were women. Most disquieting.

Judge Urquart pulled a long single hair bristling from his thick eyebrows. Counsel looked weary—Sabbattino, Sarah van Loon, and Otto at the defense table; Mahler and Landowski at plaintiff's table; the plaintiffs, neatly dressed, in the first bench. "You may begin," he said.

Mahler had been waiting with closed eyes. He was weary and sensitive to every nuance in the courtroom. An elderly messenger in the first bench sat guardian to the hospital records—the entire medical history with tests and evaluations over a period of years. It was important to be calm and keep his thoughts in order, but in fact his heart was beating harder than he could remember. A last-minute call that morning from Yarberry requesting delay— a surgical emergency of some kind—had upset a plan to begin with crushing medical evidence. It was, however, not essential. A dozen neighbors were present to lay a foundation for the medical evidence to come.

". . . begin," the judge repeated.

Mahler glanced at Sarah and strode forward, arms folded, thinking of his opening. There had been a last chat in the hall, polite regrets that they had not settled the case, but this was put aside. A full valise of notes and depositions on the counsel table was a parade of diligence. Names, addresses, points were indexed and available. A large white chart with a multicolored flow of symptoms was a detailed visual statement of the medical clashes to come. The truth was that he was looking forward to the fight. He had to remind himself that this was a civil matter, not a criminal prosecution, that he represented not the public interest but a sick woman and her husband, that he was in strange territory. He turned to the rail and began.

The jury would hear a case of negligence, he promised, done in an operating room of the city hospital by two doctors who since had mysteriously disappeared. For that reason the proof would come from the hospital itself—its records, its employees— and from its victim, her neighbors and private physicians. All this would be followed by a distinguished medical authority who would testify that the operation, useless to the patient in her condition, was a departure from a proper standard of medical care.

On that basis alone she was entitled to a verdict against the hospital for malpractice. But there was more.

"Mrs. Shroeder charges by this complaint that these doctors made a wrong diagnosis and acted wrongfully when they willfully or negligently—it hardly matters which—told her she had cancer to get her consent to the operation. They removed a large part of the left parietal lobe of her brain which controls sight, touch, and her ability to walk and function like a normal woman. She's partially lost her memory and part of her speech. She's got exaggerated sensitivity in all those areas and other distressing problems for a delicate and sensitive woman to live with. Her seizures are worse than ever and often are followed by a total temporary paralysis which lasts for hours. She can't read or write or concentrate. Sight and hearing are compromised. She feels disfigured by the scar in her skull where the bone has partially eroded. Her personality has changed and her emotions altered. She has wrong and inappropriate reactions. She laughs when she wants to cry. She cries when she should laugh. Her feelings have changed toward her husband and child. . . ."

Sabbattino was standing now.

Mahler went on imperturbably, staring at the unseen culprits who had committed these crimes. "The main thing is that these surgeons treated her so high-handedly and so incompetently that the interreaction between the organic damage to her brain structure and the reaction to the false and irresponsible horrible statement that she had cancer caused her to collapse into a mental depression that sent her to an institution for psychiatric care. I'm sure you know what that means. . . ."

"Objection!" Sabbattino said.

"Yes," Judge Urquart ruled.

"In other words," Mahler went on, "that these doctors have left her with extreme and continuing pain and anguish and all sorts of disabilities. She can't take care of her house or child.

She can't live as a woman with her husband. Life is dull, drab, and miserable to her, and a living hell. All this because the absent neurosurgeons recklessly and deliberately misstated the need for the operation and its risks and went ahead in disregard of every medical standard that would govern . . ."

The procedures, diagnosis, and damage were described in further detail no less vivid for the matter-of-fact tone in which the horrors were described. He ended with an appeal for open minds and a fair impartial verdict based only on the evidence and the testimony of the medical experts without sympathy or bias in the matter.

During the opening Sarah had come alert, startled at the rancorous tone. A dozen scribbled notes went to Sabbattino, who nodded at some, ignored others. He rose to make objections and launched into his own opening. He expressed sympathy for the Shroeder family but urged that all procedures were done in good faith by qualified neurosurgeons to save the woman's life. Of course there was distress—a brain operation had to produce damage—but was there malpractice? And after all the injuries, if any, being invisible, functional, were easily exaggerated. How much of that was neurological and how much imaginary—and financial? That was for them to say. In their selection as jurors, he reminded them, they had promised to decide the case neither on sympathy nor prejudice but on the evidence alone. He was confident of their vote. He thanked them and sat.

"Proceed!" Judge Urquart said.

Mahler rose. "If the Court please, I have these hospital records to mark for identification. . . ."

"Are they complete?" Judge Urquart asked.

"So the certificate says," Mahler said. "I'll have to examine them and make sure. But I have Dr. Grimes, who can answer that question."

"Oh, really!" The stony face was eloquent of disapproval. "Can the records be stipulated?"

"I'd rather have Dr. Grimes," Mahler replied.

"Very well," Judge Urquart said shortly.

"Dr. Andrew Grimes!"

Grimes rose and tiptoed forward with an air of bland deprecation. A plump manicured hand rose to take the oath. He smiled glassily at the newspapermen, glanced obliquely at the medical charts and illustrations across the room, and turned to meet a head-on charge.

At the end of the day the records were in evidence together with a damaging picture of faulty hospital procedures, slipshod hiring practices, and other shortcomings wrung from unwilling lips. He tottered from the stand and paused to whisper murderously that Mahler was a bastard to have embarrassed him with matter imparted in confidence.

Mahler smiled silkily. After a moment he turned to a crowded bench in the rear. "Mrs. Czeisler, please?"

Mrs. Czeisler began with spirit. "Well, the poor soul was on the floor when I got there. The bacon was burning, you know? That's what attracted me, the smell. She was out cold and shaking like a leaf. It—the fit, I mean—was the worst ever. And the baby was crying in the corner. It was heartbreaking. . . ."

"Objection!" Sabbattino cried.

At City Hall a knot of uneasy officials had met to consider an embarrassing matter in the Department of Hospitals. Notice of audit of Lewiston Central Hospital, served by the American Association of Hospitals, could have come at no worse time. A spot check showed that over one thousand medical histories, perhaps more, were incomplete and had been left unsigned by the doctors in charge. Efforts to complete records or get signatures had failed. Attendings had neglected to comply, and former residents were scattered to the four winds. The *Chronicle* had sent a reporter for comment. Who was feeding the newspaper all that stuff?

Mayor Oliphant, handsome as an Arrow collar ad, was bewildered at the scene of civic unrest in the plaza below. Pickets were out chanting slogans of protest. What did they *want?* he wondered plaintively. Promises? Concessions? That had been tried—and now that damned lawsuit was no help. He took his city attorney aside. Public washing of dirty hospital linens could not be more inconvenient. What did that outsider Mahler want in hard dollars and could it not be managed? he wondered.

"I wish we knew," City Attorney Hubert Potter grumbled. "He's asking for the sky. Sabbattino tells me we're better off with the jury—and the court. Judge Urquart's always been good to the city, you know."

"He'd better be. He's up for election soon too," Mayor Oliphant said grimly. "Who's talking to Mahler for us?"

"Sarah, from time to time. They're friendly, you know," Potter replied.

"So, I hear. Well, finish it before they get too friendly," Oliphant said sourly. "I wish this were a bigger city. They get away with murder. Look, team," he said, coming back to the meeting, "let's get up something for a statement. What about this: we're setting up a special task force to study the problem in depth? No?" Heads were shaking. "Then how about this: we're calling in a panel of outside consultants . . . ?"

The chanting of pickets was louder than ever.

"Call your next witness, sir."

The white suffering faces of the Shroeders were drawn with anxiety. Mahler smiled reassuringly and walked across the well of the courtroom to face the jury. It was a theatrical device to set the stage, to compel attention, to justify a strong, loud voice. Both counsel tables stood between him and the jury box. Sarah had placed a small handbag before her. She seemed cool and immaculate, and that in the courtroom grime was a source of wonder. She caught his glance and looked off.

"Mrs. Shroeder, please."

There was a rustle of expectation. Manya rose and with a marked limp walked to the stand. She was wearing a simple black dress with a white collar. Much thought had gone into that costume, and it seemed just right for a poor man's wife. A small crucifix was a sole ornament. She wore no makeup. A sole incongruous note—or was it incongruous?—was freshly set hair. She could have been any woman in the room as she raised her hand to take the oath. Her fingernails, as the third juror, a woman factory worker, noticed, were splintered and gnawed.

"I do," she said inaudibly.

Sabbattino was up to ask for a bench conference. In the huddle, he said nastily, "Judge, I want to know if she's had medication. If she throws a fit for the jury, I'll ask a mistrial."

Mahler said, "She's had the medication, mister! Do you think I'd let her come without it?"

"I'd like a medical certificate," Sabbattino said.

"If the Court asks it," Mahler replied.

Judge Urquart sat back reflectively. "I don't want anything prejudicial to happen, Mr. Mahler. If she gets sick in court, I don't know what my ruling would be. Proceed."

Mahler swallowed an angry thought and went back to his post. His voice was warm with confidence and reassurance. After preliminary questions to establish a convent education in Poland, he came down to her marriage. "Mrs. Shroeder, tell the court and jury, in your own language, when you first had occasion to see a doctor for this condition."

She was inaudible.

"Will you speak up a little louder?"

She smiled timidly at the jury and wet a dry mouth. "In my first pregnancy I went to see Dr. Schlomm in the neighborhood. I was frightened by my first attacks, which began with my tongue swelling and tingling and a dizzy feeling and headaches. Like migraines, I believe. The main thing was this feeling of being terribly frightened. Dr. Schlomm said I most likely had something like, well, brain fever, I believe. Or a head accident in Poland as a child. I didn't remember any such thing, of course. So he said I had probably always had the condition. He called them spells or fits or attacks at different times, but then he said they were the little kind called petit mal."

Mahler nodded encouragingly and she went on. "Dr. Schlomm sent me home with medicine. I lost the baby but I was all right for a year. . . ." She trailed off.

"It's getting stuffy," Judge Urquart interrupted. "Jerry, will you open the window just a crack? Not too wide. I don't want any of the jurors to catch this virus that's going around." It was judicial levity and everyone laughed.

"Go on," Mahler said, "and will you remember to speak up so everyone can hear?"

She stirred. "The headaches kept coming back and about five years later got worse. Then without warning I began to black out, but that was because I stopped taking the medication. That was when he sent me in for tests. On that occasion I had five days of headaches with vomiting and backaches. My legs were weak and I kept running a temperature. . . ."

The stenotype ribbon was folding into its container, fold on fold through the following years. It was essentially the story Mahler had heard on the day of his first visit.

At the end of the day, Mrs. Czeisler and other neighbors gathered, full of congratulations. Manya looked lovely, it was agreed. She was making a wonderful impression on the jury. After a short rest, she'd do even better, they were sure.

Supervisor Rose Kernochan was iron-jawed, hostile, and belligerent to a satisfactory degree. A log book was identified and entered in evidence. In her twenty-six years as operating room and supervising nurse she had never made a mistake, not an error, not an oversight. Every person in the operating room was listed including physicians, residents, interns, medical students, circulating and scrub nurses, even the student nurse. Everyone listed was in her own handwriting. The book covered a period of three years.

What was that question again?

Yes, the supervising surgeon would sign the log personally. Yes, always. That was the rule.

Had she gone back for three years as requested while waiting to testify? Yes, she had.

In that period had the supervising surgeon ever failed to sign the book?

Not to her recollection.

Yes, she had the question.

Oh, the answer. No, Dr. Bellinger had not signed the book that particular day.

Well, there always had to come a first time.

But that did not mean he was not the most brilliant surgeon she had ever seen. What had happened was a shame.

Well, persecution and discrimination and things she'd rather not go into . . .

Fair was fair.

That didn't mean . . .

Well, if . . .

She had never in her life been asked to tamper with official records . . .

Yes, she'd heard of that.

But . . .

Well, yes, she had gone off at five.

Five o'clock was not a suspicious time to start surgery. It took that long for Dr. Ling to get available . . .

Dr. Tatum didn't want an anesthetist. He wanted an anesthesiologist. There was a difference. . . .

Come again?

No idea where Dr. Bellinger might have gone during the operation . . . Presumably he'd be on call.

No reason to question Dr. Tatum . . .

Well, he was the chief resident and a very good doctor.

Dr. Tatum was rated A every month by Dr. Bellinger except once when he got rated B.

No explanation that she knew for the B.

No, she was not biased in their favor.

Yes, she had said that the lawsuit against them was a disgrace.

Yes, a disgrace!

Because every patient got the best treatment anybody could get . . .

She was crying because it was so unfair . . .

What the hell was that supposed to mean? Influenced by what masculine charm?

Supervisor Kernochan glared. "You dirty son of a bitch!" she exclaimed, and threw the log book at Mahler. Mahler, who managed to look hurt and injured at the same time, rubbed a bruised arm and with sweet dismay and regret had no more questions of the witness.

Nor had Sabbattino.

The witness waited an uncertain moment, clamping her mouth. "I don't want to be the patsy, Judge," she burst out. "Dr. Tatum always gave me the operating schedule. How was I to know anything was out of line?"

"Nobody's suing you," Judge Urquart said.

"They'd better not," she said grimly, "or I'll have a few things to tell myself."

As the witness stalked out and managed to slam the door

Mahler examined his nails and looked to the ceiling, satisfied indeed.

The voice was speaking.
". . . feel well?" it said.
She opened her eyes and turned about with a timid smile. "Yes, Your Honor," she said weakly. "I can go on."
"If not, just speak up," the judge said. "We don't want to tax you in any way, but the last juror must hear you, you see?"
"I'll try," she agreed.
Days had passed since she had first been called. It was an unending ordeal. When she tired, Mahler or Sabbattino would suggest a recess, depending on tactics of the moment. Other witnesses relieved her from time to time. She had done well. The slightly guttural European accent was pleasing. She spoke modestly and with restraint. She was often inaudible and flat and when asked to speak up excused herself in a soft, apologetic voice. She had given her difficulties with obvious sincerity. She had covered a dozen hospital admissions by Dr. Schlomm for a variety of symptoms and painful and fruitless neurological studies. The problems of a disturbed child—bed wetting, nightmares, listlessness, loss of appetite—seemed to impress the women jurors. And the marital problem which brought out her blushes emphasized the discomfort of a decent woman faced with distressing, uncontrollable impulses.
"I don't sleep," she said apologetically. "I just lost all feeling for my husband."
"And why is that?" Mahler asked.
She sighed, dabbing her mouth. "I—I feel like dirt since they opened my head. Who would want me for a minute with this thing inside me? It never leaves me. I sit around waiting for the end. Only it never comes."
"Yet you seem to be smiling?"
"I tell myself, Manya, keep smiling. What else can I do? It's only a front. I can't get it out of my head my days are numbered. So I smile. So lots of people smile. So what does it prove?"
"Do you resent Dr. Bellinger?"
"Maybe I should. I don't."
"Dr. Tatum?"

188

"No." She shook her head dumbly.

"Do you resent any of the doctors or anything they did?"

She stared at space, biting her mouth. "Well, I don't think Dr. Tatum should have told me I had cancer. Cancer! How could he do a thing like that?" The flat, uncomplaining tone was infinitely touching. "I feel changed," she said falteringly. "The music . . ."

Mahler looked up. "What music?"

"I sometimes hear a song," she said. "I can't describe it. It's men singing." She smiled hesitatingly at the fifth juror—a housewife of German background. "I think it's a German song. Maybe Swiss. It's a funny song but I don't like it." She closed her eyes. Frank's eyes were averted.

Mahler glanced at the clock. It was her fifth appearance on the stand. "Would you like a recess?"

She nodded, wordless.

When she returned, the chamber had a different smell, she thought.

Mahler said, "When Dr. Tatum told you that you had cancer, who was present?"

"An old Yankee lady. She was from the Methodist home but I understand she died."

"May we have her name?"

Sabbattino rose as though to object, glanced about at an almost empty courtroom. The trial was losing its audience. "I didn't hear the answer. What was the old Yankee lady's name?"

"Mrs. Kidder," Manya said.

"And what day did you have that conversation with Dr. Tatum and Mrs. Kidder?"

"I'll fix the day," Mahler said.

"I wish you'd leave *something* to the witness," Sabbattino said.

Judge Urquart tapped. "Gentlemen, please. No, Mr. Mahler, I won't admonish anybody. Mrs. Shroeder, answer the question, please?"

Manya was staring at the clock. The request was repeated twice. She looked up apologetically. "I'm so sorry, Your Honor. I was watching the time. I just can't seem to . . ." She trailed off in dreary humiliation.

"Maybe we should recess for the day . . ." Judge Urquart said.

Sabbattino broke in. "What time is it, madam?"

Manya again glanced at the clock. "Three," she said before Mahler could intervene.

"Isn't it five after the hour?" Sabbattino said swiftly, dropping his voice.

"Yes," she agreed.

"So you can read the clock? And you heard my question?" She nodded. Sabbattino's voice dropped lower. "Even though I'm almost whispering?"

"Sometimes I hear too well," she said.

"And other times not at all?" Sabbattino shouted suddenly. "Which do you do?"

"It depends on how I feel," she replied.

"All right, all right," Mahler said angrily. "I've got my objections to these tactics noted, Judge. It's absolutely unfair and prejudicial . . ."

"Then don't let her volunteer! If she can read the clock at sixty feet," Sabbattino retorted, "why shouldn't the record show it?"

"What can we expect?" Mahler said.

"Let her answer!" Sabbattino said.

"About Mrs. Kidder?" Manya asked. "I forget what day that conversation took place."

"But you just remembered the question?" Sabbattino said.

"That's different," she replied.

"I'm sure it is. You haven't missed church more than three times in six months. Isn't it true you read the missal?"

"Yes, I read."

"And shop at the supermarket?"

"Yes, I can do that."

"And count change?"

"Yes."

"And do everything other women do?"

"Yes, but I am suffering," she said.

Sabbattino stood back with scorn. "You remember to say that? You remember conversations with Dr. Schlomm ten years old? In fact you remember all sorts of things for Mr. Mahler. But you don't remember anything at all for Mr. Sabbattino? Is that because Mr. Mahler has come up here all the way from New York City to show us how they do things there?" Sabbattino sat and turned to Sarah. "Mrs. Kidder died ten days before the surgery," he said audibly behind a cupped hand.

A fine wrangle broke out.

"I'm sorry," Manya said piteously. "Somebody should have told me. I'm not myself."

"She doesn't sound confused to me," Sabbattino said aside. "And she walks all right when she forgets to limp for her lawyer from New York City."

Judge Urquart ruled. "Madam, you're excused for the moment. Mr. Mahler, call another witness."

The suffering groan was Frank Shroeder's.

16

Over the weeks a queer sociability had grown up in the halls.
The lawyers, grown haggard, wandered like wounded animals
under the strain of making notes, studying transcripts, preparing
for trial, and researching into the endless nights. In the noon
recesses, they ate at Flynn's where trial tactics were discussed
in low tones at separate tables. What the jury thought was the
subject of endless speculation. They met at the coffee dispenser
and gathered at the telephone booths. Mahler and Sarah came
out of the booths at the same time.

"Don't look so damned smug," Sarah said. "It's still not malpractice. You've only put in a partial case. We haven't heard any
medical testimony yet—if you've got any to put in."

"Be sure of it," he replied.

She studied the heavy features. The lines had cut deeper at
the determined mouth. His temples were gray. "Have you got
a cigarette?"

"I think so," Mahler said.

They strolled to the window at the end of the corridor overlooking the plaza. The poplars below were in leaf. "Phil might
be ready to talk settlement," she said.

"Would he? Why at this point?" Mahler asked.

She recalled something from that afternoon at the Oak Room.
"Because he usually does just before the medical proof goes in.
You may not want to risk what he might offer. It's his psycho-
logical moment too . . ." She broke off. "Oh, it seems pointless."

"What does that mean in dollars?"

"I'm not bargaining," she said.

Mahler leaned back against the wall, frowning. "I'd like to finish up my medical proof first. He's got to improve the offer a lot more before I'll come down. Still . . ." He shrugged. "If you bring me my figure, I'll take it up with the clients of course."

"Come off it," Sarah said irritably. She was not sure he was joking. "The Shroeders will take your advice exactly. They've become completely dependent on you. Really, Will. Oh, hello, Phil," she said, breaking off suddenly as Sabbattino approached. "I've been telling Will we might be ready to talk money if he'll make an offer. Is that all right with you?"

"Sure, always. If I don't have to get into telephone figures," Sabbattino said with suspicious joviality. A glance of irony took in the awkward moment. "Can I buy you guys a Coke?"

O'Dwyer, who had been guarding the courtroom, made a signal. "Judge is waiting," he said.

"All rise!" Clerk Rorke announced.

Mahler: Dr. Feke, who brought you that tissue specimen?

Dr. Feke: A student nurse. It weighed about thirty grams, which means about a whiskey measure. As I said, the frozen section showed focal hemorrhage—blood—which is perfectly compatible with surgical trauma and does not imply a primary lesion of any nature whatsoever. Nor did the slides I made from that same specimen.

Mahler: It was not malignant then?

Feke: Absolutely not.

Mahler: Your witness.

Sabbattino: No questions.

The Court: The witness is excused. Call another witness, sir.

Mahler: Mrs. Ponsonby, please. Then if the Court please, I'll recall Mrs. Shroeder.

The Court: Manage your own case, sir, but I would like the jury to hear some pertinent expert medical evidence soon or I'll entertain a motion to dismiss the complaint.

Mahler: So I understand.

The Court: I can barely hear you.

Mahler: Sorry, I'm hoarse. It seems to be a virus. I said I'll be ready tomorrow.

The Court: Swear the witness.

Mahler: I see Dr. Goldfarb is here. May I call him now instead?

The Court: Call whomever you like.

Mahler: Mrs. Ponsonby, don't go away. Dr. Goldfarb, please?

The Court: But I'm getting tired of this. Recess for fifteen minutes.

The interminable business was going on.

Manya sat forward, knitting her brows. "Can you repeat the question?"

"I want the exact language," Mahler said. "What precisely did Dr. Tatum tell you? Don't look at me. Tell it to the jury in your own words."

She resumed with an effort. "He said, 'CA.' I said, what does that mean?—although I knew, of course. Everybody knows what CA means. He sat on the bed and took my hand. Then he said, 'Now, don't let a word frighten you, Mrs. Shroeder. It's only a word.' I said, 'You can be wrong, can't you?' He said, 'I don't think so. I wish I had better news.' He repeated that several times. Then he said, 'But I'm convinced I can help you get well and better, Mrs. Shroeder, well and better, if you let me remove the condition.' I remember that look in his eyes and those funny words, 'well and better,' like a character out of Dickens, I thought. I suddenly didn't like him. I pulled my hand away, thinking that, well, in a way, I was glad. It would be over soon. It was nothing I could help and I was ready to die and have it done. I remember how my pillow smelled—stale and sweaty—and I gagged. I can't stand strong smells, that's one of my problems, of course. Anyway, I told him I didn't want to hear more and to let me alone. Oh, dear. Oh dear," she said, lapsing into silence.

"Then what?"

"I was shocked. I said I didn't believe him. I said he was just trying to get me to sign the consent form. I got upset and said things I didn't mean."

"What sort of things?"

"Things."

"Go on."

"He called me a fool, and gave me a time limit to decide. He said he'd do anything for a real woman, but not for an ingrate.

He said I was stupid, thinking impulsively, trying to kill myself without regard for others, and did I think he'd mislead me in something so serious? He was talking for my good, he said. He said no doctor in the city would touch me if I refused to let him save my life, that I had no idea what the operation was costing him. He said if I didn't sign he'd wash his hands of me and walk out. He was very angry." She paused. She looked infinitely sad.

The brain! The gruesome brain! Otto intoned to himself. She's murdering us, he thought, glancing at a transfixed woman juror.

Manya went on with an effort. "Afterwards he told me I'd need another operation. That—that thing is still in there." She touched her temple. "But if he was wrong . . ." She paused, strangled by grief. "I'm a dead woman. I can't get it out of my mind. So why can't I die?" The dreary flat voice was accompanied by a vapid smile.

"Your witness," Mahler said.

Sabbattino rose to cross-examine, poisonous with irony. By afternoon Manya's brain surgery had become, he insinuated, a blessing in disguise. He pointed a finger. Now about so-called claims to new uncontrollable sexual impulses . . .

Manya stiffened.

. . . long before the brain surgery had there not been trouble with her husband which had sent them for family counseling . . . ?

The subject was worried to death. Manya blushed and hesitated as the questions became more direct, more brutal. Shroeder hung his head, clenching his hands, staring at the oiled flooring. He was on the verge of tears. Sarah had left the room.

"No more questions!" Sabbattino said with disgust.

Manya apathetically faced the clock. She shivered and stepped listless from the stand.

Mahler turned to Landowski and winked. His opponent had got nowhere.

"Will counsel step to the bench?"

The talk was blunt with unconcealed anger. "I'm warning you both," Judge Urquart said testily, "especially you, Mr. Mahler. This isn't New York. We're not used to acrimony, or insults, or conduct verging on contempt, and it began, sir, with a jury opening of unparalleled stridency and bitterness. Now the Court wants a real effort to settle on a fair basis. Fair to these people, yes, but fair to the city. Now go back and see what you can do. We'll adjourn for the day. . . . No, sir!" he said with asperity. "Not another word. You will fix a definite time to produce your medical expert, sir, or the Court will entertain a motion to dismiss. When will you have him?"

Mahler said, "I expect him tonight. Mr. Landowski will meet him at the airport."

"I want him here, not at the airport," Judge Urquart said ominously. "Very well. Let's finish up."

As they returned to the counsel table, Mahler was smiling grimly. From the feel of it, he confided, putting himself in the city's place, the figure was over seventy-five thousand dollars. Perhaps more.

Landowski sucked in his breath. "What makes you think so?"

Mahler studied the heap of medical books before him with weary satisfaction. "Mainly the way that judge is bearing down. Well, let's see if we can't get that figure to improve. Eh?"

Shroeder sat stifled, knotting swollen arthritic knuckles. A cheap new suit felt uncomfortable and scratchy. He was conscious of patched broken shoes and a fresh shaving cut which had bled into his shirt collar.

Mahler was speaking. ". . . loud enough so that Mr. Herkimer, this gentleman, can hear you?"

Shroeder glanced at the twelfth juror, a red-faced apple grower, and nodded. A deep sigh shook the large gaunt frame. "Oh, God, God, God." His voice was without tone. "How do I explain this? When Dr. Tatum told me cancer, I didn't know what to think in there. I mean, these attacks were killing her. Eight days she had this status epi—epileptius . . ."

"Epilepticus?"

"Yeah, that. Eight days it went on. First the hand, then the arm, then the whole side. It seemed to mean something, being she was always right-handed. Okay. So she was out cold most of the time. No letup. No letup. It was terrifying. Misery. I went in there and told her, Manya, these are specialists. Maybe they're right. Maybe you need an operation. An operation cured this G.I. friend at the Veterans' Hospital. Why not you? She kept saying, 'My God, Frank, I got CA.' She wanted to put her head in the oven. I did a lot of praying, I can tell you."

A juror was staring, transfixed.

Shroeder drew a breath. "Yeah, praying. I begged her to string along with the doctor and she did. I should never have listened to that queer, but he made it seem so easy. I said to him . . ."

"Him? You mean by that Dr. Tatum?"

"Yeah. Him. I said, 'Suppose you're wrong about this cancer? Then what?' If no cancer, he said, he promised to close her up with no problems. It would be only to explore, he said, so how could it hurt? And we were looking to him for a miracle." The heavy face worked convulsively.

"Were you asked to sign a written consent?"

"What consent? What did we know?" Shroeder exclaimed. "Let the man come here and deny it. Let him face twelve people and deny it on oath. Yeah, let him do that and we'll see who they believe. Why ain't he here to explain what he did to the woman? A wife and a mother!" The strong features were convulsed with rage and grief. "Yeah! Why ain't he here?"

"Yes, why?" Mrs. Wendkos, a neighbor, exclaimed.

Sabbattino erupted, spouting smoke and ashes and flames. The courtroom was almost empty.

"That's almost it," Mahler said, smiling wearily. "We'll wrap up the medical proof tomorrow, then see what they've got to say. Good job, Frank."

Shroeder waited dumbly. "I don't think we can stand any more in there. I thought the judge would kill me he was so sore."

"Who really cares what the old son of a bitch thinks?" Mahler said. "He was against us at the start, only now he's begun to show his hand—letting Sabbattino get away with murder. Well, let him. Those crude tactics boomerang. Sabbattino's an idiot to pile it on. Those jurors believe Manya and not a word yet to justify the operation. Frankly I don't see they've got any answers." His voice softened. "And, Manya?" he said, squeezing her shoulder. "Take it easy, huh? You did fine. Leave the rest to me."

They dispersed, stumbling with fatigue.

Mahler was in shirt sleeves at the Shooler Building office jotting items for the folder marked SUMMATION. The telephone rang unexpectedly. It was Landowski at the airport. Yarberry had not arrived on the six o'clock flight from New York.

Mahler glanced at his list of witnesses. "Well, he did say he might not make the flight. You go home and take it easy. I'll call his office."

Landowski rang off, worried indeed. Mahler put through a call to Featherstone and ran up against slurry-voiced indifference at the hospital switchboard. "Miss, don't tell me you're just doing your job," he said savagely. "You find Dr. Yarberry and tell him I'm awaiting his call. Pronto."

A sudden constriction was unbearable.

He left for the men's room. When he returned a thin, smiling man was waiting in the deserted office.

"Remember me?" the man said.

The bluff grin, a smell of bourbon, stained fingers, and a sly manner were familiar. "Oh, yes, um . . ." Mahler said.

"Baldwin. Horace Baldwin."

Mahler lit a cigar. "Sure, Baldwin. The adjuster."

Baldwin had been following the trial and wondered how Mahler felt about it.

"We feel good," Mahler said. "We think the jury's got the picture. Just a few days more."

Baldwin winked. "You're doing a beautiful job, Mr. Mahler. Beautiful. Judge Urquart thinks you're amazing. You know the rules. Why, when you make an objection, you give the reason. He finds that unusual." He stuck a cud of snuff into his cheek. "You were very hasty with me last time," he said reproachfully. "Very hasty. And unfair."

"You still think I need help?" Mahler said.

"Ayeh. This can be settled, sir. I've got a pretty good idea of the value." The beady eyes were intent, watchful.

"And that's because you know your way around the men's room, I seem to recall?"

"That's one place. Ayeh."

Mahler felt his jaw. "I'm not sure I need an adjuster. How much did you have in mind?"

Baldwin wet his lips. "Say two hundred thousand?"

"Could that go higher?"

"I'm not at liberty to say." An expressionless stare made the man uneasy. "It won't cost anything unless I deliver. You don't have to take it."

"I don't have to take anything," Mahler said. He turned to the window and the muddy canal below. Over a year had passed since his first arrival in Lewiston. It seemed a lifetime. "Ten points is a lot of money."

"It'd be worth it," Baldwin protested. "Suppose something goes wrong? This way it's guaranteed. You don't have to face an appeal. They can keep you waiting, you know? And deduct for old hospital charges . . ." He was beginning to sweat. "What can you lose?"

"Nothing maybe." Mahler's eyes were dead. "I'd have taken that figure a year ago. Right now it's not enough. It's a real case. We've done work. It's solid."

Baldwin scratched uneasily. "I think that's the limit. What figure would you want to consider?"

"I'm not ready to say." Mahler showed his teeth. "But actually I don't think you know anybody. I think you're trying to horn in. So here's what I'll do for you. I'll forget you ever came here. Or I'll call Sabbattino and ask what he knows about you."

"Now just a minute . . ." Baldwin protested, alarmed. "Let's not be hasty, Mr. Mahler. Now, look . . . please! I was only . . ." He stumbled out, faster than he had come. Mahler laughed, refreshed. He flexed his muscles, amused, and noticed that the office had grown cold. Well, at least he had some idea of their latest settlement figure.

The telephone crashed through.

"How's it going there?" Yarberry was jollity itself. "I've been reading all the materials. You ought to collect. How do you stand?"

"Pretty good." Mahler sighed with relief. "We're hoping for a top verdict, say something near five hundred thousand dollars. That's been the range in this area. All we need now is your testimony. When can you get here for sure?"

"Didn't your associate Curtayne tell you?"

"Tell me what?"

"I've decided against it. I'm sending Fred Eckstein instead,"

Yarberry said cheerfully. "He'll get up there tomorrow some-time early." A pause. "Say, I did warn you not to count on me."

Mahler was in a cold sweat. The room had tilted, it seemed. "You haven't changed your medical opinion?"

"No, no! Nothing of the kind," Yarberry said. "Don't worry about Fred," he went on. "Fred's got all the *schmalz*. He's now associate professor here at Featherstone with the latest jazz at his fingertips. I'm doing you a favor. Look!" he said impatiently, cutting off objections. "He'll knock those yokels for a loop. If I didn't think so, I wouldn't send him."

Mahler drew a breath. "What changed your mind?"

"I just don't want to bother. Okay?"

A long moment passed. "Okay, like a fresh hole in the head," Mahler said shudderingly. "Very well, Doctor. But you took ten years off my life. I'll do as much for you one day."

Yarberry chuckled and went off the line.

Ages later, his last cigar gone, Mahler gathered his papers and left for the hotel. He was still shaking. Christ! What a narrow margin to disaster.

He stalked through the crowded lobby to the desk, blind to the black man in the shabby astrakhan expostulating excitedly with the bellman. He heard his name spoken and turned to a face contorted with anger.

"Tatum?" Mahler said with wonder.

"Yes, I'm Tatum!" the man burst out. "What are you doing to me? How did you get those people to lie about me? Why wasn't I asked to be heard?"

Chaka choked, falsetto with rage. "Man, don't fool with the motherfucker! It's below your dignity. Let the people handle it."

"Oh, shut up, kid," Mahler said. He took in the threadbare suit, the unkempt hair, the wild eyes. "Doctor, if you want to talk, I'll be glad to oblige." He turned to the clerk. "Let me have a sheet of paper." He wrote swiftly and with precision the words of subpoena to require Tatum's presence in court forthwith. "Tomorrow morning. Be on time," he said with grim satisfaction.

The paper was served.

17

The Municipal Building showed a single light on the sixth floor. Cigar butts and sodden paper cups with coffee dregs were strewn about Sabbattino's oversized office. The newscast of Tatum's appearance had brought about a hasty council of war on the question of settlement. Sarah took a dim view of the matter, urging that the city open talks. Sabbattino was still looking for a weak point in Mahler's case. He was not ready to panic.

"Let's not panic," City Attorney Potter echoed, harried. "Let's see how it goes tomorrow. Sarah can sound him out meanwhile and let him know the present limit."

When they met, the city's formal offer had gone to one hundred thousand dollars.

Mahler said, "Half a million and you've got a deal. And I'm being reasonable."

And so it stood.

The courtroom, which had grown empty and somnolent except for the handful of regulars, was again crowded to the walls. It was now a pleasant early-spring day with a bright sun in a clear blue sky. A window was open, but despite the warm breeze the courtroom was fetid.

"May I have a moment?" Mahler said.

"Take two moments," Judge Urquart said. "But get on with it. I've been patient enough, sir."

Mahler turned about for a low-voiced conversation. "You don't mind this now, Manya?" Mahler said gently. "Because you can wait outside. Or lie down."

"I'm all right," Manya said.

"You've taken your medicine?"

"Oh, yes. Ask Frank."

"That's right," Shroeder said miserably. "Jesus Christ, Bill, I want to tear him apart. How can I hold it in?"

"They'd like nothing better," Mahler said. "Now look, Frank, the jury's with us. Let's keep it so. One day more will do it."

Landowski said, "Don't spoil it now."

"All right," Shroeder said.

Mahler sat closer to the woman. They were inches apart. "You don't mind facing this man?" he said gently.

"I trust you, Bill," Manya said.

Their glances met with understanding. "And I'm trusting you," Mahler said. He touched her hand reassuringly. She smiled wanly.

At the defense table Sabbattino was a study in scarlet. "How in hell did this happen to us, Sarah?" he muttered.

"I don't know," Sarah replied. "But maybe Tatum has more answers than we know. I feel nervous."

"Dr. Percival Tatum!"

Tatum was seated on a rear bench crowded with angry people. He was huddled in his old chesterfield, a shabby thing. Although the court was warm, he shivered.

"Dr. Tatum!" the harsh voice repeated.

He folded his coat with care—"Mind that!" he said to a spectator—and strolled forward with rigid dignity, swinging his key. The high vaulting nose and sprouting steel-wool horns of hair were tilted at an arrogant angle. A paper had been left on the chair. He put it aside like a leprous thing and took the oath. It was an amazing performance and quite offensive.

Mahler said, "Do you recognize Mrs. Shroeder?"

Tatum turned to the white tense face in the first row. "I see her," he said with grim intent. "And her husband. I'm not sure I recognize them." The challenge went through the court. "They were my patients. I can only imagine what influenced them against me."

Manya lowered her eyes under the reproachful stare. Shroeder returned the stare with interest. Tatum turned to the bench. "Your Honor, I want to say something."

Judge Urquart interrupted. "Do not volunteer, Doctor."

"I'll say it anyway," Tatum retorted. "We gave that woman good medical treatment. I came here to have that established. Even if no one wanted me to come."

Sabbattino leaped up. "Just a moment!"

"No, sir!" Tatum cried. "Your people—Mrs. van Loon, Detective O'Dwyer—interviewed me months ago. Why did I have to come at my own expense? Eh? Well, that woman"—the winged nostrils flared—"that woman had the best possible treatment we could give. We saved her life. Now they want to turn that into money at my expense. I won't stand by and let that happen!"

It was an astonishing outburst. He was shaking with rage. Mahler waited with arms folded, unmoved.

Sabbattino broke in. "One question: didn't you tell Mrs. van Loon and Detective O'Dwyer in Queenshaven that you had saved your patient's life?"

"Yes, I did."

"And you refused to come to court at our request?"

Tatum sat forward, indignant. "Your interests are not mine, sir. The hospital would settle—" A flurry of objections interrupted. The jury was excused. "I said I'd never consent to that on any terms—and that, sir, was the last I heard from your office!"

Judge Urquart said, "Doctor, this is not your lawsuit to decide."

"I think it is," Tatum retorted.

"You're coming close to contempt," the judge warned.

"Maybe I am, but I won't be gagged and bound."

Judge Urquart looked about. "What's he talking about?"

Sabbattino was standing, facing the disturbed witness. "Very well," he said. He sat, wary and bemused.

The jury was recalled.

Mahler strolled forward, arms folded, and noted for the record that Tatum was under subpoena and would be treated as a hostile witness.

"Most hostile!" Tatum laughed.

"Hostile to which side?" Sabbattino called out.

Tatum's humorless bray brought a squabble of objections and rulings.

. . . .

Mahler said, "In any case, you agree that brain surgery should be done only by experienced surgeons qualified in that specialty?"

"Yes. Certainly," Tatum said with contempt.

"A stomach surgeon doesn't work on the brain?"

"No, he doesn't. Nor vice versa."

"Because each takes its own skill?"

"Yes," Tatum said superciliously. "If I may enlarge on that?"

"No, you may not," Mahler said in a relentless voice. "You're still on my case. Were you qualified to do brain surgery?"

Tatum stirred restlessly. "I was. I was chief resident in my fourth year in charge of the service. I had extensive experience in general and traumatic surgery prior to my first residency—"

"*General* surgery." The emphasis was heavy.

"Yes, general surgery," Tatum replied. "And that doesn't call for that face at the jury, sir. Not too long ago it was only the general surgeon, particularly the traumatic surgeon, who did neurosurgery. Half of New York City was covered by one neurosurgeon before the last World War. Actually it's not the most difficult surgery—"

Mahler interrupted. "We're not talking about the Dark Ages. We're talking about today. Did you in fact ever have any real prior experience in general surgery?"

The question was evaded. "I did as much general surgery as possible from the time I interned at Yeats Memorial Hospital."

"Yeats Memorial Hospital?" Mahler said with overtones of insult. "Up there in the piney woods?"

Tatum sat back. "There were pine trees. I don't know what that has to do with medicine." He added, "It was a rotating internship. We did everything."

Mahler folded his arms. "Let's go back a bit. Tell us about your education. Where did you graduate from high school?"

"What relevance has that?"

"Is there any reason not to tell the jury?"

"Well, no. I graduated from Cherokee County High School," Tatum said after a moment. "I went to night school, in fact."

"What was your major study?"

"We didn't have that system. It was a general course of studies. Is that important?"

"Perhaps not," Mahler agreed, and went on. The witness had

worked his way through a state college. He had no clear recollection of his application to medical college, where loans and scholarships had put him through. He had worked summers behind a soda counter. As to grades, he had no clear recollection. Mahler strolled to the blackboard and studied a column of medical terms written in bright orange chalk for the jurors' benefit. He said, "Let's return to your internship. How many beds were there at Yeats Memorial Hospital?"

"One hundred," Tatum said.

"Not very big?"

"Big enough."

Mahler accepted the statement. "And I daresay you got a smattering of everything?"

Tatum adjusted his bifocals with a precise gesture. With somewhat more confidence he described the establishment by the miners' union welfare fund of a string of hospitals in the coalmining region stretching from West Virginia to Tennessee to bring modern medicine with up-to-date offices and equipment and ancillary services and specialists into the area. Yeats Memorial was the base hospital.

Mahler let the flow go on to exhaustion, then said: "At the time you appeared at Yeats Memorial had this ambitious program yet been put into effect?"

"No. It was beginning."

"What specialists had been recruited?"

Tatum thought back. "Well, Dr. McDonald was chief of surgery. Dr. McDonald was a graduate of Charleston Medical College."

Mahler said, "Is it fair to say in fact that Yeats Memorial then had only two staff specialists—an internist as chief of medicine and Dr. McDonald, who was only a general surgeon?"

The sarcasm brought an angered response. "That's misrepresenting the situation. Yeats was organizing then for group practice. We had on call a good urologist and a good radiologist, experienced men, at Mullen, about thirty miles away, and a pediatrician at Cow Hollow. We did everything including minor surgery and assisted at major surgery. But we also were taught to treat the whole patient."

Mahler explored the limitations of a small hospital in Appalachia in some detail. He said with emphasis: "Was there much clinical material for brain surgery?"

"As much as one might expect," Tatum said.

Mahler seemed satisfied. "How was neurosurgery handled at Yeats while you were an intern?"

Tatum hesitated. "Dr. McDonald did all that work. You're making too much of specialization, sir. This degree of specialization is only recent. Even today in many areas the general surgeon still does everything. In fact even general practitioners do their own general surgery in many parts of the country—at least so they did until recently to my knowledge in Corpus Christi in Texas even though a fine surgeon from St. Louis is practicing there. The question of specialization is misunderstood. Our great problems today are not so much screwing medical science to impossible peaks as to deliver good cheap medicine where it's needed. I am impressed by open-heart surgery for the few. I would be happier to change an inadequate, obsolete system for delivery of health services to the poor—to arouse communities to reject inequities in our system—and to end a rigid bureaucracy which responds too slowly, or not at all, to the real needs of people."

During this statement, pedantically delivered, Mahler had waited with an air of patient courtesy. Behind him there was a sudden stiffening attention and expressions of approval. He waited for silence. "Does that mean we have prevailing lower medical standards for the poor in city hospitals than for the rich in the best voluntary hospitals in the country?"

"No, of course not," Tatum replied. "The goal is good medicine for all, but don't be impressed by shining facades and a parade of titles and the emphasis on research and administration. A big title once meant clinical skill, the working surgeon. Now the research people get those titles. You'd be surprised how little clinical competence there is today in those institutions. Clinical skill takes practice."

Mahler said, "And that's what you were seeking through your Lewiston residency? Practice in neurosurgery? On the poor?"

Tatum gave this thought. "Yes, but in the context of human needs and concerns."

Sarah glanced aside at Sabbattino with rising hope.

206

Mahler waited for a murmur of approval to subside. He shoved his spectacles up to a washboard forehead, sardonically ridged. "Let's get back to Dr. McDonald. On how many occasions did you manage to assist in brain surgery?"

A long moment passed. "On eight occasions," Tatum said reluctantly. "Perhaps nine."

"Did those occasions involve removal of tumors?"

Tatum was uncomfortable. "They were highway or mining accidents. Removing bone fragments. Decompressions."

"I see, I see." The sarcasm was fine. "Did you leave Yeats Memorial on good terms with Dr. McDonald?"

Lawyer and witness exchanged unfathomable stares.

"I did not," Tatum said shortly.

Mahler said sympathetically, "Didn't get along with him? Was that it?"

"It was nothing personal," Tatum said.

Mahler strolled about the well of the court. "Was it not because he refused to promote you or to recommend you for a surgical residency at Charleston Hospital?" he asked suddenly.

A squall of interruptions brought a ruling to leave that subject. Tatum sat blinking throughout. "Dr. McDonald refused to help me because he thought I'd be turned down."

"Why did he think that?" Mahler asked.

Tatum said, "For reasons I found inadmissible and irrelevant to medicine."

"Do you claim those reasons were racial reasons?" Mahler asked in a hard voice.

It was a challenge not taken up. "I never said so then," Tatum retorted. "I won't now. I wanted to be treated solely as a doctor. Dr. McDonald thought I'd be knocked out after the first year on some pretext. I didn't see why. I wanted to test it out. He thought I was foolish not to take his superior advice. It had nothing to do with my medical qualifications. I managed to get my residency elsewhere without his help."

"After a quarrel with Dr. McDonald?"

"I wouldn't call it a quarrel."

"You wrote a letter denouncing him for arrogance and paternalism, didn't you?"

Tatum sniffed. "Dr. McDonald *was* arrogant and paternalistic."

"Because he thought you'd have trouble in *South Carolina?*" Mahler stressed the name of the state with incredulity. He walked off, satisfied, having had no response.

The goading tactics brought a scowl of worried anger from Sarah.

"But I did have a residency in neurosurgery," Tatum exclaimed. "You cut me off."

Mahler halted. "Oh, yes. Where?" He affected surprise. In fact he had a clear idea of a two-year residency at a Kansas hospital with seven hundred beds. He searched his notes. "Yes, yes, yes! So it seems. Well, did you ever complete *that* residency?"

In a deepening silence, Tatum admitted that he had left after a dispute with the chief of service. A problem of unfair assignments had led to that quarrel, he conceded after some prodding. He had gone to a small nearby city of ninety thousand to practice neurosurgery in private practice. No, he had not completed his residency in the specialty, but that was not a legal requirement. Yes, a fuss in the county medical society on a public health matter had been unfortunate. He had closed down the practice when referrals failed to come. He wiped his mouth now, decidedly uncomfortable with the line of questioning.

Mahler pondered his clipboard. He made a check mark and glanced at the jury. And then what had happened?

Tatum said, "I entered the United States Army as a medical officer. I had extensive practical experience in traumatic and general surgery and even some obstetrics"—a smile momentarily appeared, then vanished—"in Germany and Korea and other theaters. I did whatever came along—including neurosurgery."

Mahler made a show of searching for a document. "Did you get an honorable discharge?"

"Yes."

"But not without trouble?"

Tatum stared at something unpleasant. "I had some disagreements, but I can show my certificate."

Mahler returned to the desk, plucking a heavy mouth. He picked up a folder. "Did you bring an action in the United States

District Court for Northern California to compel the military authorities to issue that certificate?"

Sabbattino was rising with hand up. "Now, really, what's that got to do with this case?"

Tatum's angry answer cut through the objection. "The Army agreed to enter judgment in my favor. It was not a medical dispute. It had to do with Vietnam."

Mahler glanced at the second juror, survivor of Normandy, whose interest had been sharpened, and went on to worry the witness through a series of minor medical posts, including jobs in the prison systems of California. It was not an impressive record—at least it did not appear so. Each post had ended in troublesome recriminations over credits and transcripts and breaches of alleged regulations. A few questions, carelessly put, indicated a troubled marriage—but this matter was left hanging under Sabbattino's objections. A picture of turbulence and quarrelsome indiscipline was beginning to emerge.

"Objection!" Sabbattino said wearily. "This background has nothing to do with this case, Judge."

"But I was board eligible," Tatum broke in, "by the time this came along. If someone will let me say so. I was qualified to do the procedure."

"Really, this must stop," Judge Urquart said querulously. He swiveled. "Doctor, what do you mean by board eligible? Eligible for what?"

Tatum was breathing hard. "Eligible to take my boards—that is, examinations to become a diplomate of the American Board of Neurological Surgery." The qualifications were described. One was required to work up through assistant residencies of increasing responsibilities with credits in neurology and basic sciences such as neurophysiology. Beyond that lay requirements of actual practice and the examinations. "One then becomes a diplomate," Tatum said precisely.

Mahler waited for silence. "And your fourth year as chief resident at Lewiston Central Hospital would complete those requirements? How old were you when you took up that residency?"

"I'm not sure," Tatum said after a pause. "About forty-five, I think."

"So you're now past fifty?" Mahler rocked, studying the witness. "Well, it's late, but it's not ninety," he drawled, and got some laughter. "Did you in fact ever take those examinations?"

The question was a jolt. The atmosphere was changed by his quick distress. "Well . . ." Tatum began.

Mahler stepped closer. "Yes?"

"Well, you see, there was some question as to the hospital's accreditation as a teaching hospital in neurosurgery," Tatum said slowly. "I couldn't seem to get that straightened out. And of course no other accredited hospital would recognize my credits." Something bleak shadowed the small eyes behind the bifocals.

Mahler let the moment grow. "Lewiston Hospital was not an accredited teaching hospital? Did I get that right?" Astonishment was registered.

"Not in neurosurgery. But . . ." Tatum began.

"In fact it was in danger of losing its general accreditation when its deficiencies in medical records came to the attention of the accreditation committee of the American Hospital Association," Mahler said with sudden passion. "In fact it was put on probation for one year?"

"As for that, you had better ask Dr. Grimes," Tatum retorted. "I had warned of that danger but no one listened."

The gavel was tapping.

Sabbattino turned to Sarah and Otto, conferred quickly, then stood. "We'll stipulate to that—" he began.

Mahler broke in angrily. "I don't want concessions. I want the jury to hear from the witness how an unaccredited hospital among other things let a mere resident with a spotty record do brain surgery without adequate tests or explanations of risks— and on misinformation as to the pathology. And I want that on the record!" In the quivering silence he turned back to the witness. "Was that because Dr. Bellinger too was not a diplomate in neurosurgery either? That his credentials to teach the specialty were insufficient?"

The gavel crashed.

Judge Urquart exclaimed, "Mr. Mahler, what do you think you're doing?"

"Proving my case," Mahler said, "if you'll let me." He stared at the witness. "Isn't that what you just described?"

"No, it was not!" Tatum exclaimed.

"Objection!" Sabbattino howled.

The gavel was banging. Everyone was talking at once. "I can't get it," the stenotypist exclaimed, throwing up his hands. "I just can't get it!"

Everyone halted. Without those nimble fingers, it was all a nonevent. It began again, stopped, resumed. Mahler, apparently recovering, apologized for the breach of decorum. "Don't let it happen again," Judge Urquart said.

"Yes, Judge," Mahler said, unmoved.

"Mrs. van Loon has a point," Sabbattino said.

Sarah rose to cite cases in an icy, trembling voice to head off the line of questioning. The license to practice medicine gave its holder discretion as to the kind and range of medicine to practice under proper safeguards and regulations, of course. The law did not require diplomate standing to practice the specialty in question. It was not for the courts to limit that right—

Mahler broke in. "It's the doctor's competence, not his rights, the jury wants to know about!"

"I am addressing the Court," Sarah said with fury. "Let me go ahead."

"Just so we're clear!" Mahler retorted.

Judge Urquart tapped. "Go on, please."

Sabbattino broke in with added clamor. Mahler leaned back on the rail, riding the squall, arms folded, jaw set. He was back in his element in a violent lawsuit for a cause larger than himself. It was wine. He glanced at Manya and smiled faintly. If only his legs were not quivering.

"Be quiet, Mr. Sabbattino! You talk too much. You too, Mrs. van Loon. I want to get to the bottom of this," Judge Urquart exclaimed. He was staring unpleasantly at the jolted witness. Tatum somehow had lost a button. The steel-wool hair was unkempt. "Not a diplomate? Well, well, well, well. Doctor, were you licensed to practice medicine in this state?"

"I was not," Tatum said thickly, "but I was licensed in . . ." He dropped this. "No, I was not yet licensed in New York."

The judge frowned. "Are you licensed in this state now?"

Tatum was brought up short. "I didn't bother to take the examination. I'd rather practice in Queenshaven."

"Oh, why?"

"Because there I'm a doctor. My patients look to me for medicine and they get it." Tatum touched a handkerchief to his tight mouth. "I was more than qualified," he muttered.

"But *not* a diplomate?" Judge Urquart pondered. "Proceed, Mr. Mahler!" He swiveled about, puzzled. What exactly did it mean?

Mahler spent an agonizing time flipping notes on a clipboard. "Were you aware that in this state an unlicensed doctor by law may not practice in a municipal hospital unless supervised?" He smiled pleasantly at Sabbattino and waited for the answer.

Tatum stared. "I was not aware of any such law," he said slowly. "But what has that to do with the operation? And I was supervised."

Sabbattino was standing, wordless. Sarah was scribbling a note. Otto, flipping through a dog-eared copy of the *Education Law*, was moving his mouth like a goldfish forming bubbles. A vital point, hanging in the case since inception, was now before the court.

Mahler said, "Supervised by Dr. Bellinger?"

Tatum said, "Ye-es."

"Was Dr. Bellinger present at the start of the surgery?"

A pregnant moment passed. "Not at the start, no," Tatum said. Under probing, it appeared that Bellinger had arrived from New York City later than expected. Yes, while the operation was an hour in progress. Yes, someone had telephoned that Bellinger was in his office on three minutes' call, if needed. Well—it was Miss Storrs.

"H'm. I see. Notified by Miss Storrs. Resting, I suppose. Well!" Mahler glanced at the jury. "Good place to rest, I reckon. And there you were alone with two interns, three nurses, and a student nurse, plus our missing anesthesiologist, Dr. Ling of Korea— all scattered now and gone with the wind—while Dr. Bellinger was otherwise occupied?" A gesture cut a retort short. "How long had you known Dr. Bellinger?"

"We were classmates at medical college," Tatum said sullenly.

"Friends, would you say?" Mahler was bland.

Tatum hesitated. "I was his friend. I'm not sure he was mine."

"Ah, friendship!" The sarcasm was broad. "Do friends examine each other's credentials?"

"I don't know what that means," Tatum said.

"Don't you? Let's see." Mahler turned back to the counsel table. There was a curious mood in the chamber. Shroeder was staring at the floor, clasping his broken hands.

The clock had swept past eleven.

"Let's have that paper, Gene." Mahler came back to the rail. A juror's breath was whistling in his ear. "Doctor, I show you a photographic copy of a paper entitled 'Application for Staff Position at Lewiston Central Hospital' and ask whether in fact it correctly sets out your educational background. Did you in fact graduate from Cherokee County High School as you claimed . . . ?"

Judge Urquart interrupted. "Shouldn't it be marked?"

"Withdrawn. We'll come back to this," Mahler said ominously. "Doctor, weren't you actually roommates, not merely classmates, at medical college? Wasn't Dr. Bellinger admired and envied by you to the point where you said you meant to emulate his success and become his partner in time?"

Sabbattino was trying to break in.

Tatum burst out, "That had nothing to do with the medical issues here!"

"Nothing? Nothing?" Mahler was astonished. "Didn't Dr. Bellinger give you extraordinary latitude? Weren't you running the department with a free hand in his absences, which were frequent, and in effect supervising yourself?"

"It would not be the case," Tatum retorted.

"People thought so?" Mahler insinuated. "That you were almost his alter ego in the job?"

Tatum was frozen. "That's of no concern to me. I had his confidence, yes. Rightly so."

"To the point that he accepted your Kansas residency as valid, although incompleted?"

"It was only technically incompleted," Tatum retorted. "He knew the circumstances. He was satisfied."

Mahler looked up with a grin. "Did he call you 'Doctor' or 'Percy'?"

"I regard that as frivolous!" Tatum said angrily, "But you, sir, will call me Doctor. And I had done hundreds of these procedures before this one came along."

"How many in this state were unsupervised?" Mahler said with a lurking smile. He walked off like a matador after a veronica, glancing stealthily at the jurors. He wheeled and stabbed a finger. "But you both knew you needed minimum clinical experience to become board eligible and qualified to go out to work on patients elsewhere? And this operation would go far to make that come about?"

"That had nothing to do with my judgment."

Mahler stood stock still. "Well, isn't that for the jury to say? Or doesn't single-minded obsessive ambition influence doctors when it comes to the moment of decision?"

"As it influences lawyers," Tatum shot back. "Unethical lawyers, if I may say."

Mahler threw up his hands. "Q.E.D. Exactly!"

Bang. Bang. Bang.

"Jury will disregard. Gentlemen, step forward," Judge Urquart said in a choked voice. The huddle formed, warnings and cautions were made clear. Mahler waited stoically, unmoved by reprimands most justly given. A ten-minute recess was taken. They went out to smoke.

Sabbattino scowled. "What the hell are you trying to pull, Bill? He's your own witness. You can't impeach him like this."

"I'm not impeaching. I'm showing exactly what happened to that poor woman," Mahler said, "I've only just started. If you don't like it, come up with an offer."

Sabbattino said, "Cut the bullshit and take what you can get."

Sarah was white-faced. "Well, I hope you're enjoying yourself," she exclaimed. "That man's a doctor, you know. Not one of your criminals. You don't seem to know the difference."

"I'm not impressed," Mahler said. "You two had this background on him months ago and you're still stalling a decent settlement. I feel sorry for the guy, but the more he talks, the more outraged I feel. Why shouldn't I use what I've got? If you don't like it, settle."

"We can't. You want too much."

"You're hooked on doctors. I'm hooked on victims. Come on, now!"

"Oh, damn!" She walked off, holding back most unlawyer-like tears of fury.

"Christ!" he muttered, torn and perplexed. He forced a gray smile and joined the Shroeders, who had taken in the strange exchange of views.

They entered the crowded courtroom without a word. Mahler waited for the signal, breathing hard, concentrating with single-minded ferocity on the dangerous path still ahead.

Tatum sat forward, dry-mouthed.

The question came from outer space, a harsh voice in an echo chamber reverberating in time. How curiously like Dr. McDonald's peremptory voice it was, he thought.

". . . think to do a Bárány test?"

A voice, his own, croaked, "Yes, I did. And it showed the presence of a tumor."

"Is that test anywhere to be found in this medical history?"

"Perhaps not. I might have failed to enter it. You'll find a thousand incomplete medical histories in that hospital."

"So we have only your word the test was done?"

"Not only mine. Ask Mrs. Shroeder if she doesn't remember being whirled about and tested for giddiness and nystagmus—involuntary eye movements."

Manya's shaking head was eloquent answer. "I don't remember that at all," she whispered.

It astonished Tatum that the clock had not yet reached one.

18

Dr. Frederick Eckstein was a pleasant-mannered, hard-working doctor with an optimistic outlook on life who enjoyed his wife, three small children, a house in Connecticut, and his career, almost in that order—all of which made him pliant and yielding to Yarberry in matters of convenience. Yarberry was a grasshopper, a creature of impulse and enthusiasms, so it had come as no surprise to Eckstein to find the Shroeder matter dumped into his lap on one day's notice.

"So how can it hurt you?" Yarberry said. "Come on, Fred. They have my solemn word of honor I'll testify. You've got to get me out of it."

"We've got theater tickets," Eckstein protested.

"So what about theater tickets?"

"My marriage hangs on taking Josie to the theater. She'll divorce me if I don't."

"Tell Josie it's for me," Yarberry said. "No, don't. She hates my guts, doesn't she? I don't give you boys a chance at the private work. Right?"

"She's sure you'll never give up a boil, not till the day you die," Eckstein agreed.

Yarberry chuckled. "Bail me out and you'll do the next boil. Now what's bothering you?"

"You're going in on the wrong side," Eckstein said.

Surgery was going on at Featherstone.

Next day after the morning conference in which brain sections looking like sliced cauliflower were passed for review, Eckstein left for the airport, taking the Shroeder materials along. By touch-down he had the case in hand. He was mildly excited at the prospect of testifying in court.

"Something wrong?" the taxi driver said. "You're talking to yourself."

"I'm going to be a witness in a case," Eckstein said.

"Oh, that!" the driver said.

A sweep of road brought them to the Civic Center where pickets, separated by sweating police, were exchanging taunts. A moment later he was at the courtroom door.

The guard said, "Sorry, but nobody gets in, mister. I suppose you'll say you're a doctor?"

"Actually, I am," Eckstein said.

"Everybody's a doctor," the guard said. "But there's no room." Eckstein explained his mission.

"Oh, well, squeeze in, Doc," the guard said. "I'd go in myself but it's all Greek to me. And I'm Greek. So who's to tell? Just heart-wrenching what those bastards did to her."

"Watch your mouth, man!" a community worker said.

Eckstein entered the warm, smelly chamber and squeezed into a rear bench of intent viewers. As though on cue, Mahler turned and nodded. Other eyes—Mahler's opponents, Eckstein imagined —noted his presence. A tall, broad-shouldered lawyer, Landow-ski, came back and introduced himself. "Glad you made it, Doctor," he whispered. "Have a good flight?"

Everyone was watching, Eckstein felt. "Oh, sure," he said. He studied the scene with interest—a craggy judge, a stenotypist with clawed fingers—it was like the television. "What do you want me to do?"

"Just listen. Tell us later if this testimony makes medical sense. It's been going on for two days," Landowski said wearily. "If you need anything, send up a note. . . ."

A bushy-haired youth—it was Chaka—turned about with pene-trating suspicion.

A court officer came shushing.

Landowski went back to his post.

Mahler resumed an angry, muscular prowl. "Very well, Doc-tor . . ."

The black man in the witness seat sat forward. Studious, hostile, bitter with contempt.

". . . let's go back to that first day in Emergency. You took it upon yourself to work this woman up," Mahler said hoarsely. "Why?"

Tatum's voice was equally hoarse, tired, laboring under the strain. "I wanted more tests to determine exactly her condition."

A hand went out. "But even there, down in the emergency room, you decided she had a tumor, did you not?"

"I thought a specific physical cause likely which would include the possibility of a tumor, of course," Tatum said tiredly. "I have said that more than once now."

"And you were suspicious at once?"

"Yes. I was suspicious."

"Why so?"

Tatum hesitated. "Experience. Call it intuition. I had a feeling. The sense of other patients before her."

Mahler accepted this with utmost incredulity. "And is that all you brought to this problem—intuition? Didn't you consider the prior history and make tests?"

"That too, of course." Tatum asked for a fresh glass of water. He was near exhaustion.

Mahler waited, rocking on his toes. "You had the specific objections to surgery by Dr. Gates, didn't you?"

"May I refresh my recollection?" A page of medical records was handed up. "Yes, I had a family doctor who insisted that the seizures were purely hysterical or psychiatric. Not unusual these days." Tatum snuffed with derision. "Instead of confessing ignorance, it's easier to label real organic illness as psychiatric even when it exposes the patient to continued neglect of the real condition. Often people appear to be neurotic or emotionally sick precisely because they are physically sick. When the doctor talks about psychiatric or functional symptoms, because he can't make a physical diagnosis, it may be time to get another doctor."

"Good!" a woman spectator exclaimed audibly.

Mahler said, "But you have agreed that seizures can be hysterical or psychiatric in origin?"

"Yes, yes!" Tatum said. "But in this case I also found a history of prior hospital admissions which showed strong efforts by the hospital doctors to find a physical basis for her symptoms. If so, a tumor would be highly possible."

"Did those doctors ever find such a physical basis?"

"No, but clearly there was the suspicion."

"Which was never proved, you'll admit?"

"Not by them," Tatum said with heavy irony.

Mahler studied the clipboard for instruction. "Doctor, how did you propose to determine the specific physical cause? Or did you use snap judgment?"

Tatum knitted his brows. "Actually it's a process of elimination. There are almost a score of physical or organic explanations for such seizures. It could be a congenital malformation, for example."

Mahler looked up. "Was it congenital in your opinion?"

The smile was faintly a sneer. "No, because the seizures began after her marriage. The congenital form would show up in childhood—although it's not invariant. Nothing is invariant."

"If it were congenital, surgery would not help?"

"I don't imagine so."

"Then why bring it up?"

The reply was classical. "You asked me."

Mahler stonily checked his clipboard, "What other physical cause might you suspect?"

"Well, encephalitis, brain fever, for example, which might be picked up from the history. That would affect the brain in a general way."

"In that case too surgery would not help?"

"I agree."

"And in fact her first doctor, Dr. Schlomm, thought she might have had brain fever, or a brain injury, as a child in Poland. Did you learn that?"

"That was his conjecture."

"But his reasoned conjecture?"

"If you like, but not controlling, since the condition could change. It was a continuing possibility." Tatum removed his spectacles with his precise air. "However, my impression was Jacksonian seizures, that is, one-sided, or focal seizures on the right side, coming from a specific area of the brain, cause unknown. Since I had no indication of encephalitis, the location, I felt, was

219

almost certainly in the left parietal lobe. I had enough to call for a complete work-up before resorting again to medication. A routine work-up consists of X rays on the suspected side, or sides, to visualize the arterial tree or the air spaces inside the brain. That is, arteriograms and pneumoencephalograms. Also an electroencephalogram, an EEG, to measure the brain waves. The spinal fluid is tapped and tested and normal blood count procedures carried out as well."

Tatum paused, staring ahead as though at something learned almost by rote. "All that was done. Well, if we had no clinical indication of focal signs—that this was on one side or the other of the brain—then we'd go back to medication to control the symptoms. Focal signs mean we are dealing possibly with a specific single lesion. Not always, but at least we should know this before anything else. It may be a congenital A-V. anomaly. It might be a patch of scarring. It might be a tumor. These are the best possibilities. The last was the most likely."

"And in that case what do you usually tell the patient?"

Tatum sank back into himself. He was avoiding the patient and her husband. "Usually we say that we want to find out what's causing the trouble. That we won't know until we have carried out the tests. That there's no point in listing possibilities, all of which are very serious. Not to cross any bridge till we get there. Then we can discuss it."

Frank Shroeder shifted angrily, but at a stern glance from Landowski subsided, glaring.

"Then it would not be good medical practice to tell the patient she has cancer?" Mahler advanced a step, then with deliberation put aside a page of notes as something to return to. "Never mind that now," he said. "Let's take one step at a time. Now the earlier EEG's were not revealing, were they?"

"I don't agree," Tatum said. He asked for the record and called attention in prior hospital admissions to certain slow brain waves in the temporal area, discovered five years prior to the surgery in question, which in his opinion might well have been signs of a benign glioma.

Mahler studied the record in turn. "Weren't those earlier brain waves within normal limits?"

"Yes," Tatum said with a sneer. "But your question has no real medical meaning. Many vital signs—high blood pressure, rapid pulse, blood chemistries—can raise suspicions even within normal limits. The usual question is one of change from a prior state. In that sense these waves were unusual enough to be suspicious."

"And again, maybe not?" Mahler stared at the restless jurors. "And on an EEG five years old and well within normal limits you decided to operate?"

"Not on that alone. On the history and all the evidence."

"Including the X rays?"

"Yes, of course."

Eckstein sat forward with interest. The X-ray evidence was again worried between lawyer and witness to mutual anger and exasperation, not for the first time, he judged.

Mahler's voice was rising. "But in fact all prior examiners at most found a general disorder, perhaps hysterical, for which surgery was not indicated. Wasn't that the case?"

Tatum shook his head impatiently. "To say a general disorder is negative, like saying a sick brain, or an acute abdomen. It means nothing except perhaps to cover unnecessary surgery. It's more important to make a reasonably positive diagnosis." He gripped the rail. His eyes were watchful.

The stare was unwavering. "It is always dangerous to open the skull, isn't it?"

"You mean a craniotomy?"

"I mean to open the skull," Mahler said.

Tatum wiped his mouth. "Every operation is dangerous," he said.

"And not to be done unless in accord with standard neurological diagnostic practice, do you agree?"

"I agree," Tatum said.

"And certainly surgery for a woman merely with hysterical or psychiatric seizures, or for seizures of unknown origin, would not be good practice?"

"Yes, I agree."

"And without a positive diagnosis of an operable condition, it would not be wise to order a craniotomy?"

"It would depend on the degree of suspicion," Tatum said after a moment. "That's why you explore—to verify the suspicion and give therapy—in case of a scar, extirpation; of a tumor, surgery, if possible; radiation, if not. Or perhaps nothing can be done. Let me give a humble example. Five percent of all cases of acute appendicitis cannot be diagnosed. To operate may be wrong. Yet not to operate might be fatal. A good surgeon might prefer to risk delay rather than to risk early surgery. Another may not. Yet if he errs, you can expect the lawyer to question his judgment to save the patient's life. What do you want at the bedside—lawyers in residence?"

Eckstein smiled.

Tatum went on. "In this case we had reason to suspect a deep midline lesion of some kind, though we could not absolutely localize a tumor as such. Neither could we exclude it. We might have found scar tissue, or an old calcified abscess, or a clot. We could hope to deal with the scar by referring the patient elsewhere—but a tumor could be treated by us with surgery or radiation. That was the reason to explore." He sat back and wiped his mouth. "I was sure, however, it was a tumor."

Mahler made a note. "Still, one doesn't just guess?"

"One uses judgment," Tatum replied.

"But I am puzzled," Mahler went on. "Why do you insist it was a tumor?"

"Because of frequency and because of something intangible," Tatum said hesitantly. "When one has convulsions, the maxim is that one must always suspect a tumor or the danger of tumor, even long before other symptoms appear. It's a red light. You must remember that tumor is the most common cause of seizures, especially at this patient's age. That does not mean that all tumors cause seizures or that all seizures are caused by tumors or that all tumors are malignant, but the chances are there. But I did not actually insist that she had a tumor—merely that she had a high risk sufficient to require exploration."

Mahler came to a halt, facing the witness with irony. "Then in fact you were *not* sure of a tumor?"

Tatum drew a breath, goaded. "Not in that sense," he admitted.

Manya smiled pleasantly. The discussion was passing over her head. She was a spectator at a tennis match.

Mahler paused, rocking on his toes. A point had been scored. "Does she have a psychiatric condition now?" he demanded suddenly.

Tatum stared a long moment. "I think so," he said slowly.

Mahler stood back. "Which is it? Yes or no?"

A long moment passed. Tatum said, "Yes, she has a mild depressive condition, an emotional reaction I'd rather not describe further. Obviously. It might well be phobic, but it was not caused by the surgery."

"Not caused by the surgery?" Mahler repeated heavily. "Then did this psychiatric condition *precede* the surgery?"

"I think so, yes," Tatum said.

"Which might fully explain the seizures?" Mahler pointed a quivering finger. "And if so, surgery was useless?"

"No . . ." Tatum attempted.

Mahler broke in. "Isn't it the fact that she had only mild hysterical symptoms which this treatment aggravated to a full-blown phobic disturbance?"

"I can't say that either," Tatum retorted.

Sabbattino stood.

"Then what do you say, Doctor?" Mahler flung out insultingly.

Tatum retorted. "I say that both kinds of seizures might coexist and be hard to distinguish. For that matter there's no actual proof of prior hysteria or of a psychosis—"

Mahler broke in. "What do you call proof?"

"A clinical note of nervous breakdown or admission to a psychiatric hospital. Crying fits. Adolescent hysteria. Some such euphemism. I should add—"

"Do you think a note is essential?" Mahler exclaimed.

"No, I don't," Tatum said.

"So the condition could have been there?" Mahler said. Tatum was silent. Mahler sat back against the rail with folded arms. "Did the surgery *help* her condition?" he asked with irony.

"It had to be done!" Tatum retorted. "I did not explore for seizures but for the tumor with its specific danger. Yes, obviously she's depressed. But suppose you're right? Suppose the seizures *were* psychiatric and not organic? Then how can you attribute the present phobic condition to surgery and not to ordinary development at her present age? You can't have it both ways." He stared with a flicker of resentful mockery. "I understand that's your great claim for damages here?"

"Ah," Sabbattino sat, satisfied.

Mahler said, "By the same token, do you claim her seizures were *not* emotionally induced? That she was *not* a psychiatric problem when you saw her?"

"I don't say that either," Tatum replied, "but I repeat that something new had come along which I decided required more drastic treatment than anyone else was willing to give. I took the risk."

"*You* decided?" Mahler folded his arms, digesting this matter, and walked across the chamber. He looked up into the staring face. "Are you infallible, Doctor?"

"Not infallible. Right!" Tatum struck the rail.

"So right that when Dr. Gates begged you not to operate, you had to call her a meddlesome bitch and all the rest?" The question brought some smiles, an intended effect.

Tatum retorted, "Dr. Gates used intolerable language. I have no apologies for that woman."

"Good enough—" Mahler began.

"And besides, she was talking out-of-date Freudian nonsense," Tatum went on. "These seizure disorders are not so exclusively functional, involutional, or sexual to the degree she seemed to imagine. To look for the basic cause of convulsions merely in disembodied psychic disturbances is absurd—just as it is to seek the cause of insanity in the same source. It's the existing primary defect in the pathways of the brain that must be cured—and by surgery, if at all. A normal brain doesn't produce either convulsions or psychoses." He remained staring a long moment.

"And that's what you learned at Gorham Medical College?" Mahler said with incredulity. "Brushing psychiatry as a branch of medicine aside entirely?"

"What do you know about Gorham?" Tatum flared, stung. "It's turned out more competent graduates—" He halted, biting his mouth. "No, no! I'm not taking that bait," he said, recovering. "I'm resting on one of the outstanding clinical authorities of our times."

Mahler glanced at his notes. "Are you referring to Dr. Theodore Wyatt's treatise on brain tumors and their treatment?"

Tatum's sarcasm was broad. "You've heard of him?"

A copy of *Brain Tumors and Their Treatment* by Theodore Wyatt, M.D., was displayed.

224

Mahler said, "Are you aware that Dr. Wyatt published that work forty years ago based on earlier training and clinical experiences and that it represents a purely deterministic view—questioned by other authorities since then?" He turned to the jury with incredulity. "And that was the basis of treatment given in this day and age in the state of New York?"

"Dr. Wyatt was the outstanding man at Johns Hopkins," Tatum retorted. "I audited his lectures myself. It was the medicine we were taught. He is still an authority. If you read that treatise with understanding you'd find his clear view that in suspecting the diagnosis of brain tumors, the chief emphasis must be on common sense, especially in the early stages. Sudden headaches, progressive signs, sudden changes of personality, and a suspicious electroencephalogram raise a great suspicion of tumor—if only because tumor is the most frequent cause of those symptoms. It's folly to wait for destruction of vital function or other signs of pressure. I was taught that the earlier the diagnosis, the earlier the removal and the better the surgical result. In the late stages of the disease, the dangers to function and life can only be enhanced."

He broke off, closing his eyes. The court waited. He sipped water and waited for the next question.

Mahler said, "In the years since you studied Dr. Wyatt's treatise, haven't diagnostic techniques advanced . . ."

"Yes, they have—" Tatum interrupted.

" . . . to the point," Mahler went on, "that tumors can infallibly be located without exploratory surgery if proper tests are done?"

"Nothing is infallible! As you have taught us," Tatum retorted.

The two men, witness and lawyer, faced each other a long moment. Mahler went back to his reasonable voice. "But, Doctor," he said with soft menace, "doesn't Dr. Wyatt himself require adequate and revealing tests to localize the tumor before surgery?"

The thick mouth was working. "It's never that cut and dried. The tumor is always a danger to life. Tumors can grow unsuspected to baseball size in the silent portion of the brain without obvious symptoms. A tiny tumor, scarcely larger than a pinhead in a vital area, can be devastating and still defy all tests. Sudden coma and death are just too common. In one year Dr. Wyatt—

if you read that far!—saw five patients die without warning in a taxi, in bed, on the operating table, on the toilet, just because of a slight increase of intracranial pressure. Yes, medicine changes, but not that much. And what happened to Wyatt's patients can also happen to the patients of a doctor in a city hospital. And they're so helpless, so dependent on what we do—or hold off doing. I know that only too keenly . . ." Tatum broke off. "My Lord! What gives anyone the right like this to question me, or any doctor who must decide these questions?" He was shaking, panting with pent-up bitter feelings.

The outburst was received in a silent court.

Judge Urquart stirred. "Go on, Mr. Mahler," he said quietly, "if there are no objections."

"No objections," Sabbattino said. He whispered to Sarah. "Not too bad. Keep your fingers crossed."

"I wish he'd make fewer admissions," Sarah said.

Mahler walked forward with ominous intent, kicking the floor. "What comes through, Doctor, apparently, is a concession that your diagnostic data were too meager and uncertain to satisfy even Dr. Wyatt's standards?"

Tatum stared with hate. "Dr. Wyatt also states the maxim that the inexorable law of growth of brain tumors makes their early removal imperative to prevent loss of function and death. Surgery is the only hope of cure. It is not up to lawyers to decide what data are enough. Why didn't I run more tests? What more could I do with what I had at my disposal? Ask for expensive, sophisticated electrocorticography diagnostic tools when we were short of soap and toilet paper? Send her back to a family doctor with a bias for Freudian explanations that fail to explain? Ship her to one of those emporiums with more obvious cases to pick and choose from? Would they take her? All she ever got there was wait and see. All very well for them but for a city hospital with its needs and pressures . . ." He paused, working his mouth, staring. "I had to use my judgment. And I did. And I was right." He sat forward, gripping the rail with quivering hands. "No, don't stop me, Mr. Mahler. You promised to let me talk. That woman was in serious trouble. Someone had to do something." He turned to the jury in direct appeal. "I agree of course that for years the seizures were general and always in connection with pregnancies or other sexual, hormonal, and chemical disturbances. What we might call intensifying effects. That's why those seizures were always diagnosed as hysterical or possibly classical epilepsy. . . ."

He paused to wipe his mouth. He was not making a good impression, if one could judge from the jurors' frowns. "Yes, I admit I saw a psychiatric component. I also saw seizures that had become Jacksonian, focalized, right-sided. That meant that the neural discharges marching across this area of the brain"—he thumped his skull—"were producing increasingly frequent convulsions in the right side of the body. The hand, the wrist, the arm, the entire side were thrashing about and the eyes were glazing. . . ." The illustration was grotesque. The jurors sat back, repelled. He was on the verge of hysteria. "In my opinion a tumor had begun to show its effects. It was creating new symptoms imposed on former symptoms. Even psychiatric patients grow tumors, you know. And in fact often do."

He looked up, staring. "On this occasion, she had come in with status epilepticus—repeated attacks without regaining consciousness that had lasted over a week. She had blinding headaches. She was in extreme misery and had threatened to kill herself. Her husband begged me to help her. He wanted an operation, something, anything in view of the hardships and the misery at home due to her extreme disability. Oh, yes, I had misgivings. I wanted to send her home to wait—but for what? For someone else to act—too late? And who? And when?"

He swallowed. "That's not why I became a doctor. No!" He was hoarse, strained by grief and rage. "I did the best I could in unspeakable conditions. I got to know her. We talked. I learned things about her life and the conditions at home. She was begging for relief. And I suppose, like a fool, I told myself no one else would ever be interested enough to help her but me. Finally . . ." He halted, fighting an overwhelming feeling. "When you have hands and fail to use them . . ." He gazed about helplessly. "Does anyone know our most desperate problem? It's that no one cares. You can scream and no one comes. I never abandoned a patient in my life, and I wouldn't start with her. I knew everyone was hoping I'd trip, but what else could I do? And now. And now . . ." He covered his face and wept. "Fool! Fool!"

The silence was embarrassing.

Tatum blew his nose. "Sorry," he said, rimming his eyes.

Mahler polished his spectacles, unmoved. The man's head was lowered like a stuck bull's, he thought. They were both breathing hard. He clamped his spectacles on and glanced up with savage intent. "Well, let's see. You say you observed status epilepticus? Can't a psychiatric patient show false seizures, false symptoms even of status epilepticus?"

"Yes, she can," Tatum agreed slowly. "I don't think I'd be deceived."

"But you *might* be deceived by a clever patient?"

"Not in my opinion," Tatum said stubbornly. "Well, perhaps a patient might get away with it for a time, but that was not this case."

"But it's possible?"

"Yes," Tatum said reluctantly.

"So all that proves little," Mahler said in a loud aside. "You relied too on questionable EEGs and on X rays taken under your supervision . . . ?"

"Plus her history," Tatum interjected.

"Yes, her famous history," Mahler said. The quarrel with Dr. Cassidy was painfully, tortuously brought out. "But Dr. Cassidy, your own chief radiologist, told you that the X rays showed nothing. Did you disregard that?"

"I would disregard anything Dr. Cassidy had to say," Tatum exclaimed with venom.

Mahler read the testimony of Dr. Cassidy, given earlier in the trial, with emphasis. He put the transcript aside and folded his arms. "In other words, you were determined to ignore Dr. Cassidy's opinion? A radiologist of over thirty years' experience?"

"Forty years," Tatum said with contempt. "In my opinion, Dr. Cassidy was an incompetent who should have been retired years ago. I never got an affirmative opinion from him. He was most antagonistic."

"Really? About what?"

"Ask him. He was running a slovenly service—a slovenly service, I repeat. I had complained about him more than once."

"That *would* account for his antagonism," Mahler agreed.

Tatum flared. "But not behind his back. I told him so more

228

than once. It wasn't the only instance of substandard work. It was the general condition—" He broke off wildly. "I remember one poor devil in orthopedics who almost lost a leg because no one took time to loosen a cast. I saved the leg, but I doubt they ever forgave me. Was that wrong?"

Sabbattino stood to object, scarlet.

Tatum lowered his voice. "Dr. Cassidy picked the quarrel," he said sullenly. "I didn't. I wasn't wrong—only impolitic." He paused, fighting for control.

Mahler said, "You were about to say?"

Tatum shook his head. "I saw a disturbance indicating a mass pressing on the ventricle. Nobody can tell me I didn't. Certainly not doctors hired to testify in a dishonest lawsuit. I saw that mass." He broke off again, staring. "Well, that's it. I removed a tumor. That's what I came here to say. I'm being well repaid. I can't say I wasn't warned against it."

"Warned? By whom?"

Tatum looked about. "Dr. Bellinger," he said with wonder. "He said this would happen to me one day. I should have listened." His eyes were suddenly awash with tears of self-pity.

Sarah looked off in despair.

As he had throughout the day of heated exchanges, Sabbattino entered strenuous objections in the record.

"I'm giving him latitude," Judge Urquart ruled. "Doctor, try not to get emotional. Just answer the questions."

"I'll try," Tatum said.

A flapping shade broke the silence.

Mahler walked forward slowly. "Did Dr. Bellinger see that mass?" he said pointedly.

"I—I don't think he really looked," Tatum replied, blinking.

Mahler turned to the opinion written by Herlihy that the X rays were technically so poor as to be worthless and that, such as they were, no abnormalities could be visualized. Did the witness disagree with that distinguished authority too?

Tatum was laboring. "If the X rays were so poor, how could he tell anything about them? How could he say there was no tumor? Dr. Herlihy is being arbitrary. Elsewhere he says he saw no convincing evidence to show organic seizures. He overlooks my written note that I saw the tumor and sent tissue to the pathologist. If his notes are evidence, why not mine?"

Mahler nodded slowly. "Well, let's see if the pathologist bears you out. As to that tissue you sent down to the laboratory . . ."

Sabbattino was standing, poised, expectant.

Mahler held up a hospital record in evidence. "Who is Mrs. Longfellow?"

"I have no idea," Tatum said, wiping his eyes. He blew his nose and waited.

Mahler said, "It appears that a Mrs. Longfellow brought thirty grams of brain matter to Dr. Feke for a frozen section to report the nature of the tissue. Did that happen?"

Tatum's face softened. "Oh, the student nurse. Gertrude. I suppose so. Yes."

"You also sent the slides made by Dr. Feke from that specimen to a dozen leading laboratories around the country? Did you receive any report whatsoever that the tissue was malignant?"

Tatum was wordless, transfixed.

Mahler went on. "Is Dr. Feke also an incompetent in your opinion?"

A long moment passed. "No. He's competent enough."

"Did you wait for his report?"

"No. Dr. Feke could take weeks to report. I couldn't wait. Once I saw what I had, an infiltrating glioma, I took it out with surrounding tissue." Tatum burst out, "I can't account for Dr. Feke! If he missed the malignancy, I didn't. I felt tumor—like the soft part of a peach—and saw the soft tissue. It was unmistakable. I saw it."

"You saw what you expected to see?" The overtones were strong.

"No! I saw the pathology and cleaned it out," Tatum retorted, stung. "I had made no mistake. You have no grounds to say otherwise."

"Except that no one has agreed with your interpretation of the X rays and all competent pathologists reported normal tissue. On which you staged another quarrel? As you quarreled with every doctor you ever met—who ever came in contact with this case?" The shout was thrown at the witness. Mahler pointed a shaking hand. It was a moment frozen in time he would never lose or forget. His voice was hoarse, his tongue thick. "And on that naked, reckless, egotistical opinion you dared to tell this poor sick woman she had cancer—that more cancer remained to be taken out? With all the trauma inflicted in her weakened emotional state? And you say no grounds?"

Lawyer and witness eyed each other. Tatum burst out, sputtering, choking. "Take that back, sir! I never told her that—never! Never!"

"And that's as true as all the rest of your testimony? Never? It's in the record!" Mahler, now scarlet, shouted.

Chaka was bouncing with excitement in the rear.

Frank Shroeder was up. "You lie, Dr. Tatum! You lie!" he repeated through the banging gavel. "You're not making a liar out of us," he said passionately. He turned to the jury. "Who are you going to believe? After what he did? Us, or him?"

The gavel was banging, banging.

Sabbattino was a thundercloud. Sarah was staring at the medical terms printed in bright orange on the blackboard display.

Manya's eyes were unfocused. Her right hand was rhythmically convulsing.

19

She was made comfortable in a room lined with books and the stern portrait of a judge in robes. She felt disgrace and waited for an end to things.

Shroeder placed his hands flat on the inner door. It was a gesture of resignation and finality. He waited a moment and left for the hall. He found Mahler about to step into an empty room assigned for his use.

Shroeder said, "I was out of line in there, huh?"

"Yes. Just don't do it again," Mahler said. "Why? Something on your mind?"

"Not really. Only maybe you're asking too much. Why bust a gut holding out for more when you say you already got a good offer?"

Mahler lit a cigar. He was irritated by the dull, heavy manner. "I'm busting a gut too," he said sharply. "Manya's come this far. Can't she hold out a bit?"

"If you say so. Only I got to tell you something," Shroeder said guiltily. "I'm not sure we can keep it up in there."

"Oh? Why not?"

Shroeder looked aside.

Mahler shook the man's shoulder. "Frank, you're upset, but don't blow it now, for Christ's sake! We're in good shape and they know it. They're considering an improved offer, and if not? We'll get it from the jury. Now I've got to talk to this doctor. Okay?"

"If you say." Shroeder sighed.

The conference room was a bare cubicle with a table bolted to the floor. A calendar was the sole decoration other than an improbable spit box in the corner. It took a moment to settle down.

Eckstein said, "Quite a show, Mr. Mahler. What happens now? Do I testify, or what?"

Mahler was breathing heavily, drained. He rubbed stiff, aching muscles a weary moment, smiling faintly. Yes, it had been a good show. A last-minute walloping effect for the jury to sleep on. He said: "It's too late now, of course. I've only started on Tatum, but we'll hold him off in the morning to let you testify first thing. Can you stay overnight?"

"If I'm absolutely needed," Eckstein said.

Mahler nodded. "Well, I'm relieved. Yarberry almost gave me a heart attack. We have time to prepare. What did you think in there?"

Eckstein said, "I sympathized with the doctor. I could see myself in his place."

Mahler stared. "Oh." He lit a cigar, puffing slowly, considering something not quite right. "At least it got some response. Judge Urquart is pressing them to settle. The old bastard finally moved over to our side. Supposedly we're considering a latest offer of what they call a lot of money." He winked at Landowski. "Didn't I call this shot, Gene?"

"Ayeh," Landowski said, grinning. He was calculating the rate of interest on a large sum of money.

Mahler yawned and scratched. "Jesus, I'm dead. I can't wait to get a drink." He yawned again, eyeing the young doctor.

Eckstein was intensely interested in the novel situation. "How much were you just offered?"

Mahler smiled darkly. "More than before. Less than what I think the jury will give. Still . . . I'm not entirely easy. Tatum is suffering. You never know about jurors. He might even wind up with enough sympathy to cut the verdict. It'd be a joke after all this work, but that's what makes verdicts and maybe that's not bad. Let's get down to cases." He smoked thoughtfully. "Was Tatum justified to explore?"

Eckstein shook his head. "I didn't think so. I'd certainly want those tests repeated first. Without real proof, we were taught to treat the symptoms first and live with the possible tumor as long as possible. You don't operate until you must."

Landowski made a face. "Live with a tumor?" He shuddered.

Mahler gave this thought. "And you can go in tomorrow and testify to that in court?"

"Oh, yes." Eckstein returned to an earlier thought. "Of course to be fair I can see why Tatum was worried. Headaches and epilepsy are signs of brain tumor. He wasn't wrong in that respect. I can't say he was."

"Oh?" Mahler frowned. "Please explain that."

Eckstein's manner was precise. "Tatum didn't look good under your cross-examination"—a faint smile appeared—"but his reasoning wasn't bad. He had a thirty-five-year-old woman with a history of progressive seizures which had changed and now had a focal signature attached. She had intractable headaches and severe psychiatric problems and the rest of it. She had staring spells, and the seizures had failed to respond to medication. So his hunch wasn't unreasonable."

Mahler was trained in a hard discipline to withstand the worst surprises with composure. "Is it good practice to go ahead on a hunch?"

"Of course not," Eckstein replied. "You showed that. But it was more than a hunch. He had a serious life-threatening situation. The husband thought it was. Maybe he couldn't wait. I don't agree with the action. On the other hand I can't fault him for acting on strong feelings. Many clinicians have strong feelings they cannot justify objectively. If that's how he felt, that's how he felt." He smiled, pleased with the neat and unexpected thought. "The old-time clinicians used to walk in and smell different disease entities—diabetes, tuberculosis, some kinds of cancer. We laugh, but it was true."

Mahler stared. "You're not putting me on?"

"Why should I?"

"Can you do that? Smell cancer?"

"No. We're trained to rely on the equipment. But they could." The same pleasant smile appeared. "You must realize he had something there no one else has had."

"What's that?"

"The patient herself," Eckstein said simply.

Mahler walked across the empty room to the far corner, rubbing his jaw. "Oh, Christ," he said. He turned to Landowski. "Gene, will you see what's happening out there?"

Landowski went out to the hallway. He returned to report that the opposition seemed closeted in a heated discussion.

Mahler said, "How's Manya doing?"

"Still resting," Landowski said. "Frank wants to take her home when she's ready."

"So let him!" Mahler said. He turned back to the doctor and picked up the thread. He said worriedly, "So Tatum smelled cancer. The pathologist said no. In the usual routine, aren't you obliged to accept the pathology report?"

"Oh, sure. Very important. Pathology's fundamental to study this disease. It's the final answer."

"Would you expect a good pathologist to make a mistake?"

"Not likely." Eckstein considered the matter. "You take it for what it is. On the other hand, you have Tatum's notes in the record. He wrote that he found a tumor. I'm sure he made those notes in good faith."

Landowski interrupted. "What makes you so sure of that?"

Eckstein looked up with wonder. "Why else would he remove so much tissue from that area? What are you suggesting?"

Landowski said uncomfortably, "Oh, only that he was wrong and covered up."

"Isn't that the question?" Eckstein said. "How do you know?"

Mahler continued to stride the room. Landowski's suggestion had been hanging in the case since the first interview. The young doctor's intonation had blown it away. He was walking suddenly along a dangerous precipice. "Doctor, let's not speculate on motives. I'll suppose good faith. On the other hand, we established that he sent slides taken from that same specimen to a dozen laboratories to reverse the pathologist's opinion on the frozen section. I grant he wouldn't deliberately invite negative results, but he was frantic to get confirmation. It also shows uncertainty. Why was he so anxious to get proof? Every pathology laboratory we know about sent back negative reports. Walter Reed, Howard, Bellevue, Mt. Sinai, Harlem, and others, maybe some we haven't traced. If he had just one favorable opinion to show malignant tissue, it'd be another ball game. But he has nothing to back him up. If he did, he'd say so."

"That's true, I suppose," Eckstein said.

Mahler came to a halt. "Forget the instant case." He scowled. "A surgeon and a pathologist disagree. Which would you believe?"

"Oh, the surgeon," Eckstein said.

"Why? Because you're a surgeon?"

"No, because there's no reason not to. The pathologist only knows what comes to his hands. The surgeon knows what he's seen. A small tumor can be missed in taking the sample. Or go down the suction. Or be discarded. You saw how much tissue gets taken out. In fact, why should he wait for the pathologist's report? At that point, he's almost committed to go all the way."

"Committed? Why?"

"Because there you are and you're stuck. You're thinking of the usual biopsy, but a biopsy is itself fraught with danger. If it's abnormal tissue you might as well clean it out. It's doing no good anyhow—not like a breast or arm where you dare not move without the pathologist's advice. That's why we don't favor exploratory surgery for this purpose. Unless you're going in with purpose and not to fiddle around you don't even begin. And the pathologist isn't infallible. Only recently I got a negative report myself and two months later the patient was dead. Conversely after a bad report the patient may live for years. This patient had a bizarre history. So her future in fact may be very good. I'll have to say all that if your opponent asks me on cross-examination."

Mahler gazed off distantly. "Oh, he'll ask, he'll ask," he said grimly. "Look, doctor . . ." he began. An unreal echo returned.

"Yes?"

Mahler drew a breath. "Wouldn't a tumor have to show up on the X rays?"

"A small tumor in that area—" Eckstein began.

Mahler cut this off. "No! Don't say it! I know!" He collected his thoughts. A hundred scribbled notes, random thoughts, outlines of the case made over the toilsome months swam before his eyes. The implications were devastating. He glanced up angrily.

236

"If I put you on the stand tomorrow morning, could you truthfully say you didn't like the tests?"

"I could."

"I have to know this: would you concede Tatum found a tumor if you're pressed on cross-examination?"

"Not a bit. As I indicated, all those negatives make it doubtful to me. I mean only that I'd have to consider his note that he saw a tumor—like the one Yarberry showed you that day. Maybe he mistook a cyst. That's possible but I can't say. He was there. I wasn't. It becomes a question of credibility."

"Do you believe him?" Mahler demanded.

Eckstein smiled pleasantly. "Is that a proper question?"

"No!" Mahler snarled.

He prowled the dreary room. "But a resident! A lousy resident," he burst out. "Can he operate unsupervised?"

"In his fourth year?" Eckstein shrugged. "Well, I did. At that point you're supposed to be independent in diagnosis and treatment. How can you learn with the attending always breathing down your neck? Some attendings will scrub when they see the resident going ahead. Some won't. But this is realistic practice, because in an emergency the attending can get there in three minutes, clean his hands, and don gloves. That elaborate scrubbing isn't always necessary at all. It's enough for him to stand by."

Mahler said nastily, "Is it? And if he's not in condition? I'm not finished yet. Tatum's hiding something and I know what it is. Bellinger came back from New York drunk. He was sleeping it off in his secretary's lap. That's why Tatum started so late—and not the only time."

Eckstein said, "Why didn't you bring it out?"

Mahler said gloomily, "I didn't want to overdo it. I thought I had enough. Maybe I'll have to get into it after all. I don't know."

Three men in an empty room contemplated trial tactics.

Mahler stared with growing anger. "So what the hell does that leave us with? The cancerphobia?" he burst out. "The son of a bitch told her pointblank she had cancer! In her condition was that good medical practice? Is that what you're going to tell me?"

"Not at all," Eckstein replied. "Ordinarily there are better ways to break the news, sure. And Tatum stated them. But . . ."

"But what now?" Mahler exclaimed.

"Well . . ." Eckstein halted. "You only have that information from her. She's intelligent. But she's unstable with poor insights, schizophrenic. She might even be telling the truth in a way—and maybe it had to be done to get consent. But she has impaired judgment and her interpretation may not be trusted. Ideas of reference are common. She is aware now of her problem and has incorporated the thought of cancer into her life system. While Tatum might have told her the facts of life to overcome her fears of the operation, it's equally possible he didn't. My guess is that she invented the conversation. Especially as Tatum denied it."

"Invented? Oh, Jesus! Look, her husband supports her story. She was reasonably intact until the surgery pushed her over the brink—"

"I thought the psychosis supposedly was always there causing the original seizures," Eckstein said.

"We don't actually know that—" Mahler began.

"But isn't that your claim?" Eckstein broke in, faintly irritated now. "You're in constant paradox. You adopted hysteria or a psychosis to explain the seizures. Now you want the opposite to preserve her credibility as to the cancerphobia—as though it's one or the other. But it's not.

"See here," he went on, noting the unhappy, baffled expressions. "This woman had multiple causes for seizures and learned them all well. Tatum had to reason that the one masked the other —that years of testing and medication had gotten her nowhere. He could have sent her home, but he might have felt that she'd get no better treatment elsewhere—I'd have to agree with him there—until she reached a point of no return. As I see it, he thought he had to save her life. If the question is sincerity, no one can prove otherwise, except to take his testimony as untrue. That's up to your jury, of course. But he's too obsessive—too compulsive, too much the meticulous nit-picking doctor to believe that."

Landowski groaned.

"All right!" Mahler burst out. "So he was sincere. What's your own opinion of the case?"

"My own impression is that the phobic disturbance, the cancerphobia, so-called, is not related to the surgery. But don't take my word. I gather Dr. Herlihy thought otherwise. Call him as a witness. What exactly do you want from me?"

"I'm not sure I know anymore," Mahler growled. "Well, I want the truth, of course," he said after a pregnant moment. A significant glance was exchanged. "The only thing is . . ." He paused uncomfortably. "This is a shock, Doctor. We put in a strong case. I think the jury is with us, subject to your testimony. But all this coming from you—you, our own witness?" He shook his head. "You sure gave me a sour can of beans to eat."

Landowski was gray. "Doctor, can't you reconsider . . . ?"

"Please, Gene!" Mahler snarled. He recovered. "Look, Gene, suppose you find Frank? Tell him I want to talk to him alone?" He returned to Eckstein, studying the intelligent face. The doctor was not as young-looking as he had recalled. Those blue eyes, clear, pleasant, unyielding, saw the whole gestalt. "It's not just this woman I'm considering," he said after a moment. "I think her husband will do something desperate, abandon her, kill himself, something. There's a child too. Money, a verdict, is their only hope. . . ." It was his jury speech, rising from a well of emotion. "The life problem didn't just stop in the operating room, you know!" he said savagely.

Eckstein waited. "I know that."

"I don't ask you to stultify yourself. I can't and I won't. But in an area of mere opinion . . ." Mahler rubbed his neck, scowling. "Well, those views can destroy that family as effectively as Tatum's knife. Jesus! Don't you see that?" He was standing on an abyss.

"What can I say about that?" Eckstein said.

Landowski returned, agitated. "I've got Frank waiting in the little room—"

"Oh, shut up!" Mahler snarled. He eyed the doctor with respect. The surgeon's hands were thick, stronger than his own. "Never mind what Tatum thought he had. On the direct case, what can you say that could be helpful? Was there a tumor?"

"I strongly doubt it," Eckstein said. "No."

The stare was piercing. "What else can you say that's helpful?"

Eckstein smiled faintly. "In my opinion on the total picture, the chance to find an operable tumor was not good enough to warrant the procedure. I can say that, if you like."

"What else?"

"Oh. Well, an element of good medical practice, as you know, is the proper selection of candidates for surgery. This patient in my opinion didn't meet that standard. I can say that too."

Landowski mopped his neck.

The baleful stare was unwavering. "And yet you seem to justify what Tatum did. How would you explain that? Is there more than one standard?"

"Oh, no! Only one standard, but we have different conceptions of that standard. It depends in the last analysis on the doctor. Some doctors will take any risk in a life-threatening situation even where the chances are poor. Others won't. They want good cases only. I don't suppose lawyers take any old case that comes along, do they?"

"Apparently some do," Mahler said with feeling.

Eckstein shrugged. "Ultimately it's a matter of philosophy. It comes down to the surgeon's temperament and how he deals with life itself. I would guess that's true of everything."

A court officer looked into the room with word from Mrs. van Loon that the other side wanted a meeting. "In a minute," Mahler said. His glance was on the doctor. "That's not what Yarberry led me to believe," he burst out. "Hearing all this, how would Yarberry testify? And please! No more surprises."

Eckstein smiled. "Oh, he's got absolute standards. As far as he's concerned, this hospital's a joke. If you can still get him here, he'll testify it was butchery without qualifications. Almost a crime. But I can't say that. You see, I saw that doctor's look of concern and alarm when the woman threw that last fit in the courtroom—and that's influenced my view of the matter. He's a sensitive doctor. I doubt he could be brutal."

He adjusted his glasses with a precise gesture. "I do think he used poor judgment to operate on a woman of borderline psychological status. I completely disagree with what he did, but there's one sin he didn't commit—the sin of omission. I couldn't swear it was so bad as to be malpractice. Sorry."

Mahler stared at the floor. "All right, all right. That's one man's opinion. I heard it. I wish I hadn't." He looked up. "We'll get Yarberry up somehow. Meanwhile let's buy some time. Gene?"

"Ayeh?"

Mahler hesitated. "Ask Sarah to wait a few minutes, while I talk to Frank. Then we'll see what they have to say. And let's button up, eh? No loose talk." He turned to Eckstein, who was rising to leave. "Anything else, Doctor?"

"Well, actually, there's the surgery itself. If Tatum could remove that much tissue in that area and leave the woman with a fairly intact personality and only mild deficits, he did a good job. I'd have to say that too, if asked."

Mahler shuddered.

Shroeder looked aside guiltily. "I tried to tell you before about the cancer. Tatum never told me she had the condition directly. I got it from Manya."

"Christ!" Mahler shook his head in despair. "And you had to volunteer all that crap? What got into you? Manya's testimony was good enough as it was."

Shroeder blinked. "I had to back the woman up. What else could I do?" he said sullenly.

Mahler continued to stride, considering the implications. "All right! Maybe you were confused. Not so terrible. We'll go back and fix up the record—if we still can. Or dare. Don't you realize what you did?"

"I'm her husband," Shroeder retorted. "So I looked for a few lousy bucks! What the hell do I care for anything but her? And don't tell me a smart guy like you didn't figure it out."

Mahler recoiled. Really, there was no decent reply. "I'm on notice now. Before, I wasn't. Look, how far do you think I can go?" He stood glowering. "On the level now! Did Manya really get that story about having cancer from Tatum?"

Shroeder was silent. "I don't think she knows herself. Do you want me to go into that?"

"No! You said enough!" Mahler exclaimed. So stupid, so unnecessary! he thought. A case shattered by nonsense, by faulty preparation, by a lie at its heart.

His own lie.

It stuck in his craw. The courtroom was before him—black man, white woman—a stolid, unthinking jury who would take his lead. To what?

And yet, and yet.

He planted himself before the miserable man, weighing the remorseless years against living needs in the balance.

The room was silent.

Shroeder looked up wanly. "I'm glad I told you, Bill. I feel better. You'll know what to do."

Judge Urquart was staring moodily at the darkening plaza. His secretary tapped to advise that a strange ritual was drawing to a close.

"Bring them in," Judge Urquart said.

Almost a dozen people—lawyers, stenographers, secretary, court officer—gathered about his desk. The meeting had a curious formality. They sat tense, facing each other in stiff anger, masking thoughts, feelings, information. "Have you agreed on a figure?" he asked.

Sarah was tired. The last hard session of bargaining had been exhausting. Sabbattino who had thrown the ball to her, was seated apart, silent and resentful. "I'll want something for the city," she said with ragged feeling. "We want a statement that malpractice is not admitted."

"That's understood," Judge Urquart said.

"We want it on the record when you discharge the jury. It's important for our doctors. If not, there's no agreement."

"I see no problem," Judge Urquart said.

Mahler said, "We're prepared to state that Dr. Tatum had the patient's interests at heart—no matter how far he departed from the best standards."

"What does that mean?" Judge Urquart asked.

Mahler said, "Oh, there's enough ambiguity to justify compromise. Our clients agree to accept two hundred and fifty thousand dollars only because they accept the doctor's good faith. Right, Gene?"

Landowski nodded solemnly, dazed by the sudden end of things. "It's better this way," he agreed. "I'd have taken ten percent of that figure if the city had been human—"

"Let's not start that again," Sabbattino began testily.

"Gentlemen, gentlemen." Judge Urquart was admirably stolid. "Well, if everyone's satisfied! Congratulations, Mr. Mahler. Of course you others, Mrs. van Loon, Mr. Sabbattino, did very well too. For a while out there I was quite worried. It's a lot of money."

"A lot of money?" Mahler said.

"Why, yes!" Judge Urquart said. "It seems a lot of money to me."

Mahler stared at the remote man across the limitless desk. The case in all its aspects was before him. "Oh, sure. They can buy a house in Florida and live on the interest," he said. "The interest on their share may come to what a welfare family would get—without a hole in the head to pay for it—just because a hospital was underequipped and a doctor got desperate. Yes, it's a lot of money."

The message was for Sarah, who flushed, more than for anyone else.

"Well, everyone did well," Judge Urquart said. He was flustered by the note of underlying rage. "Let's discharge the jury and put that on the record. It'd be nice if both sides were to thank those men and women for their patience. All that listening and nothing to show for it. My!"

She retreated from the faraway place. Something was shaking. A voice screamed. "Wake up, Manya," Frank said gently. "It's over. We're going home."

New York City's weather was at its best. A chill wind was in the air, but the straw-colored sunlight falling on the park was warm. The Oak Room at the Plaza was filled with a drinking crowd at the end of the day. The mood was genial.

Mahler was having cocktails with Sarah. She seemed abstracted, not sure of herself. She looked fresh in a smart tweedy suit over a crisp blouse with white scalloped collar. Her hands were animated as she finished a description of events at Lewiston in the aftermath of the Shroeder case. Judge Urquart had retired. City Attorney Potter had become a nuisance about punching the time clock. . . .

"Phil sends regards," she said. "He's not too sore about the trimming we took. After the usual editorials about taxpayers' money, things settled down. But it did bring some reforms. We've had a special commission working on a study of our hospital system.

Medicine's too important, if I can say it without groans, to leave to doctors. Terribly emotional, immature people." She smiled over the cocktail glass. "I had O'Dwyer sound out the jury after you left the building, you know?"

"Oh? I didn't have any heart to stay around." Mahler was feeling warm. None of this held any interest. He was thinking only of how to get her to bed. Damned hard, he thought fretfully, with a woman who meant to talk forever.

"Are you interested in the result?"

"I suppose I am. What would the verdict have been?"

"I'm ashamed to say this, considering how much we paid out. At that point we actually had six votes. You had six votes too with indicated verdicts ranging from twenty thousand to three hundred thousand. Of course they hadn't yet had your matchless eloquence—or the final medical testimony." She sipped her drink. "You were expecting to put Dr. Eckstein on in place of Dr. Yarberry, weren't you?" she asked casually.

"Dr. Yarberry was expected," Mahler said stolidly. He had no intention to go into that last conference with Eckstein.

"Well, I don't suppose it matters now," she said. "It was a dangerous case, but we felt we could hold the verdict down to a reasonable figure since Manya's difficulties were not visible to the eye. After a few weeks her story lost its impact. At least so we thought. But after that last business with Tatum, we had to raise the ante. That cost us one hundred thousand. I hope it went to good effect."

Mahler said, "I got a card from Fort Lauderdale. The family's living quietly. So I'm satisfied. Do you know what happened to Tatum?"

"Not really. Very bitter that we paid a cent. He can't see why we did even though we protected him down to the end. Difficult man." Sarah called for another drink. She seemed to be sparring for time. "Did you know why Jane Gates was so reluctant to testify?"

"I'm afraid to ask," he said.

"Well, she wasn't trying to defend the hospital. Actually, she had all the background on Manya's psychiatric past in Poland from that Dr. Schlomm. She was trying not to give the show away —that Manya had a number of so-called childhood hysterical

244

episodes after the war. Nazi bit, you know. So her testimony was not reliable." She eyed him curiously. "But of course you didn't know that, I'm sure."

"Not in any formal way," Mahler said without expression. "I had other things on my mind. I thought the jury felt the weight of Tatum's sincerity. I couldn't risk the verdict with so much on the table. And, who knows which way those six votes might have gone? And another thing . . ."

He looked up. "The negative pathology report left me in doubt. It still does. As it is, we'll never know whether Tatum saved her life or mutilated the woman without good reason." He glanced at marvelously swelling breasts and a flushed handsome face and smiled. "Well, that's why we settle cases, I suppose." He glanced at his watch. "What about dinner now and a sexy show, if I can keep you in town for the night? Would you like to change your dress, or something?"

She sat back quizzically. "Dinner sounds good, but I don't see the point to the sexy show, do you?"

Mahler nodded in appreciation of a moment long deferred. He said: "On that solemn note, Counselor, I rest my case."

Young Dr. Longfellow emerged, panting, from the attic of his new house and clattered down three flights of stairs to the room set aside as an office. A baby was asleep in the nursery.

"Darling?"

A pretty girl looked up from the trunkful of papers, books, and scientific instruments which had followed them from Lewiston for several years. "Yes, honey?" Her face was smudged.

"What are you doing?"

"Hanging up your certificate. Getting rid of junk."

"Useful junk?"

"Junk junk. Just crap."

Longfellow entered the littered room with a frown. "What kind of crap?"

"Papers, slides, comic books."

"Not the comic books." He kissed her nose, eyes, forehead, neck, and became passionate. "Let's go upstairs while the baby is asleep," he whispered, nuzzling a fragrant neck.

"Now, quit it," she said, returning the kisses, then yielded. "All right, but keep the telephone off the hook."

An hour later Gertrude Longfellow, ex-student nurse, returned languidly to the task of putting her new house in order. Among the items for disposal was an old slide made by her talented husband as a medical-student exercise from an extra lump of brain tissue given to her on a forgotten day by an indulgent surgeon in the operating room at Lewiston Central Hospital. It had been a routine act too trifling to be noted or remembered.

The classification was unmistakable: gliomatous, malignant.

The slide was thrown out with the trash.